Return to Beechend

H Jane

written by

Hannah Jane

First published in the United Kingdom using KDP
2022

Print ISBN: 979 8 43918 370 8

This book is a work of fiction. Names, characters, businesses, organizations, places and events are either the product of the author's imagination or are used fictitiously. Any resemblance to actual persons, living or dead, events or locals is entirely coincidental.

Look for more books at
https://www.amazon.co.uk/~/e/B096NV6BQG

Printed and bound in Great Britain by KDP Amazon

To my sister and brother, you gave me the praise and support to do whatever makes my heart soar.
Thank you for believing in me when I struggled to believe in myself.

Prologue

Darren

The smell lingered in the air causing Darren's nose to twitch in disgust. The dampness of the flat was getting worse now that November had arrived. He hated it here. The neighbours were the worst kind, and his girlfriend's sheltered upbringing made him anxious when he saw the discarded drug paraphernalia in the corridor opposite their front door.

He knew that Sadie didn't think of herself as a spoilt rich kid. But sometimes, the reality of the world made it glaringly obvious that she was definitely out of her comfort zone. He was aware of her very sheltered up-bringing, but that had all changed a few years earlier. He had met her several times. Mainly when he had tagged along to Ewan's parent's house. They had made him feel welcome and although he hadn't grown up in such a grand home as Owersby Hall, he had been privileged in other ways.

Somehow, and Darren wasn't sure how, but Sadie had begun to develop more of a backbone over the years. She was made of tougher stuff, he knew, but he hated that she was here in this place because of him. This was all they could afford at the moment, he felt a failure for not providing what he thought she deserved.

"Darren, don't you need to get up? What time does the gig start?" Sadie called through to the bedroom where he was pretending to sleep. "You told me to wake you. I've heated some soup and there's one slice of bread left if you want it." Darren's grunt of acknowledgment travelled the short distance and he knew she would hear him moving around. He was desperate to get her out of this place.

He watched her as she gently stroked her round protruding stomach. This was the reason Sadie hadn't been home to Beechend. What would her parents say if they knew? He could already imagine what words would be thrown at them. None of them nice.

Darren emerged from behind the curtain that created their bedroom area. He turned his nose up at the soup sitting on the table, instantly hating himself when he saw her reaction. She bit her lip to hold back her tears. The truth was, he had used the last of this week's pay for the rent on this dump.

He sat down and started to eat regardless. They had stopped talking about their situation. Six months pregnant. Sadie had dropped out of University to get a job so that Darren could focus on the band. They were going to be huge she had declared to all who asked.

Now, they were facing winter and without realising, the money was almost all gone. She didn't sing her praises anymore. In fact, she barely had a smile for him, between working and band practice.

His phone trilled breaking the silence. Sadie sighed. Her lack of patience was etched on her face which was like a dagger to the heart. The neighbours were having a blazing row and they could hear everything through the paper-thin walls.

He answered his phone, not recognising the number.

"Oh, My God!" Darren was on his feet, the tomato soup forgotten. "They want us to tour with them! This is amazing." Sadie smiled and the woman he knew came back to the surface. Her beaming face made his day. Then as fast as the happiness appeared it began to evaporate as her face became stony.

"What about me and little blip? Are we going on tour too?" Their relationship had been rocky over the last few months. Money was in short supply and then the news that she was expecting had thrown a real spanner in the works. Why couldn't she let him have this moment.

He hung up and then beamed at her. "It's a five-month tour. The second had to back out because of family commitments. So, they've offered it to us. The band. This is our big break!" Darren paused for a breath. Sadie failed to put on the smiling happy face. "Can't you be happy for me? This is what we've dreamed about for the last two years!" The woman facing him was not someone he knew. Darren wasn't sure when this had happened, but in that moment he realised that their relationship wasn't what he wanted anymore.

"When does the tour start?" Sadie tried to show an interest. He had never laid a finger on her and he hoped she knew that he never would. But their lack of communication was getting to be a problem for them. He buzzed on about the dates, somewhere he mentioned them signing a contract and leaving tomorrow. "Saturday!" Her eyes widened in shock. "I don't think I can get everything sorted by tomorrow. It's such short notice." Darren's face took on a bewildered expression. "Darren, what's wrong?"

He stood stock-still and Sadie twisted her hands together. He didn't want another row. He was hungry, tired and she was supposed to be going to work again this evening. "No girlfriends on the tour." Darren stopped and let it sink in. "This is our big break."

He watched as something inside Sadie seemed to snap. They had never argued like this before. He had told her he wasn't ready to be tied down. She had told him that nothing was stopping him and that he should leave. So, he did. Slamming the doors so that their windows rattled. He never saw how she had then broken down in a fit of sobs that had consumed her body and soul.

The instant the ice-cold rain hit his face; Darren began to cool his temper. But how could she not be more excited? This was everything they had talked about. Their dreams of his band making it big and touring the World. Granted it was just touring the Northern half of England. But a tour was a tour. He was still mad at her and the way she had reacted.

He had regretted saying he didn't want to be tied down. He hadn't meant it. But her actions had stung and in the heat of the moment, he had wanted her to feel some of that pain. It wasn't true of course. He was looking forward to being a Dad. Then it hit him. Five months touring. But little blip would be here in less than four months. He was an ass. Sadie was right.

Darren groaned. I'm such an idiot. She is never going to forgive me for this!

He flipped open his phone and hit Ewan. It wasn't late and he hoped that he would answer. Ewan would know what to do to fix the royal mess he had made.

"What's up Daddy to be?" Ewan sounded jolly down the phone. He almost didn't want to tell him what he had said. "Darren? Is this another pocket dial? Hello!"

"Hey, Ewan." God his voice sounded hoarse and scratchy. "I messed up." He then told him everything.

"You are a prized pillock!" Darren hung his head in shame. "It's simple really, head home, apologise and take your head outta your ass!" Ewan chuckled. "Mate, the tour is a great idea, but to be honest it's shit timing. You are gonna be a DAD. Start acting like it."

Darren knew that he was right. He couldn't wait for little blip to arrive, but it was hard letting go of his childhood dream.

"Look, there is a job going at the office. It's crummy and low paying, but I'm guessing better than you are now. I'll put in a good word for you. You and Sadie can crash here until you get on your feet."

Darren was so full of emotion. He had the best mate anyone could ask for.

"You'll get this chance again, but don't mess up your chance with Sadie, you guys, you're meant to be, right?" Darren nodded into the phone.

"I've been an ass!" It was Ewan's turn to agree, and they both burst into laughter. "Shit, she'll be at work." Darren was already walking back to where he had abandoned his car.

"Just be honest with her. Tell her you love her, and you'll do anything to make her happy. Girls love that sappy stuff." Ewan laughed at his own attempt at a joke. "Message me when you make your plans and I'll make up the spare room for you both."

"Thank you, it won't be for long." Darren sighed.

"Don't mention it, take care and I'll speak to ya tomorrow." Ewan hung up and Darren made to cross over to his parked car.

"I should probably get her some flowers or chocolates." Darren was talking away to himself in the now torrential rain. He never saw the black sedan. But he heard the screech of the brakes and the tyres as they locked and skidded on the rain-soaked road. It was too late. He didn't even have time to turn before the impact. His last thoughts were for Sadie and their baby. He wondered, boy or girl. And then he was gone.

Chapter One

Sadie

The smells of summer still drifted through the air. It was almost the end of August, and the tourist season would soon be over. Sadie sighed absentmindedly as she loaded her shopping into the front basket of her bike. She was starting to regret the extra bottle of detergent that she had seen on offer, but it was just too good to miss out on. Decidedly weighed down with her purchases, she started on the slow trek back to her little cottage. The afternoon sun lay low in the sky warming her back as she cycled onto the brow of the next hill.

Her naturally wavy haired was loosely tied at the nape of her neck, whisps had escaped and framed her almond face. She pouted from the exertion of cycling the incline that led back into Beechend.

The trees and hedgerow lined both sides of the narrow lane and meandered up the hill. Dappled light cascaded through the trees and warmed her face.

Without much warning, a gleaming red car

screeched and swerved across the road narrowly avoiding her in the process. The top-heavy basket became too much to handle, and Sadie wobbled dangerously to avoid the collision. The shopping, including the parcel she had collected from the post office, toppled, and crashed to the ground as she skidded into the hedgerow.

The scream didn't have time to leave her lips as she screwed her eyes tight and braced for the inevitable impact.

Realisation slowly dawned. Sadie was half in the hedge, half under her bike. She was shaken but could tell that she wasn't seriously hurt. Thoughts of how she was going to get out of the hedge flashed through her mind as she silently cursed the unknown driver into oblivion. Sadie tried to move but found it near impossible to manoeuvre out of the thicket of thorns that were gradually puncturing her soft pale skin. She winced, realising moving was only making it worse. Great.

"Oh my God! Are you alright? What were you doing in the middle of the road?" The voice was stern and authoritative yet had a slight softness that she could not quite place.

Male, the voice was definitely male, and she could hear him getting closer. "You shouldn't be riding around these lanes on a pushbike. Are you trying to get yourself killed?" A large hand reached towards her and pulled Sadie out of the bush. Bits of twigs and leaves scattered around her. He continued to ramble about the dangers of country lanes as she made to start gathering her items, some of which had rolled back down the hill. The largest bottle had split open on impact with the hot tarmac. A purple liquid oozed out and trailed after the now bruised apples. "Are you even going to speak?" His tone showed that he was quickly losing patience.

She turned to face her accident-causing rescuer. Her anger rose to the surface at his ideocracy. "I have every right to be on this road!" She declared haughtily.

His lips were full and not at all happy to see her. His eyes were obscured by the oversized sunglasses covering his face. Sadie stopped dead in her tracks taking in the sight before her. It was clear that his toned body was very well cared for. Instantly a blush crept over her face as she realised, she was staring.

Sadie quickly changed tactics, she needed to get home. She didn't need to get into an argument with a complete stranger. "You were driving too fast." She mumbled, her voice softer than before. The man was collecting the bread and half a dozen broken eggs. He placed them into the basket as she held the bicycle steady.

He was standing a mere foot away from her and she could feel the electricity tingle between them. "You really should drive more carefully around here... children are playing nearby not to mention this is a quiet country lane!" She avoided looking directly at him this time. Keeping her eyes averted to the meagre contents of her shopping.

"Are you hurt?" His voice had softened and she braved a glance up at him. He was nodding to her left arm that had taken much of the impact from the hedge. "You're bleeding." He reached out to her, but she quickly pulled away. The tall dark stranger stared at her intently slowly lowering the glasses, she caught a glimpse of the brightest blue. For a fleeting moment, she felt that her soul was exposed. It was unnerving, she didn't like it. "I think I know you…" He smiled, it reached his eyes and lit up his whole face making him appear a little younger than she had first thought.

Sadie ever the independent woman that she was, was having none of it. Determined to leave, she deposited the last of her shopping into the basket.

"No, I don't think so… people I know, have a better respect for their environment. They don't race around country lanes in their sports cars. My arm is fine. It's a scratch." She felt slightly unsteady on her feet and thought twice about getting back on her bike. Yes, it was better to carry on, on foot.

"Stick to the side of the road and cars won't have to swerve to miss you in future! It's been a delight to meet you, miss…" His comment dripped with sarcasm. Sadie didn't turn to face him again as she gingerly walked away. She merely raised her hand to wave goodbye before thinking twice about it and continuing her journey home.

Rhys

The car roared back into life, destroying any peace there might have been in this side of the valley.

"Rhys! Are you there bro?" The voice on the speakerphone was deep and had a sense of laughter running through it. "What happened?" The driver used a few choice words before setting back off down the lane, albeit at a much slower speed than before.

"I almost hit a cyclist! Some crazy woman in the middle of the road on a blind bend!" He tutted loudly before remembering her warm hazel eyes gazing up at him out of the hedgerow. He had seen those eyes before, and he was certain that the woman was full of sass and loathing just for him if only he could remember…

"You what, you're breaking up…"

"There was a brunette cycling over the hill. I only just managed to avoid her." He shook his head trying to clear it.

"You trying to keep that bad-boy image from your former days little brother? I can't believe you've gone back there! Better you than me!" Rhys's older brother laughed before telling him to take it easy. The call ended as the car sailed past the sign announcing, 'Welcome to Beechend'. This was it. He was back. The home of his misguided youth. Ten long months stretched in front of him. This was going to be interesting, he thought as his car slowed to a snail's pace.

The little cottage was at the other side of the village, but he needed to collect the keys first and sign the last of the paperwork. He hoped that he could survive his time here, heal and then maybe move back to the city as an improved man.

The place of his childhood seemed to be frozen in time. Rhys slowed even further as he drove along Main Street. The village green perched on the left, the duck pond was surrounded by reeds and green shrubs. The pub façade was worn and faded, but an air of community lingered as he watched a group emerge and gather at a rickety table.

As the road veered round to the right, he noticed the butchers and the old sweet shop he had frequented with his pocket money. There were new shops too, that were unfamiliar, and he was pleased to see that the place had adapted a little. This gave him hope that the villagers would be accepting of the changes he would soon propose.

For the remainder of his journey, he struggled to focus on driving. He was looking out for the petite yet curvy cyclist. Deep down he was hoping for round two. He didn't make any effort to conceal the smirk on his face.

Sadie

The rage burning inside her made the rest of the journey go by in a flash. What kind of stupid idiot drives like that? Sadie batted it around over and over, all the things that could have happened. She took a few deep breaths before walking through the front door. Calming her nerves, she didn't want to be seen in a wrecked state.

"Mum! I thought you would be home ages ago." Tabby, what an angel! She had started the dinner. "Chicken and chips ok for tea?" The teenager half-turned as her mum walked in but didn't notice the bits of hedge in her hair. "I wasn't sure what you wanted... Mum?" Tabby spun fully to take in the sight of her mother. She gasped and rushed across the clay tiled floor, pulling out a chair and helping her into it. "What happened?" Sadie shrugged. But now that the adrenalin was wearing off, the pain was setting in. She ached. A lot.

"Stupid driver in a flashy car. Probably a tourist. He was driving too fast around Sweet Pea Lane." Tabby's face showed pure shock and terror and her eyes began to water. "I'm ok. He didn't hit me. I swerved and lost control." She shook her head at the thought then unwillingly laughed. Tabby joined in as she went to fetch the first aid box.

"How did you get all these cuts?" She pestered as

her mum breathed in deeply. "Wait, mum, there are leaves in your hair!" She sniggered, and instantly Sadie felt the laughter was therapy for the soul as well as her bruised ego.

"I landed, somewhat ungracefully, in the hedge." Tears of laughter were now streaming down her face. They hugged and made a cuppa whilst the dinner finished cooking. Tabby helped to sift through the dregs of the shopping, salvaging what she could.

Despite the events of the afternoon, the subject of the mysterious driver didn't come up again. Sadie couldn't stop thinking about him though. He had seemed so familiar to her. Like a prince from a far-off dreamland. A person from another life that a long time ago existed in her world. If only she could place that voice.

Rhys

Although the cottage looked quaint from the outside, almost idyllic, the interior was nothing compared to what he was now used to.

The charm and enthral of the archaic oak beams lasted mere seconds. Shortly after taking the moment for admire the aesthetic created, he collided with them when attempting to look around the downstairs rooms. Rhys would have to adjust the way he stood if he was going to survive here. He found himself stooping his way around downstairs. Instantly missing the open plan living space he had in the city. Had, had in the city. It wasn't his anymore. Well, he supposed it was, but he didn't want it. The thought was alien and yet a comfort at the same time.

Mentally shaking himself, he set about gathering his cases from the boot and moving them into the house. Rhys needed to make this place home, if only for a little while.

He was pleasantly surprised to find that the essentials had been stocked up in the kitchen and a list of emergency contacts was on the fridge.

The window above the sink looked out onto a modest back yard that would barely fit a lounger. A few plant pots were dotted about and appeared to have a few plants fighting to dominate. On the kitchen side was an invitation to a BBQ just around the corner. The thought of mingling with the villagers filled him with dread, but he needed a fresh start and maybe getting in with the locals would make this stay more bearable. Besides, maybe, if he was lucky, he would run into the brunette from earlier.

Her eyes were imprinted on his brain. It had taken him a while to realise who she was. Sadie was not eighteen anymore. Those eyes. They hadn't altered. They still had the power to captivate him. Rhys was kicking himself over how he acted less than thirty minutes ago. He could have seriously hurt her. What had he been thinking? Damage control. First thing tomorrow he would need to make amends and hope she would forgive his foolish city ways.

The girl he knew, would forgive anything. A hopeless romantic who fell in love with someone who wasn't him. Bitterness would not be his friend he scolded as he looked around the remainder of the cottage.

Sadie

Later that night, in another part of Beechend, the traumatising nightmares had returned. Each time the dreams portrayed the same event. This time was no different; the road was wet, and the car took the bend too fast. As it spun out of control the world appeared to slow down and almost stop. Darren's eyes were wide with fear as reality caught up with him. The explosive sound of crunching metal woke her immediately. She was a tangled mess of sheets and pillows. Gasping as she tried to eradicate herself from her self-made prison. A soft whimper escaped her lips, as the tears tracked down her face. He was back. Haunting her dreams. Her biggest regret tied up neatly in her subconsciousness. If only she knew the truth about what happened almost seventeen years ago. Maybe she would stop torturing herself.

Experience taught her that there was little chance of her sleeping now, Sadie tiptoed across the landing to check on her sleeping daughter. In her haste, she forgot about the loose floorboard and the creaking sound echoed into the night. She paused and slowly lifted her foot from the culprit that lay under the carpet. Tabby was a mess of curls, but she slept soundly. At least she could keep the demons away from her daughter, she thought to herself.

In the kitchen, Sadie made herself some camomile tea and sat petting Bruno, their affectionate golden retriever. He often sat with her in the moments after waking. His company soothed the panic that inevitably flowed through her each time she dreamt of the crash that took away Tabby's father.

Her life had changed in an instant that dark and rainy night all those years ago. Sadie had been forced to return to Beechend. Heavily pregnant and unwed, her well-to-do family were ashamed and made plans to keep the story hidden.

The first two years of Tabby's existence had been spent at Beechend Manor. Her ancestral home was anything but. One of two large estates that surrounded the village of Beechend. She had despised their customs and the aspirations they had for their only child. Sadie new that she was different from a young age. Her thoughts and ideas were constantly in conflict with her parents rules and expectations. Returning there had been her only option at the time and she still regrets allowing them back into her life.

Their lives were controlled from the moment she stepped over the threshold into the cold yet opulent foyer. Over the weeks that followed, Sadie had begun to believe that she would never get out from the suffocating existence. She had scrimped and saved all she could before finally landing a job and finding somewhere else for them to live. Things hadn't been easy, but she hoped that the life they had built together was one of happiness and that Tabby would always know unconditional love.

Chapter Two

Ewan

Ewan is one of those people that you can't help liking the moment that you meet him. He is tall, dark and handsome, but mostly and more importantly he is kind, gentle and generous. Among his many friends, he is affectionately known as the gentle giant. At well over 6 foot and broad-shouldered, he can look imposing but with a beaming smile and soft hazel eyes, he can make you feel both at ease and safe to spill all your deep dark secrets.

For Ewan, this was both a blessing and a curse. He had been friend-zoned more times than he could count. Always viewed as a great guy or my 'best mate Ewan'. He had had enough of searching for the one. Now pushing forty, he had watched as many friends, acquaintances and colleagues had all taken the leap, walked the aisle and set up home in the fashionable area of the time. Now on his twentieth year since moving to the city, in order to make something of himself, he felt weary and restless. Well over half of the marriages had come and gone. He had continued to work hard on mass his fortune, but for what? Was he happy with his life? The truth, no, he was no longer content.

"Ewan, old man! You sneaking out early?" The voice belonged to one of the interns he had interviewed two or three years ago. He couldn't remember his name. He had always been good with names, but he had seen so many come and go, they all seemed to blur into one. Ewan smiled and nodded his acknowledgement. Was it Simon? Steve? "I'm working on the Dixon account, so won't be home before midnight by the looks of it." He remembered the grunt work of his early days. Four years of slogging away before he got his first promotion out of the pits.

"I heard about the mix-up, looks like you'll be working all weekend." He was relieved that this wasn't one of his accounts. But then his team would not have made such an obvious mistake. "John up in the office still?" John's team were notoriously the worst in the whole department. With one too many mistakes under their belt, they were at risk of being disbanded and let go. Not his problem, but he felt for the rest of the team. He knew it was the leadership that was the real problem.

"He's already headed out. Left us to it." He shook his head, "My kid's first birthday on Sunday, I promised Diane that I'd be there, then this happened!" His eyes were pleading now. The big, puppy dog look.

"Ok, Steve,"

"Si, or Simon if you prefer." He smiled as Ewan

sighed.

"Simon. I don't like to step on toes. I will look at the account and send some ideas to point you in the right direction. If you have a grievance about the situation, please speak up and go to HR. I'll look it over this evening at home. Forward the latest reports. Put the work in tonight and you should have no problems about making it to your kid's birthday on Sunday." With a slight smile, Ewan nodded at the thankful Simon and left the building.

He always enjoyed his walk home from the office. The streets were a hive of activity and the park that he cut through to the apartment building was small but perfectly formed. Edged with a crop of overhanging trees and filled with lush green grasses and winding paths and benches. There was almost enough open space to trick you into thinking you were in the country. Almost.

Today was different. He wasn't looking forward to returning home. For the last three days, his home had been the central hub for the start of a war. The battle wasn't his, but he'd waded in regardless. Now he felt uncomfortable in the one place that should be his sanctuary. He sighed again. He had been doing that a lot since the discovery on Tuesday evening.

Here they were, just seventy-two hours later and his safe haven was no more.

Ewan pondered when it had all gone wrong. He supposed if he was honest with himself, it was probably well over a year ago. Heaven knows, he didn't need the money but with most of his friends moving out of the city and him still single, he had decided to get a flatmate.

He had the space; the income would be a tax write off. It made sense. His brother's girlfriend knew someone looking for a place. He was in finance, not a playboy, knew how to cook. On paper, Cole was just what he was looking for.

In fact, once he'd moved in, Cole was everything Fiona had said he was. Funny with a dry sense of humour, he liked to go out. Picked up after himself and liked to cook elaborate meals in his spare time. In the seventeen months that Cole had been living here, they had formed a bond. Dam it, he had classed him as a friend. They socialised together. They were like brothers. No. They weren't brothers. And now he knew they were never really friends.

His phone began to buzz against his chest. Without faulting a step, he reached in and retrieved and answered it. "Hello?" Instantly his broad smile returned. "How is life in sleepy Beechend? Have you been drinking in the graveyard? Handed in your homework yet?"

"You are hilarious Ewan! And no, I've done none of those things. Besides, I didn't do the drinking in the graveyard. My friends did!" Rhys was so naïve back then. Ewan held in the snort of derision as he thought of the group they had hung out with. Where were they all now? He stopped himself, thinking about it hurt. Even now.

"So how is it, really?" He rounded the last corner and headed straight through the park.

"Nothing seems to have changed much. All flowers and hedges, grass and trees."

"Sounds like heaven!" Ewan sighed again; he was almost home.

"Why don't you come down next weekend? Heaven knows I could do with my big brother right now." Rhys chuckled softly down the phone. "I just mean, it would be nice to see a friendly face."

Ewan nodded knowingly, "I'll make the arrangements and see you in a week. Think you can cope until then?" They both laughed, deep and surprisingly alike. "You know, you can come back to London, any time."

"Thanks, I think I'm exactly where I need to be right now. Funny thing is, I'm not that shocked or heartbroken. What does that say about me?"

Ewan took a moment before he answered honestly, hoping that his brother would take his words to heart. "I think your reactions and your emotions speak more about your relationship with Fiona and your amazing ability to give your all. I think, deep down, you knew she wasn't the one. You're right, take the time. But don't forget that you don't have to stay away, you have friends here, you have me."

"I know, I'm just grateful for the change of scenery. This job will last at least ten months and the timing couldn't be better. I'll see you next week."

"See you Friday." The call ended as he walked into his building and began climbing the stairs. Bracing himself for what was to come, he let himself into the apartment. It was quiet. The tell-tale signs of being empty. He didn't waste his breath calling out Cole's name. Ewan neither wanted to see him nor speak with him.

After making himself a drink, he fired up the laptop and set about reading the report. It was bad. There was no mistaking it, but there were a few tricks up his sleeve that could save the account. He sent the email over to Simon and closed the laptop.

It was at this point that he first noticed the half-filled boxes in the corner of the room. He felt a pang, he was losing a mate. The rent was inconsequential, but the friendship, was harder to replace.

Cradling his tumbler, he allowed himself to consider his future life in the city. It wasn't what it used to be. Maybe his little brother had the right idea. Getting out of London was sounding more and more appealing.

Chapter Three

Sadie

The sound of laughter rolled off them. Sadie looked up at the heavens in mock jest, she secretly loved the sight though. They looked so happy, even though it was yet again at her expense.

"You fell in the hedge!" More laughter sounded as Mae gasped to get her words out between fits of delight. "I wish I had been there with a camera! Classic." Tabby caught her mother's eye as she hung the last of the bunting in the already elaborately decorated garden. 'Sorry' she mouthed in her direction. They both knew there was little point in keeping secrets from her Auntie Mae.

They weren't related in the conventional sense unless you counted their shared passion for tea, chocolate and creativity. Mae was Sadie's rock. The one person that she truly relied upon. They met on Tabby's first day of school, oh so many years ago. Her lad, JJ, was a year older. A chip off the old block. Mae had taken Sadie under her wing when she saw her sobbing. Whilst her little girl, who was oblivious to her mother's distraught emotional state, had waved her goodbye and headed into the classroom with a beaming smile.

Sadie had been thrilled to discover that they lived across the village green from one another. Since that day they had been through everything together. Friends to the end.

Mae was a true inspiration, and Sadie was certain that her friend had a strength and compassion inside her like no other. Her ability to console and support others over the years and in turn, showing her how to do the same when the time came. Mae's husband of almost a decade, Mike, had passed away eight years earlier. It had been a devastating shock, the whole village grieved and rallied round. Sadie had been there to help her as she cried. She tried her best to hold their families together, whilst Mae mourned the love of her life.

Three years later, Sadie had opened her shop 'Craftiness'. Mae had been her very first customer, she couldn't knit and told anyone who would listen that she wasn't even sure she liked woolly hats. But she had been there, supporting and bolstering her each time there was a knock back. Over the last two years, their relationship had settled in to an equal partnership. Each knew the other so well that often there was no need for words.

They had shared many cups of tea, glasses of wine and laughter sessions. They were two peas in a pod. Sadie wasn't sure where she or Tabby would be now without her. She very much doubted that she would have had the gumption to go after her dreams and attempt opening a shop without the slightest understanding of how to run a business. But she had, with the support and encouragement Mae had so loving provided. Sadie now felt like a whole new person.

It had been a blessing to see that it wasn't just the two women who had hit it off. JJ had instantly taken Tabitha under his wing. Adopting her as a little sister, they had played together, and their bond was still going strong.

Now JJ was leaving in a few weeks for university, something they were all having mixed emotions about. It seemed only fitting that they had an end of summer bash to send him off to uni life in style.

She stood in the shade of the house and watched as Mae and Tabby continued to add fabric bunting to the low hedges and picket fence that surrounded the edge of the garden. The green fields beyond led to the river that was little more than a stream during the warmer months of the year.

The high-pitched squeals of delight reached her ears on the breeze. No doubt, the local children were playing in the cool waters and swinging on the rope that JJ and Tabby had built so many years before.

Just one more year and it would be her daughter they would be sending off into the world. The thought of that terrified her. Her daughter was still so young, and she had so much more to teach her. The idea of Tabby being out in the world, being an adult made her heart ache. She made a pact with herself that she wouldn't waste a moment of the year they had left before she left Beechend.

Tabby

Several hours later and the party was in full swing. The meat had been charcoaled to within an inch of its life, and most of it had been consumed within minutes of being put out on the table. The drinks were flowing, and the music had everyone in a great end of summer mood. Tabby had finally made her wishes known about the new school year. It was going to be her year; not being hidden by JJ's enormous shadow at school. She wanted to be her own person.

She couldn't deny that she was going to miss him when he was away, but she was looking forward to seeing what life would be like without a big brother watching her every move.

"So, you're going to try out for drama club Jelly belly?" JJ raised his eyebrows at her. It was a loaded question. His eyes twinkled at her and she knew there was more coming… "Are you sure that you really want to go up against… well, you know!" Tabby stared at him with a sickly-sweet smile, even though she could feel the panic rising inside her. Acting was what she wanted to do, now for the performance of a lifetime! Doing all she could to handle her emotions, holding her smile fixed in place.

"It may come with challenges, but it's what I want." Oh gosh, Tabby's voice sounded a lot steadier than she felt. She glanced around the small group briefly, taking in their smiling expressions. JJ nodded and briefly raised his glass in her direction. See, she was a natural... if they couldn't see her nerves, she must be good!

If only thinking about being good at something made it so.

"Our Tabby has the voice of an angel; you give it all you've got love!" Mae sung out to her.

Auntie Mae was the angel. No doubt about that! Tabby let out the breath she hadn't realised she'd been holding. The air was hot and the sun's rays beat down on them causing the trickle of sweat down her back. "Go after your dreams honey, don't let haters dictate your life!" Unconsciously, her smile broadened. She wanted this year to be great. Scratch that, she needed it to be great. Her final year at school before she left for the great unknown.

"Honey, if this is what you want, go for it!" Her mum beamed at her, gently placing her hand on Tabby's arm. "I'm going to check if everyone has got drinks. Be back in a bit." Sadie made her way towards the house and out of sight.

"We've got your back!" JJ announced to the surprise of the rest of the group. "I just don't want you to get hurt, I feel bad that I won't be there to look out for my little Jelly belly anymore!" He winked at Tabby and nudged her in the arm almost knocking her drink from her hand. They all laughed, and the conversation moved on to a tale of the two of them climbing the apple trees in the orchard, in the village when they were eight and nine. Technically the orchard belongs to an extremely rich family, and they weren't really allowed to be there. But people round here seem to gloss over those details.

Despite them not being related, somehow people at school all thought they were brother and sister. It was quite ridiculous, they looked nothing alike, lived at different houses, but no one had done anything to quell the rumours. It hadn't really bothered Tabby when she was younger, she liked having a 'big brother' to protect her in the playground. But since joining the comprehensive school, things were different. Tabby was older and wanted to be her own person. JJ's 'over-protective behaviour' was more of an annoyance now. Tabby had noticed a change between them last summer. Neither of them even acknowledged it, but it was there. She felt it. She had followed his lead as always and tried her best to ignore the tingle she felt when he walked up to her. Tabby had become even quieter, not wanting to draw attention to herself or the feelings that wouldn't go away. But in doing so she had become less like herself. She wasn't truly sure who she was anymore, but she was going to find out.

She didn't want to be in anyone's shadow. She was not JJ's 'lil sis'. Not Jelly belly. She was Tabby Mirada. This year, people would see that, hopefully.

Rhys

Rhys had been braving the BBQ for about twenty minutes when he first caught a glimpse of Sadie from across the sun-scorched lawn. She was wearing a long summer dress that showed off some of her curves whilst remaining modest.

A beaming smile showed that she was in her element. Mingling with others from around the village, she was light on her feet almost as if she was floating across the garden. Rhys was not sure how long he stood staring as she made her way back and forth. He knew that he needed to fix what happened, he just hoped that she would forgive him and his behaviour the other day.

Taking a deep and somewhat calming breath Rhys tentatively stepped out of the crowd towards her. She spun around and almost danced up the path towards him. Her eyes locked with his and he smiled at her. Rhys unexpectedly felt the familiar pull in his gut. Her eyes, he could stare at them forever. She stumbled as she continued forward. He instinctively reached out to catch her. No longer making eye contact she suddenly looked uncomfortable that she had been caught staring. Rhys didn't try to hide the chuckle that escaped. Her head shot up and she silently challenged him with a look that told him all he needed to know.

"We meet again!" Smooth Rhys, not cheesy at all! Inwardly he cursed his stupidity. Strangely, Sadie continued to smile timidly up at him. "Look Sadie, I'm so sorry about the other day, I was way out of order. I blame the long drive and road rage. Forgive me?" He was rambling, but the change of facial expression didn't pass by him.

"You recognised me?" She questioned then glanced around as if expecting to find the culprit waving at her. "How? Wait…" She glanced at him again, realisation dawned, her smile crept up to her eyes, those beautiful eyes that glowed amber in the afternoon sun. They were glistening. "Rhys? Wow, you um, you are back!" Her hand reached out and grazed his arm. If only for a moment, it was like lightning. She pulled her arm back as though she thought twice about her actions. The skin seemed to tingle, and he felt his pulse quicken.

"The one and only. You look great by the way! You live here still?" Rhys wanted to know everything about her but was afraid his eagerness would scare her off.

She suddenly looked flustered, reaching up and hooking her wild locks behind her ear. No ring. Did that mean she was single or just not married? He glanced around looking for angry eyes that would probably be boring into his brain. Nope, none that he could see. Perfect.

"Thank you, yes, you are forgiven. You look great too, umm, I can't believe I didn't recognise you!" Her cheeks were flushed and there was a rosy glow on her shoulders that he was sure would transform into a warm tan over the coming days. "So, what brings you back?" She indicated that she was heading inside, and Rhys fell in step beside her, taking the tray of empty glasses and bottles that she had been carrying.

"Work, believe it or not. A commission came up at work. They said I was the guy for the job, so here I am." He may have missed out on some details, but it was still the truth. Sadie nodded as she started to sort the rubbish into different bags. She then walked around the kitchen, making herself look busy, he wondered if he was making her nervous. "What about you? You're still here, husband, kids?" She chuckled at the question, he already knew the answer to, at least he hoped that he did.

"No husband, just Tabby, my daughter." She beamed… Wow a daughter. Didn't see that coming. Although a cute little six-year-old with Sadie's hair was running around the garden, that was probably her.

"Wow, is the father not in the picture?" That was an insensitive question, she stared at Rhys wearily, only for a second before hiding her emotions. He thought she was well rehearsed at doing that. Not letting the world see what she was feeling. Apart from when she blew up at him yesterday. "Sorry, that was a little too intrusive."

"No, he's not in the picture." Sadie handed Rhys a cold bottle that she had just opened. She held onto it as he went to take it from her. "Oh, are you driving? I can get you something else." He told her that he had decided to leave the race car at home.

Her laughter sounded like gentle bells ringing in his ears, soft and delicate. They remained in the kitchen far longer than was socially acceptable, talking about the party, some of the guests, the village, the weather, the government, and the price of milk. It was all meaningless chit chat. Rhys was a gonna, and hung on her every word. If his brother could see him now, he'd tear him a new one. Thank god, he wasn't here.

"Look, tell me to shut up and I will…" Rhys paused taking a deep breath, she tilted her head to the side slightly, her gaze permitting him to continue. "I heard about what happened to Darren. I'm sorry I never made it back for the funeral. I didn't hear until almost a year after it happened. By then, coming home… it just didn't feel right…" Sadie took a long drink from her bottle. She nodded along but didn't offer a word. He felt that he had to fill the void. "Darren was a great guy! The best! I… I miss him. I'm sure you do too…"

"It was a long time ago. You've been living your life. Darren was one to live life to the fullest." Rhys chuckled as memories of his old school friend filled his mind. "You two were the fairy tale couple back then."

Sadie

He smiled warmly and chuckled, oblivious to the harsh tone in Sadie's voice that she tried her best to hide. A great guy! Those who knew Darren thought that her memories were different to everyone else's. She desperately tried to keep the façade in place. Not wanting her bitterness to seep out and be seen by those around her. But the reality of Darren and Sadie was anything but a fairy tale.

"I had best get back out there, they'll be wondering where I've got to!" Rhys nodded, his smile slipping briefly before he regained his composure. "Enjoy the bar-be-que! See you around the village." Sadie didn't give him the chance to reply, she picked up the bottle and headed back into the garden, a determined air that hadn't been there before.

As she made her way back to Tabby, she wondered how long this project was going to take, was Rhys going to be back for a while? If so, how long was a while and was she going to be seeing him regularly? He'd only been back a few days and already they had talked twice. This was ridiculous, she was overthinking things. Focus, she chastised, wanting to stop letting her mind wander to things that didn't need thinking about.

"Thanks for that Sadie, you can relax, grab a bite to eat..." She glanced at Mae, who smiled at her knowingly. "Earth to Sadie... quick Tabby, get your mam some grub before she wastes away." The group burst into sniggers as she handed her a paper plate piled high with lovely but naughty things including the cheese that was dripping down the side of the burger.

"Waste away indeed! I would never get the chance with you cooking such amazing dishes just down the road." The two grinned at each other and then Mae winked and inclined her head to something behind Sadie. She turned unwillingly to see Rhys on the other side of the garden glancing in their direction. This was not a good sign. Her nosy best friend, who was continuously trying to set her up with any guy with a pulse under the age of forty, had spotted Rhys. Not just Rhys, who in Mae's eyes fit Sadie's match description perfectly, but Rhys who was looking at her. She felt her face flush. Mae's smile widened. Not good. Not good at all.

Chapter Four

Sadie

Sunday mornings. Without a doubt, Sunday morning is the best time of the week for Sadie. Everything seems to be a little bit slower on a Sunday morning. An entire nation can be a little bit lazier (if they are lucky enough to have a day off). Unfortunately, Sadie is not that lucky, but she does start the day a little later on a Sunday. Getting up she does her normal morning routine but takes the time to enjoy the morning sun shining through the window into the kitchen. Percolator coffee, instead of her normal instant, which is by far more superior. She sits and strokes Bruno as he lies obediently by her feet. Peace, that is what Sunday mornings are. Pure bliss at the end of a hectic week.

Inevitably, the harmony of a Sunday morning doesn't last forever. An hour if Sadie is fortunate. It just so happens that this Sunday, Sadie was extremely blessed. She had a little over an hour to rest and recoup before opening the shop to the public. Tabby was having a much-deserved rest and lie in this morning, so by the time Sadie left for work, the house was still quiet and undisturbed by teenagers.

Despite the peace and quiet, that a Sunday morning frequently offers, her short opening times at the shop were often quite a different matter during the main busy season. This was great for Sadie, and the success of her business brought her a lot of joy. A quaint crafty shop in a small village, in the middle of no-where, had all the makings of a failed business. But word spread around the local area and soon Sadie had grown quite a cluster of faithful locals from all walks of life, who appeared to love crafting just as much as she did. Things had grown from strength to strength and the business was flourishing.

The 'Craftiness' shop was located down the main street that ran through the village. It was situated in a row of adorable shops that had been in the village at least a hundred years. The charm of the building was just one element that had crafters flocking in droves.

She was fortunate to have bagged such a prime spot and only the second shop that you saw as you entered the village from the direction of the nearest motorway. Unfortunately, Beechend's parking situation wasn't ideal. But her regulars never seemed to mind and new customers put it down to the idealistic appeal and joked that this was village life. Sadie didn't let the thought of bigger and better craft shops deter her on her journey.

As you drew up outside, the traditional double-fronted facade was always interesting and seasonal to entice people through the door. Rows of shelving and display cases gave perusing customers space and hopefully lots of choice. Sadie had been careful not to clutter up the space, but offered an order in service which had become popular and in all surprise, it was this decision that made her the greatest income and people liked to buy in bulk when it came to craft supplies.

Sadie wasn't rich by any means, but the income from the shop meant that she had been able to find her and Tabby a comfortable home without the support of her parents. This had been something that she was extremely grateful for.

They had moved from their rented home next to the church into their cottage near the green. In truth the move had barely been two-hundred metres, but owning their own place meant everything. Since then, they had taken the time to make it theirs. She cherished it, wonky stairs, the plumbing that had a habit of either scolding you or freezing you mid shower, and the over grown garden that had taken several summers to get back to blooming once again.

The chime of the bell brought her back to reality, "Good morning, Rosie, back again? It's lovely to see you. What can I help you with today?" Sadie was in her element at the shop. She loved to catch up with her regulars.

They often popped in and showed her pictures of the things they had made. Rosie was one such lady who loved all things wool, knitting up a storm was her second favourite pastime. Her first…

"Oh, Sadie dear, I heard about your little mishap the other day." Rosie was staring intently. Hanging on to what she hoped was going to be juicy gossip that she could lord over the other ladies in the weekly knitting group. "Quite a dishy chap I heard. And he helped you after you fell."

Sadie was not surprised by the query from Rosie Butcher. She was notoriously the biggest gossip in the whole village, well almost... there were several contenders for the top spot. After many an inquisition, she managed to dodge the conversation with little more than a shrug and an 'I'll be fine.

What did seem to catch her off guard during her short time of opening was the sheer number of ladies who seemed to have run out of their crafting supplies today. Especially as she had seen a few of them earlier in the week. They seemed to be learning new tricks from Rosie. She chuckled at the thought. They were a lovely bunch, chatty and sweet. But with not all that much going on in our sleepy village, any sort of news, including a new man, was a prize to possess.

They seemed relentless in their endeavour and by the time the end of the day had nearly arrived, Sadie never wanted to hear Rhys's name again.

Then the door chimed, a small groan escaped her lips. Who could it possibly be now, the whole village seemed to have been in during the last hour and a half. "Sadie!"

Relief coursed through her at the sound of her own name. "Mae, what brought you in today?" She beamed briefly then continued to tidy the shelves that always seemed to be so unruly.

After a moment, she halted and spun on the spot to face her. I wasn't like Mae to be so quiet, was something wrong? However, the moment she caught her eye she knew there was nothing to worry about. She had that knowing smile plastered on her face. The sheer number of inquisitive visitors that had been in today was merely the warm-up to the main star of the show. "Should I put the kettle on? Or will I be needing something a little stronger?" Sadie let the sigh escape her lips and she gathered the last of her cleaning supplies from around her and headed to the back. "Flip the sign round will you?"

The lock clicked and Mae exploded like a volcano. "I was hoping that you would have come round before opening. It's all over the village. You were seen. With a man. A young man. A young handsome man. A young handsome man who appears to be one hundred percent available. Come on Sadie. I need to know everything." It was a miracle that she had managed to keep talking like this. Sadie didn't think she had taken a breath throughout her speech. She really was something. "Are you going to speak? The village"

"The village likes to gossip if the postman is five minutes late." She rolled her eyes and shrugged. She did not get the big deal of the situation. Where did these people get their information from!

"I think he was over an hour later than usual, there'd been a traffic accident and he was held back in the build-up over the hill. But that isn't the point." Sadie finished making the tea and fished out the biscuit tin from the top shelf. She gestured towards the back door which led to what she could only describe as a picturesque courtyard that she had put a few chairs and potted plants in. "The rumours! They say that you needed stitches after he ran you down and that he gallantly carried you to his car and drove you to the medical centre for you to be seen to." Sadie had to laugh at this. "Old Mr Rivers told me that he had seen the new gentleman handling a small box that looked suspiciously like it held a piece of important jewellery." This caught her attention and made her pause.

"I did not need stitches! I already told you all about it. I do not know where these rumours come from." She sipped her tea and picked out a custard cream. "Besides, you saw me yesterday and know I am perfectly fine!"

"And the ring?" Mae questioned while searching for the last chocolate digestive. "You said nothing about a ring. I got the impression that you didn't think all that much of him. You don't waste any time!"

Sadie's mouth fell open in shock. She couldn't believe that Mae was listening to idle gossip. "I, I don't know anything about a ring!"

Mae snorted a laugh and looked at her sympathetically. "You are so easy to wind up." She shook her head. "I wish you could see your face. Granted the gossip tree likes to embellish the truth. But the outright lie of him having a ring after less than a week. That is a bit much, even for them."

Sadie took the time to ponder this for a while. Strange. There is always an element of truth to the village tales. "Did anyone actually see a ring?" Curiosity was getting the better of her now. She cursed herself for speaking her mind at the sight of Mae's knowing smile.

"Um, no, I don't think so, but the gossip circle was pretty set." Mae shrugged and managed to lose the biscuit in the tea. "I guess he's not as available as we first thought!"

Strangely, that comment unsettled Sadie. She could not see why but unease had come over her all of a sudden.

Chapter Five

Ewan

A week after his brother moved back to Beechend, Ewan was still living in a sort of limbo. He had managed to avoid Cole entirely but had noticed that the boxes had morphed from meagre to full and sealed ready for moving. It hadn't passed him by that there was no forwarding address. The whole situation had irked him to no end. He couldn't wait to be away this afternoon and heading to the country.

Ewan had managed to shift some things around at work, he'd come in early three mornings this week to make up the time owing. At noon he was out the door, heading home to grab his things then to King's Cross station.

When he reached the apartment, something wasn't right. He could hear the music from the hallway. Letting himself in he came face to face with Fiona.

"Oh!" She looked startled by the sight of him then called out for Cole. He came round the corner with a wooden spoon in one hand and a saucepan in the other.

"Hon, I need you to try this! I added less garlic than last time…" Cole stopped dead at the sight of him. The three of them stood like cowboys about to draw and shoot.

Ewan broke the immediate tension, "I'll give it a miss thanks. The garlic makes that sauce, thought it smelt a bit funny in here." The sarcasm dripped from every word. It was so unlike him. He didn't like it but somehow couldn't stop himself. He turned and faced Fiona, raising an eyebrow, he stood still, daring her to contradict him.

"I think it's best if I leave Cole."

"Great idea!" Ewan sang as he reached behind him and opened the door. Without another word, she walked out. Ewan slammed the door behind her. He was so angry. How dare she come into his home.

Spinning round to face off with Cole, he was disappointed to see that he had already walked back to the kitchen.

"What are you doing here?" Cole's question and accusatory tone made him see red. He was pleased to see that Cole knew it was the wrong thing to say. "I mean, I'm surprised that you are home this time of day."

"I am going away for the weekend. Have you found somewhere to live?"

"I have, I'm moving in with Fiona. She was here to help me move."

"So, you're moving from one Knight's house to another?" Ewan raised his brow a second time, taken aback by his former friend's cavalier behaviour.

Returning to Beechend

This time Cole had the sense to stay quiet. "I want you gone before I am back on Sunday. That should be more than enough time. That woman is not welcome here. I'll be speaking with the concierge on the way out. She is banned. Be thankful that my brother is allowing her to stay in the house. It won't be long, and you'll be evicted from there too. If I were you, I'd start looking for a new place to live." Ewan stormed out of the kitchen. In the time it took him to shower, dress and grab his bag, he had begun the road back to his calmer self. The guilt he felt for the situation was unbearable. When would this end?

On his return to the main living area, he found that the kitchen was once again immaculate, and the fresh lemony scent was doing something to mask the garlic sauce. He grabbed some fruit and a bottle of water for the train and turned to leave. "I'm sorry that my actions have hurt you." Ewan stopped in his tracks but didn't turn to face Cole. "Neither I nor Fi wanted to hurt you. It was something that just happened." After a moment's silence, Ewan continued to walk towards the front door. "I won't insult you by asking for forgiveness, I don't deserve it. But I want you to know that I'm sorry. I counted you as a friend." By now Ewan's hand was on the door handle. He waited a fraction longer then turned to face the man who had stolen his brother's fiancé.

"Do you love her?" It had been a thought floating around his head for over a week. He waited and saw his ex-roommates face light up. He looked like he was struggling to hold back a smile. Failing it came across as a cocky smirk. "Don't worry, I don't need to know.

The pair of you deserve each other. Leave the key with the concierge. I'll return your deposit after I've returned." Cole gave one short swift nod of acknowledgement before Ewan left the apartment.

Later, once he was sat on the train, Ewan took the time to reflect on the last week and a bit. The discovery had been a shock initially, but over the course of the week, Ewan had realised there had been signs. He was angry with his brother. Someone whom he had trusted had caused so much damage. Was it any wonder his brother had high tailed it out of the city? Was he much better? He didn't compare his pain to the pain Rhys must be feeling, but Fiona was going to be his sister. The betrayal stung a little.

He had told himself that he was going to Beechend to support his brother, but partly he knew he needed to get away. Maybe it was time to look for somewhere in the country. He couldn't see himself gardening and keeping chickens, but a slower pace sounded good right now.

"Ewan!" Rhys was standing in the carpark of the train station. He patted him on the back as he took his overnight bag from his hand. "How was the journey?"

"It was quiet and quick, starving now though!" They laughed and joked as they made their way to Rhys's car. It was his only extravagant purchase. Ewan hated it. Didn't see that there was a need for a car in the city. But here he saw that it stood out a mile from the other vehicles in the car park. He chuckled inwardly, "Lunch?"

"Definitely!"

They were almost through with eating when Rhys stopped talking and stood up waving at a tall brunette across the other side of the room. This jovial behaviour had surprised Ewan but in a good way. He was pleased to see that his brother was doing well. There were no outward signs that he was heartbroken. It didn't mean that he wasn't, but he was certainly hiding it well if he was.

"Mae! It's lovely to see you again," the brunette was standing at their table, when she turned to face him, it was like lightning. The woman was a goddess. He'd say mid to late thirties, her smile was captivating. "So, what brought you into town today? I would have given you a lift if I had known." Rhys clearly knew this woman well if he was offering her lifts. He wondered for a moment if Mae was the reason his brother was smiling so soon after becoming single. He couldn't tell. "Mae, this is my brother, Ewan." He stood and held out his hand. Her smile lit up her face and she took his offered hand at once. "He's staying for the weekend."

"It's nice to meet you, Ewan." She let go of his hand abruptly as a shock of static electricity surged between them. "It's this carpet, always getting shocks." She laughed at herself. Her voice was light and delicate, and he found himself hanging on her every word. "I'm only popping in to collect a few things I ordered for JJ. I came in for a cold drink before I head home." Rhys was nodding along as if this all made perfect sense to him. Who was JJ he wondered? "Did you enjoy your food? Always good in here. We try to keep it a secret mind, don't want the tourists clogging up the place!" She laughed again, she glanced at her watch, made her goodbyes and she was gone. She had been a breath of fresh air. It was only after she was gone that he realised he'd not checked for a ring. Damb it!

"Earth to Ewan! Hello? Are you going to finish those onion rings?" Coming out of his trance he pushed the dish over to his brother no longer hungry. He knew he was in trouble. "Wow! You have got it bad!" Rhys was laughing now, not having caught what was making him laugh so derisively, Ewan merely smiled and downed the last of his drink.

Mae

Rhys's brother was so tall! When he had stood and accepted her hand, she had been surprised by his stature. He was broad-shouldered and there was something about him... Mae smiled to herself as she walked the short distance back to her car. Those eyes. And so quiet. She wondered what his voice would be like. Then she mentally chastised herself for her silly thoughts. Her only child was leaving for university soon, now was not the time to be going gaga over some bloke she would never see again.

"Wake up Mae, you are a thirty-eight-year-old widow. You have lumps and bumps in places you would rather not think about. You certainly can't compare to the twenty-somethings he probably spends his time within the city." She sighed, resigned to the fact that she would never be with someone that handsome and successful again.

Once she was buckled up and back on the road towards home, she rang Sadie on the car's internal system. It was one of those modern gadgets that she had chastised Mike for at the time. Now, she didn't know how she got along without it. "Mae!" Sadie sang down the phone. "How did the shopping excursion go?"

"It was good, finally got the last of the items on the list. He has everything he could need!" She sighed again. The thought of JJ moving away tore at her heart. She had always imagined that when he flew the nest, that would be her and Mike's time. They had talked of travelling, lazy weekends, just a slower pace. Now she would be rattling round in that house all by herself. A tear escaped and ran down her face. Mentally slapping herself, she took a deep breath and focused on what Sadie was saying.

"I couldn't believe that you missed it! There were milk bottles everywhere on the main road through the village. Luckily, it appears that only a few have smashed. But the smell is getting pretty bad in this heat. Some of the ladies are out there now with buckets of water trying to rinse the milk down the drains. What a palaver!" Picturing the scene of carnage as some of the village's older generations tried to clean the milk off the street brought a fresh wave of tears to her eyes as she exploded in laughter. "No one was hurt thankfully, but Mr Winters needs to sort out the gate, that's the third time this week Betsy, his goat, had escaped."

"The poor thing, maybe she was looking for Mr Winters." She chuckled again as the laughter started to die down in the chest. "I'll pop over later and see if I can secure a new latch."

"If I were you, I'd get us all some nose plugs. The pungent smell of curdled milk is starting to turn my stomach." Sadie sounded as though she was pinching her nose for effect. Then she laughed down the phone.

"I'm just pulling into the village. No nose plugs I'm afraid, but I see what you mean about the milk bottles, oh dear. The milk float has seen better days. Ryan wasn't hurt was he?" Mae pulled up in front of her house but didn't disconnect the call.

"He'll live, just a few bruises. He wasn't going fast after all!"

Mae was nodding along. She wanted to tell her about Rhys's hunky brother but thought it would be nicer to have a long chat at the pub over a few drinks this evening instead.

"Are you up for a night at the Crown?" She heard Sadie groan down the phone.

"I am such an old woman! I'm still a little sore from the bike incident last week. I'll give it a miss. But you should head out for the night. Get all the milk float gossip!" She chuckled but Mae could tell she was dead serious about gaining intel.

"I might see if JJ wants to go out with his mum, even just for one drink." She pondered his reaction. He would, she knew, but she didn't want to stop him from spending time with his mates before he left.

"Great plan! We'll catch up on Sunday, you can give me all the gossip then." After a brief goodbye, she disconnected the call and started the arduous task of unloading the car of all the things she had collected. Sadie hadn't been wrong about the smell! Wow, maybe she would fill up the watering can and head down to help.

There were several of the village locals at the green when she arrived. They had set up a long line from the town hall and were passing the pots, pans and buckets along to dilute the milk. She found a wider gap and joined in.

In this part of the village there was a distinct lack of trees and the sun was able to beat down on them causing Mae to soon feel the effects of heat exhaustion. She was wishing she had grabbed her hat from the car.

It was after about twenty minutes of mindless water passing that she spotted the sports car. She saw him in the passenger seat. Him and his brother seemed to be engaged in conversation and he appeared to be quite animated in the discussion. He could talk then. She smiled, wondering why she was so taken with him.

Mike had passed suddenly over eight years ago. In the first year of grief, Sadie had been her rock. It took a long time for her to feel normal again. But in all the time since, no man had ever begun to measure up. In honesty, she hadn't looked at anyone like that since before she was married. She was sure that Mike would be looking down and having a good laugh at her expense right now. Oh well, C'est la vie. Maybe this was the sign that she was ready to start dating again. She did miss the closeness and security of her husband. It didn't mean she wanted to get married. But it would be nice to have someone she could rely on. A guy to continue life's journey. Thing was, Mike had been one of a kind. He had loved her for her quirky and unique sense of humour. Her weird habits and the way she viewed the world differently from others.

She had loved him for who he was too, but his acceptance of her just made her love him more.

Perhaps, one day she would find someone new

who would love her for her. She wasn't ready to give up on love just yet. Not like Sadie seemed to. She exhaled slowly, Sadie was one in a million and she wished she would give someone the chance to discover that.

"Mum!" She spun around towards the sound, her light footing making her appear as if she was flying. "What is going on?" JJ had screwed up his face at the smell as he had approached.

"Perfect timing!" She handed him the watering can and looped her arm through his. "Spilled milk!"

"Explains the smell. What was the cause this time?" She smiled up at him, always amazed that he had outgrown her a few years earlier.

"Betsy, she got out. I was going to wander over and check that the gate was secure."

"Again," JJ chuckled at the absurdity of their reality. "I'll do it mum, no worries." He gave her arm a reassuring squeeze. He was such a kind thoughtful lad.

"Thanks, I was thinking, do you fancy a drink down the pub with your mum this evening. I know it's not cool. But just the one before you go into town with your mates?"

"Great idea, I'll go check the gate. You should go take a shower. No offence, but you need one." She swatted him playfully and took the watering can.

"Dinner will be ready in forty minutes." They went their separate ways and Mae decided that she would make a bit more of an effort this evening. Jeans were so blah. Maybe one of her flowing skirts. A little perfume and she could leave her hair down. Maybe...

Chapter Six

Ewan

In most places, a bar on a Friday night would be three deep and you would struggle to get a standing space let alone a seat. Not in Beechend. The pub was quite sizeable for such a small village.

With all this knowledge, Ewan was surprised by how busy the pub was when they entered.

At first glance, he struggled to find a spare table. "I'll get the round in. You find us somewhere to perch." He slapped Rhys on the back and headed to the bar. A young girl maybe early twenties was serving. She was friendly but not flirty which was a fresh change. She made small talk, asked if he was passing through or here to stay. Some would say that the conversation could be classed as suggestive, but the tone was an inquisition, he was a stranger. He had grown up since he last stepped foot in here. "Thanks," he paid for the drinks and left her a generous tip and turned to find that Rhys had located two spare seats. The table however was being used already. He took a double take. It was the girl, no woman, from earlier on today. Her hair was down, and she looked at ease. The lad sat to her left was nursing what looked like a soft drink.

"Ewan!" His brother was standing and waving him over. "Mae has kindly offered to share the table." He nodded and smiled briefly at her. He was once again tongue-tied. "You've met Mae, this is her son, JJ." Son! Relief coursed through him. He was now wondering if these seats had been saved for the husband. He stole a glance at her hand. No ring. Interesting. Ewan sat down and completed the cosy foursome as JJ thrust out his hand to shake his. Instinctively he reached and shook his hand, surprised by the firmness and forwardness of the action by someone who was probably no older than the barmaid.

"Jacob, you're Rhys's big brother? Pleased to meet you." The lad held his gaze, it was obvious that he was trying to suss him out. Maybe he had caught him looking at his mum's ringless fingers.

"Yep, nice to meet you too." He smiled and took a sip of his beer. It wasn't bad, the taste had surprised him.

"Craft beer," Mae announced. "They've been working on this one for a while now. It's their best so far and the others were no slouches!" His expression was warm and inviting.

"It's good, this would sell in the city!" He took the time to admire the colour and took another taste. It didn't disappoint.

"So, you're originally from Beechend?" Mae was making polite conversation. "How come you left? We love it here." She stared at the brothers in turn and waited for either of them to respond.

"The usual, we both left for university, stayed away for work commitments. We lost mum and dad a few years back. So, we haven't been here for a while." Mae was nodding along as Rhys spoke. Jacob was staring at the bar. Or maybe the barmaid behind the bar. He tried to hold back the smile. What he wouldn't give to be starting out all over again.

"I'm sorry about your parents. It must be difficult to return." The sympathy in her voice was sincere and genuine. "Has it changed much from what you remember?"

The brothers chortled, "Nope!" Ewan responded. "Maybe it looks a bit smaller than I remember. But the character is the same. Does Mr Winters still keep goats?" Her eyes shone with mirth. Nodding her head, she was struggling to get the words out. "Nothing changes, it's comforting."

After another round of drinks courtesy of Rhys, they discovered all about the drama of the day. Several locals came over and regaled them the tale of the milk float swerving to avoid the local celebrity. How the bottles of milk had toppled from the back. By the fourth time the story was retold, not one bottle had survived the fall and Ryan had been thrown from the front landing in Mrs Potts' rose bush. Covered in bruises and scratches, the ambulance had taken him to the nearby hospital.

Jacob rolled his eyes at the absurdity of the truth being stretched. The reality had been that the bottles had toppled when Ryan had swerved, but only half had broken. His minor injuries had been a bumped arm and several small cuts. All of which had happened after, when he had tried unsuccessfully to round up Betsy and keep her away from the debris. The folks of Beechend sure did like the drama!

At around half-past ten, Ewan's phone began to ring. It was a miracle that he had heard it. The raucous laughter that was ricocheting around the pub he reached an all-time high. He made his apologies and headed for the door to better hear the person on the other end. On the way out, he spotted Jacob now perched on a stool at the bar, he was chatting to the girl who had first served him earlier that evening. The sight made him nostalgic. What he would give to be that age and have so much in front of him to enjoy.

"Hello?" The garbled words were sounding very far away. He moved further away from the entrance and perched on a bench facing the green. "Hello? The signal isn't too good. Who is this?" He could just make out the overly cheery voice rambling on about an accident he had been in. There had been no accident. He no longer owned a car. "Sorry, you've got the wrong number!" He hung up then proceeded to block the number to prevent future calls. What had this world become?

Ewan decided to stay outside for a moment. The air here was cool compared to the stuffy atmosphere inside the pub. He wanted to get back in to talk with Mae some more, but she was so popular in these parts that the majority of their time had been spent with him on the side lines whilst locals monopolised her time.

What he had found was that his initial impression of her had been on the money. She was bubbly and kind. Liked to laugh a lot and was some sort of advice giver. There had been no fewer than six people approaching her with their problems.

Each time she had shown a gentle smile, listened to their woes and then offered what could only be described as sage advice. Each time she showed no sign of judgement, merely leading them to the solution. The first time it had been quite something to watch. She was professional yet thoughtful and not afraid to call them out on some warped truths. Particularly one bloke late fifties said he was in trouble with the Mrs. She had set him straight. Told him that he needed to get home and finish sorting out the tiling in the kitchen. As it turns out, he had started renovating their kitchen back in March. The wife was saying that she had had enough and wanted a divorce. All because of the kitchen. The bloke didn't seem to have a clue that that was the source of their problems.

The sound from the pub suddenly became louder and then muffled again as the door closed behind Mae. He stood up and turned to face her. "There you are. I'm just heading home. It's been a long day." Mae was putting on her thin jacket as she spoke. "I'm glad I saw you, didn't want you to think I had snuck out." Ewan reached forward and helped her with the tangled sleave. "I'd only planned to pop out for one drink with JJ." Her eyes sparkled.

"He seems to be getting on well with the barmaid." Ewan's voice was mischievous. "He seems a good lad, he's a credit to you."

"Thank you, he's been friendly with Debbie for a while. Think he's finally going to do something about it. Doesn't need his mum cramping his style." She came and sat on the bench, and he sat back down on the opposite side.

"I think that most teenager's mums wouldn't be in the pub in the first place. I think it's nice that you show an interest." Ewan waited patiently, she was pensive and maybe a little surprised by his comment.

"Mike, his dad, he couldn't wait to be able to take him out. He always said that having a kid was great. But that having another adult to converse with and hang with was going to be the best bit." She paused then looked at him sadly. "He passed a few years back. So now I try to do the things I know Mike would have done. I didn't want JJ to miss out. Turns out Mike was right. We were lucky when he was little. But I am so proud of the man that he is becoming. Kind and unselfish. He was supposed to be going out with his mates. He stayed in the pub with me. Well, partly with me, I think partly to see Debbie."

Ewan let it all sink in. "Let me walk you home. It's late and dark." She laughed loudly and it ended in the most adorable snort which she hastened to cover.

"It's Beechend." Mae blurted between laughs, "I don't think anyone would dare take me on in the dark!" Regardless, she hooked her arm through his. "But it is nice to find a gentleman in these here parts. You are so kind."

"Lead the way milady…" Ewan gestured with his arm, and she burst out laughing again. They walked slowly across the village green and towards the bridge over the river. For a while, they walked in companionable silence. It was nice. Although, being this close to her and inhaling her intoxicating scent was all-consuming. Then breaking the spell Ewan enquired about the sheer number of people coming to her for advice.

"Yes, it's a little odd. But I write an advice column for a small local paper." She affectionately squeezed his arm. If only she knew what he was thinking. She would probably run screaming for the hills.

"Wow, did you study journalism at university?" He wanted to know everything about her. She fascinated him.

"Well, no, I was meant to be going to University to study Art History." She pulled a face and he indicated for her to continue. "I didn't really know what I wanted to do back then. I jumped on the year-out bandwagon as a way to avoid the decision-making process. I met Mike in the second week on a train to Berlin. The rest, as they say, is history. JJ arrived almost a year later." She stopped and then gently led him to the right. They were standing in front of a picket fence. "I wanted to go to university when JJ was in school, but we didn't have the funds for me to give up work back then. I started writing a blog." She stared up at him and he instinctively tucked the loose strand of hair from her face. "People wrote in with their problems and I would offer suggestions. Just before the accident, the paper I now write for got in touch. I left my job and now write three columns a week. It pays the bills and I have found something I enjoy that hopefully helps people."

"Based on what I saw this evening, you are a natural. I think I'll be coming to you with all my worries." Ewan had spoken in jest, but Mae had immediately picked up on it.

"You can talk to me any time if you have worries. I can be discreet." She reached up on tiptoes and kissed him gently on the side of his mouth. His body was suddenly on fire. She lingered; her eyes searching his.

In a flash, he had swooped down and covered her lips with his own. A small moan escaped her as his arm snaked around her back and pulled her body to him. They stayed locked together as she moved her hands up the front of his top. For a moment he panicked and eased the pressure of his mouth on hers. She pulled him to her, parting her lips in invitation. Mae tasted sweet like honey.

When they finally parted, they were both breathless but continued to give and take soft butterfly kisses. His lips tingled and he longed to kiss her again.

Gently, he placed a finger beneath her chin and tilted her face to him. Her eyes were dark blue, and he felt like he could swim in their depths. "I am sorry. I..." Before he could finish, Mae had placed a solitary finger on his lips to silence him.

"Never apologise for kissing someone who wants to be kissed." She had snaked her hand around the back of his neck and pulled him down to meet her lips. She took the lead. She was a Goddess.

He had never felt this before. But somehow, he knew that this is what coming home felt like.

Chapter Seven

Rhys

Ewan was an amazing brother. He had been looking out for him long before their parent's untimely passing eight years earlier. Here he was again, trying to take care of him. Rhys was grateful that he had Ewan in his corner, but he didn't always need someone else to fight his battles for him. "I think that you are in the right place here. The distance is good for you. Getting away from the City, from the crowd, from... her." Ewan was ranting on about him having left the City. He had noticed that he was yet to use Fiona's given name. It was always her or she. So many times, this weekend, their conversations had left him thinking that Fiona's infidelity and betrayal had hit his brother harder than him. Granted he wasn't a saint by any means, but almost two weeks later, he just felt relief.

Rhys was relieved that they hadn't been married. He was relieved that he hadn't sold his flat like she had wanted him to. He was relieved that he no longer had to pretend to be someone he wasn't. He wasn't happy about how it happened, but deep down, he was Okay. "This living in the country lark, I could get used to it!" Ewan had been more his old self the longer he had been here. It was refreshing to see. "Now, about you and this girl you ran over with your bike. I'm sorry I didn't get to meet her. Maybe next time? But perhaps in the meantime, build some bridges. It's your job after all!" He laughed jovially as Rhys pulled the car into the station car park.

"I don't build bridges! I design buildings, there is a big difference. But I get your point. I'll swing by one day this week." Ewan nodded along, smiling. He had been so happy since he took that phone call on Friday evening. He didn't want to pry into his brother's affairs. He had assumed it was a work thing. But the sheer joy on his face had him questioning the reasons behind the change.

"You say you know her from when we were in school together? What's her name?" They were almost at the ticket barrier. "Sofie?"

"Sadie, Sadie Mirada. But she was always called…"

"Sarah." Ewan had stopped and Rhys collided with his back. "Darren's girlfriend?" The tone of his voice was different. Gone was the calm and happy Ewan.

"Yes. She was with Darren in our last year of school. He stayed back and took a year out. Why? We knew Sadie long before then, all those Sunday teas at her parents place!" Rhys was staring intently, grimacing at the memories. He couldn't decipher his brother's expression. "Ewan, are you ok?" They heard the announcement of the imminent arrival of the train to London. "Ewan?"

"I'm fine, a little surprised, but fine." They embraced briefly and Ewan walked through the barrier as the train pulled into the station.

The return to Beechend had been an interesting journey. Rhys was taking the time to mull over the goings-on so far. His brother's reaction to Sadie being the woman he almost ran over was a surprise, to say the least. He had become pale, and he was abrupt, which was a stark contrast to the breath of fresh air he had been this weekend. He knew that Ewan and Darren had been close friends. Since Darren's death, his brother had never mentioned him. He had never disclosed his feelings about what happened. Rhys had assumed that one day he would open up about it, but he never had. Maybe he should have pushed harder, but Ewan was his big brother, nothing seemed to bring him down for long.

Ewan was right about talking with Sadie though; he was going to be in Beechend for a while and it would be best all-round if they got along instead of being awkward with one another.

The cottage he was staying in was small but had everything that he needed, he just had to remember to duck under two of the beams in the kitchen. Curse his height!

Almost running Sadie down... he chuckled to himself at the thought, not the best way to meet after all this time. But she was relatively unscathed. She hadn't lost the fire from her eyes. She was different, yes. But he had known the second she had looked up at him with those big brown eyes, who she was. Seeing her had been a bigger shock than almost killing someone with his horrible, rented car.

He was sure that he'd heard through the grapevine that Sarah Mirada had not come back after university. No one called her Sarah. He wondered if folks around here even remembered that was her name.

Rhys pondered, lost in the memories of school and their family gatherings when they had been about eight or nine. She had declared to all that would listen in the playground. 'I will henceforth be known to all as Sadie Mirada!' She had been taken to the headteacher a short while later for refusing to answer a teacher's question. She had been so full of life and confidence back then. A determination that her parents tried to squash out of her. He was pleased to see that they hadn't succeeded in their attempts.

Her fiery temper didn't appear to have changed much. But she'd wavered during their tryst the other day. The Sadie he knew wouldn't have walked away or backed down in any way.

Rhys supposed that life had simply softened her. Maybe being a mum. Whatever it had been, he had the overwhelming urge to find out. He wanted to get to know her again. He wanted to find out if the girl who left all those years ago was still there, hiding just below the surface.

Rhys placed the small velvet box he'd been fiddling with back on the counter. He sighed. His life was a mess. When had everything become so complicated?

He slumped onto the stool next to him and swept a hand through his hair. He had taken to doing this so frequently that his hair had taken on a permanent messy quality.

Rhys stopped and allowed his mind to wander aimlessly, each thought triggering another memory. He rarely if ever granted himself permission to do this, as often the pain of remembering was just too much.

He was six years old, he was running across the green grass. A wooden sword waving in his right hand. Sadie ran behind him brandishing another, his brother's he was certain. She wore a makeshift patch over one eye and he turned as they battled, the swords barely making contact as they laughed so much his side had hurt. His father had called out to him and he had dropped his weapon and happily ran to embrace him. Sadie's mother had stood waiting on the veranda, her face was fixed in a line of contempt.

They had been eleven, the Christmas after they had started boarding school. Another meaningless gathering with the well to do of the county. They had been sent to the den after Sadie had refused to wear the dress her mother had chosen. She had entered the room where he was with his mother and brother. He had smirked at the sight of her as gasps rang out about the room. She was wearing baggy jeans that sported a rip at the knee. Her top hadn't met her waist and hair was left loose and curly down her back. As she had been ushered from the room he had caught a smile crossing his father's lips. His mother had turned to him and told him he could go too. She had squeezed his hand affectionately and winked at him.

At the age of seventeen, he had attended his last function at Beechend Manor. They had finished their exams and the first weekend of freedom consisted on a garden party. Ewan was away at university and his parents had given him the option not to attend. He had known that Sadie wouldn't be so fortunate, so he had agreed to go in a hope that they could finally get a chance to talk before they both left for the wider world. He had spent the best part of an hour searching the grounds for her. When he finally found her, she was down by the stream at the farthest point from the house. This had been their favourite place to play as small children. When he rounded the trees and she came in to view, he had felt his heart break. She was with someone. In their spot. Instantly, the sight of her in the arms of Darren had made his skin crawl. She hadn't seen him, so he quietly backed away into the cover of the trees that lined the path. Nothing had ever been the same since.

What was he doing filling his head with Sadie when he was supposed to be here to get back to normal. He needed to... well, he should... Oh hell! Rhys Knight had taken this job to get perspective. His brother called it 'time to recover'. The box sat there, mocking him and all his bad decisions. He picked it up and placed it in the kitchen drawer.

He was here to do a job. But first, he needed to smooth things over. Maybe if he made things up with Sadie, he could focus better on what lay ahead.

Chapter Eight

Sadie

The delivery driver was right on time, there were no customers, so Sadie took the time to help Andrew as he unloaded the boxes from the back of the van.

"So that's everything for this week. Should I let them know at the office about the ink bottles?" He was a sweetie.

"Oh, no Andrew, do not worry about it. I spoke with them, and they agreed to put some replacements on next month's delivery free of charge." He nodded in understanding. "I hope you didn't get in any bother over it."

"No Miss Mirada just got a lot on my mind at the moment." Bless him, his wife was now just a few days from her due date. Their first.

"Of course, which reminds me. I have a little something for you." His response of 'you shouldn't have' was battered away as she brought over the basket.

"Wow! This is too much." He was a little pink in

the cheeks.

"Nonsense! There are a few bits in here. Some clothes from when Tabby was little. They grow so fast she had barely gotten any use out of them. I crocheted you a little blanket and the Knitting group have made a few more bits, I think there are hats and even a cardigan." She handed him the little hamper of baby goodies. "Give Nina our best and be sure to come by once things calm down after the baby comes." He nodded, suddenly lost for words. "Drive safe now."

"Take care, Miss Mirada, see you soon." She waved him off and returned to the shop to start checking off the order.

She was counting bags of yarn when the bell chimed again a little while later. She called out a greeting and made her way down the isle and over to the entrance.

"Rhys." Her voice had come out completely not her own and she felt her face warm. He nodded and smiled then cleared his voice. The tingling sensation that started in her chest seemed to spread over her body and she felt her heart quicken.

"Sadie." They stood still, neither of them speaking. She grinned up at him. With the low ceiling, he looked quite comical. Giants sprang to mind, and a small chuckle escaped her lips.

"What brings you by? Do you need knitting needles? I've got a new delivery of yarns that I'm sorting through if you are interested." Her smile grew with each question, then finally she stopped and raised a quizzical brow at him, waiting for his response. "Rhys?"

"Oh, yarn? Not really." His voice appeared hoarse and she nodded her understanding.

"The painting and art supplies are over here if that is what you are after." She remembered his love of drawing when they were kids. He followed her through an archway to a small room off to the side. The walls were covered in shelving and hooks. He stopped, clearly taken aback by the amount of stock and choice she had for a small village. Recognising the look Sadie jumped in. "I know, it's more than people expect from the outside. The shop is a lot bigger than people realise."

"This is amazing," She smiled and blushed a deeper crimson. "How long have you been open?" She walked to the small window seat and perched herself as he moved around the small space to look at the paper of different weights, sizes and colours.

"We opened our doors almost six years ago. Initially just yarns and things, but as demand grew, I repurposed the stock room. We have a small craft space for classes and groups upstairs. It's not ideal for access, but it's popular!" He turned, eyes wide and looked around.

"Can I see?" Rhys enquired, Sadie nodded and led the way. She jabbered on about running out of space and hoped that he wouldn't notice the nervous energy that seemed to be radiating off of her body. "This space is great!" She nodded her agreement, somehow, she wasn't sure how, but her mouth felt dry.

He wandered around the small space that housed a respectably sized table and a dozen chairs. When he finally turned on the spot and faced her, he had a broad smile that lit up his whole face. "I. It was all we had... we try to make it work for us." Once again, her voice did not sound like her own. Perhaps she was coming down with something.

"What did you say that you used the space for? Classes? Groups?" He was examining the sloping ceilings that Sadie had lovingly draped bunting from.

"Both, I hold small group classes. The Knitting ladies meet here once a week. I have dreams of a larger more accessible space. But, well... this is a listed building, so there is nothing to be done here I'm afraid." He made a sound showing his agreement and continued to pace around and smile.

A while later, the pair were sat in the courtyard outback. Sadie's one and only employee, Mrs Lynch, had arrived some thirty minutes earlier and was now running the show. The first of two classes were underway upstairs, and Sadie was finally sitting down to relax whilst she had the time.

"This place is a real hive!" He was nursing his coffee and looking straight at her. "Who knew Beechend could have such a treasure?"

Sadie's face grew hot under his piercing stare. She smiled weakly not quite able to meet his gaze.

He placed the finished cup on the upside-down plant pot which was used as a table. "The shop is great." He paused and she took the opportunity to glance in his direction. Rhys was now staring at the floor as though lost in a world of his own. Then, abruptly, and far more nimbly than she would assume he was able, he rose to his feet, collected the empty cups and made his way back towards the miniature cupboard that was the kitchen.

"Oh, you don't need to wash up!" He nodded at her and rinsed them all the same. Before she had the time to digest what was going on, he had bent and pecked her on the cheek, made his excuse and left. All of this had taken place in front of Mrs Lynch and two of the biggest gossips in the village who were momentarily downstairs to pick out some new colours. Inwardly, Sadie rolled her eyes. The village was going to have a field day with that gossip! At the same time, her stomach flipped and her mind reeled over what had just happened.

Tabby

Life in a small and remote village can be pretty sweet. For many people, they will strive to earn enough to be able to afford the idyllic life the countryside can offer. But what about those people who haven't slaved away to earn enough to live in a hamlet surrounded by goats? Tabby continued to write in her diary. She thought about how she was one such person. The teen who didn't really want the quaint life in the country. She shook her head, internally laughing at the monologue in her brain that never seemed to shut off.

Her home wasn't so bad she supposed. Everyone knew each other, and whilst you couldn't really escape their knowing everyone else's business, she knew that the people here supported one another. Tabby wondered if other places were this close-knit. From her experiences at secondary school, she thought, perhaps not.

Groaning to herself she rolled off her single bed and landed delicately on her feet. Summer was almost over. She liked school and was good at it, but that didn't mean she wanted the summer to be over.

After stashing her diary in the loose floorboard by her desk which she never really used, Tabby made her way downstairs to have breakfast. She didn't really have any plans for the day. She would probably help out at the shop around mid-day when it was normally busy. Maybe get the bus into town. She sighed again. Knowing full well that she wouldn't go into town.

Tabby's best friend had moved at the end of the school year. So far, it was torture. They promised to stay in touch, but the messages were getting further apart and far shorter replies than the long essays she had been typing.

To begin with, the replies were almost instant, and it felt like Julie was in the house down the street, just like old times. But as the summer went on the time between messages was getting longer.

What had once been about complaining how horrible it was there, their correspondence was now dominated with news of the friends Julie had made. The great dance club she had joined, and last week's messages were dominated by this guy she had met at the beach.

Julie's family had moved to the coast.

Tabby laughed out loud at the absurdity of where she lived. 'Beechend' was the absolute oxymoron. The village was nowhere near a beach and there wasn't really an end to speak of. The main road meandered through the centre of the village leading to the nearest villages in both directions. In fact, they were a good hour's drive from the nearest shore and even further from the nearest decent beach.

Julie wasn't though.

In their last weeks in school, they had talked about her going to visit, maybe spend a week or two together. Her mum had agreed and offered to return the favour and have Julie to stay.

Unfortunately, Julie's family, or rather her dad,

didn't agree. He had suggested we wait until October half term for me to visit. He mentioned house renovations and finding their feet and before plans could be finalised, they were gone.

Tabby had always been polite when round at Julie's house, but she had never been made to feel welcome there. It was nothing like her own home. She supposed that was why she and Julie always spent more time in her room together.

The summer was almost over and as bad as the holidays had been, Tabby knew that going back to school in September was going to be unbearable. No Julie. No JJ. She had wished she had worked a bit harder at widening her social circle.

Nevertheless, she plastered on her smile and walked into the kitchen pretending like the whole world wasn't baring down on her shoulders.

Chapter Nine

Sadie

"I'm late, I know." Sadie jangled the shop keys and smiled sweetly at Mrs Norris and Mrs Betts. "Have you been waiting long?" She unlocked and hooked open the door allowing them to enter in front of her.

"Oh no worries my dear. We were here not five minutes before you arrived." Mrs Betts chorused.

"We wanted to miss the mad rush." Mrs Norris informed her. "We heard that you have the colour changing yarns back in stock!"

Sadie nodded over to the yarn display in the corner and laughed quietly to herself. The order had arrived last thing the day before. She was about to close but stayed late to check and sort out the stock.

How did the ladies of this village do it? They knew and saw everything.

By the time Tabby arrived just before noon with her sandwiches she'd not had the time to prepare, Mrs Norris' prediction had come to fruition. She had not stopped, and she was doubting that she would even have the time to have any lunch.

"Wow!" Sadie looked up from behind the till. "Been busy mum?" She nodded and handed the customer her change and receipt.

"I haven't taken a break since I opened the door. Can you do me a favour, pop the kettle on and check on the class upstairs and see how many teas and coffees they would like."

When the beverages had been consumed along with the Victoria sponge, Tabby was in the kitchen clearing the dishes when her mum finally came in. "Your tea I made you is cold. I'll make you a fresh cup. Why don't you go sit in the yard and rest for a moment. I'll cover the shop for a bit." Sadie smiled knowingly at her daughter. Tabby had spent so much time in the shop this summer. She wished she could fix the situation but at the same time it was nice having her around.

"I will take you up on your offer. But only for a few minutes."

Sadie had barely sat down when she heard Tabby calling her back. She knew the different cries of her daughter and this one was not a voice of anguish, pain or despair. She slowly got back to her feet, wincing at the pain and made her way through to the shop front. Pondering on her way what she might need.

"You called." But the rest of sentence fell away as she saw the reason stooped in the shop to avoid hitting his head. She had been right, there had been a smirk to the call that she should have known. "Rhys."

"Mr Knight is here to take you out for lunch." Sadie's mouth dropped open. "I am happy to stay in the shop this afternoon." Tabby's smile widened as she handed her a purse and phone. "I think Mae might pop round later and I'm sure she'll give me a hand if I ask. So, take your time!" Her daughter, the one person that she had been thinking such wonderful thoughts of just moments ago, was now feeding her to the lions. No, just a lion.

By the time she had rediscovered her voice she was outside the shop. How had this happened? Her footsteps faltered and Rhys reached out to hold her steady. This was not good.

"I'm sorry if I bombarded you. If you really need to get back to the shop, I'll understand." He released her arm but continued to stare at her. The smile had not changed, and her arm was continuing to tingle where he had held her. "Sadie?"

"No, um, it's fine. I was just taking a break when you stopped by." He nodded.

"Fantastic, great timing!" He turned and continued to walk towards the pub at the end of the street. She found herself keeping step beside him and nodding along as he made polite conversation.

Rhys

Rhys had a lot of work to be getting on with, but he hadn't got much in terms of 'food' at the cottage for lunch not to mention he had a sudden craving for pub grub.

The Huntsman had been the place to go in his teens. It was a small village pub with a sticky floor from all the spilled drinks. It had had a small room towards the back with a pool table and the landlord was happy for the local underage crowd to congregate and spend their money on soft drinks, crisps and the twenty pence for each game.

He supposed that it was not much like that now. But he lived in hope that some of it was familiar, including the great food they used to serve.

Rhys's quiet pub lunch had been hijacked by his feet. As if on autopilot, he had found himself in the craft shop near the corner. He had stood like a lemon, not sure what to say when being bombarded with questions at an alarming rate. The questioner could be non-other than Sadie's daughter. She had her eyes and cheeky smile that Sadie seemed to be lacking of late. He dropped in to…

"Take mum for lunch!" He'd be startled by her request. Glanced around and saw that Sadie was nowhere to be found.

"Um, your mum is probably busy." Rhys's feeble response was half-hearted, and he was surprised to discover that the prospect of having lunch with Sadie made him feel warm. After bellowing behind her, she turned back to him and held out her hand. It was such a formal gesture that he smiled, taken aback.

"Tabitha Mirada." He took her hand and was surprised by the strength of her grip. Just like her father. This girl had the ability to knock you off kilter.

"Rhys Knight." She smiled again. "Pleased to meet you Tabitha."

She swatted her hand at his reply. "Call me Tabby, everyone does." At this point her mother had walked in. She looked great. Whisps of her hair had come loose and hung round her face and the back of her neck. The glorious sun shining behind her created a sort of silhouette and yet her hair seemed to glow with a radiance he had yet to find in any other person.

"You called... Rhys!" She flushed and he had found that this made him immensely happy.

The work the pair had abandoned was long since forgotten. They had been tucked away in the corner of the pub for the best part of two hours.

The locals who frequented the pub were in for a treat. Having the latest gossip was like winning the lottery in these parts. Gossip on the black market could be worth a pint and a packet of crisps at least. However, the pub was empty of locals. Only the landlord, who had greeted Rhys by name when he entered, would know.

"Then it flew straight at me!" Sadie exclaimed recalling the last time they had really spent any time together. Rhys's laughter was loud and deep. She beamed then continued with her tale of woe. "Those gulls were possessed."

"I remember you screaming, 'You win!' then throwing the whole tray of chips at them." He downed the last of his drink. "You were so mad!" She nodded, then her smile faltered briefly as she caught his eye.

"You let me share yours, so that I wouldn't go hungry." He shrugged, suddenly embarrassed that she remembered that part.

"You had gallantly sacrificed your food so that we were not attacked by vicious seagulls. It was the least I could do." His tone had meant to be jovial, but he'd failed and a serious note leaked in.

"No." Sadie recalled. "You didn't, and you were the only one who offered up your supper."

Rhys nodded thoughtfully, "Another round?"

"I'd best not, Tabby will be wondering where I am." He made to agree with her then stopped short. Laughing he gathered the glasses.

"One more, I get the impression that Tabby will be disappointed if I take you back too early!" She laughed at his confidence and a look of wonderment appeared over her features. He thought perhaps he could read her mind, 'when had the shy boy she knew, become the man in front of her'. If only she really knew.

"Just the one, orange juice please." He strode over to the bar and leaned on it casually. He watched her reflection as she stared at him unabashed and clearly believing no-one was watching. He was wearing worn jeans that had been bought this way other than caused by actual wear and tear. He chatted comfortably with Gerry as he poured him the drinks.

He thought back to that day on the beach. They had all piled into Darren's beaten down car and headed out. It was the last time they were all together before they went their separate ways after school. His brother had been home. It was the last time that they were all together. Rhys didn't come home for almost three years, preferring to stay at University or going travelling.

Sadie had been loud and often outspoken. Her and Darren were a perfect fit, everyone said so. But years later, he wasn't so sure.

"Penny for them…" She startled at the voice that was right next to her. When had he sat back down? She reached out for her drink and took a sip. He tilted his head and looked at her quizzically.

"Lost down memory lane." She shrugged and changed the subject.

Rhys hadn't been certain of what happened whilst he was at the bar. He just knew that something wasn't right. Sadie's smile wasn't reaching her eyes and she seemed to have her mind elsewhere.

Not wanting to ruin what had been a great afternoon, he offered to walk her back to the shop.

"I'm sure you've got lots to be getting on with." Sadie chorused as she gathered her purse. Whilst he stooped awkwardly with both hands thrust into his pockets. He nodded, trying not to show his disappointment that the afternoon with her was over. "See you around?"

"Yep, definitely! Maybe we should do this again some time?"

"Um, yes, maybe." She showed a half smile and was out the door before he could make any plans. He turned round at the deep chuckle that sounded behind him.

"You my lad, have not changed!" Gerry pointed his thick finger at him. Rhys's reaction was a picture and Gerry took it as an indication to continue. "You have been smitten with Sarah since you first came in here."

"You called her Sarah!" Rhys perched on the bar stool as Gerry poured him a half. "I didn't think anyone remembered her name. She's gone by Sadie for so long."

"She will always be Sarah to me." He went back to wiping glasses, not missing a beat. "She's single you know."

Nursing the glass in his hand, he sighed deeply. "She doesn't think of me like that. She never has." He snapped his head up and smirked. "She isn't seeing anyone?" Gerry shook his head returning a broad smile.

"Miss Mirada is never seen out with blokes round here. If she has a fancy man, no-one in the village is aware. So, if my Mrs doesn't know about it, it isn't happening. A right gossip if ever I knew one!" Rhys laughed, everyone knew that Gerry moaned about his wife all the time, but anyone who saw them together knew they were meant to be. "Take some advice from an old man like me."

Rhys looked up at him. His face had taken on a seriousness that he hadn't seen before. "Snap her up!"

"Oh, right! 'Snap her up!' If only it was that easy!" He shook his head in defeat.

"Did you ever think about just going for it? You aren't the lanky kid you once were. I think she might even like ya!" Rhys downed the last of his drink, placed the money on the bar including a generous tip. Nodding and thinking about what he just said.

"How do you know? Why do you think that she likes me?" Rhys thought that Gerry might be losing his touch.

"Did you see the time?" With that, the pair turned and looked at the old clock on the wall. Almost half past four. Wow, they had sat in here all afternoon. "Don't wait. Make a move before someone else does." Gerry had given him a lot to ponder. Did Sadie like him like that? He did not think so. She was intoxicating when they were teenagers. But he never said or did anything to make her think he liked her. Maybe just having her as a friend, after all these years, maybe that was for the best!

After all, he had a lot on his plate right now. He did not have time to be thinking about romance with his teenage crush.

Besides, he would have noticed if she liked him like that. She did not. They were just old friends.

Sadie

As the Bell chimed, a sing song voice rang out, "Well look who decided to show up!" Tabby was happy. Her sing song voice carried through the shop as she entered. "Don't worry. I've cleaned upstairs, restocked the yarn that arrived this afternoon and I've just closed and counted out the till. You don't need to do anything." Sadie stood in the shop, shock washing over her. The place was spotless. Looking at the floor, she had also put the hoover round. "What shall we have for dinner this evening? I was thinking, maybe take out?" Sadie nodded nonchalantly.

"I'm so sorry, I never meant to be out all afternoon! I don't know what happened." There was a note of panic in her voice. "It won't happen again." Tabby snapped up and stared at her. Mouth open then she frowned.

"Mum, I can run the shop occasionally for the afternoon." Sadie shook her head. "No complaints and I enjoyed it!"

"I am sorry that I abandoned you for the afternoon." She shook her head again as it trying to clear it. "Don't know how I lost the whole afternoon!" Tabby smirked and nodded knowingly.

"You must have had a nice time!"

"Yes, yes I did."

"Good! I want to hear all about it."

They packed up the last of their things and made

the short walk back to the cottage. It wasn't until later that evening that Tabby made the suggestion that they invite Rhys over for dinner. She had sensed a moment of weakness on her mother's side. Her defences were down. She went in for the kill.

"Well, he knew Dad. I'd like to get to know him!" Sadie sighed; she knew that she couldn't deny Tabby this simple request. "Please mum, besides, he seems nice."

"I'll make some arrangements, but he'll probably be busy, so don't get your hopes up."

Knowing she had won, Tabby smiled. She looked like her father when she smiled. She had seen some old photos. She wished her mum smiled more. "Thanks, I'm sure he won't turn down an invitation from you. I'm going to practise my piece upstairs for a bit. Love you."

Sadie took the time to reflect, not on her experience at the pub with an old friend, but rather the memories that had been triggered. As motherhood had mellowed her, she had reflected on her relationship with Tabby's father. It had been explosive, passionate and turbulent most of the time. They were always disagreeing and falling out. She supposed that was what teenagers did. But now that she had a teen of her own who was calm and collected most of the time, she wondered. Had they really been a good fit. She had loved him, he was her first love, but she often thought about what life would have been like if he hadn't got in the car that day. Would they still be together, married, more children? Or would they have continued to fight and gone their separate ways? And if so, did that mean that there was someone out there better suited to her? Someone who knew her better than anyone, someone who made her heart leap. She had always thought so when she was younger, but he had never reciprocated her feelings. Never shown more than the love two best friends would share. Besides, where had he been all these years? He was a stranger to her now.

Chapter Ten

Tabby

The roads were strangely quiet as they made the short journey out of the village. Tabby was sat in the front passenger seat of Mae's car; she was humming along with the radio. She couldn't remember the name of the song or the artist who sang it. But it had a good beat and her mum seemed to like it. They could have walked to her grandparents' house, but they ran the risk of being forced to stay over if they didn't have the excuse of a 'safe' journey home after their traditional weekly dinner. So, her mum had borrowed the car.

Tabby loved her grandparents. After all, they were her grandparents and there was this built-in expectation. But despite the affection they showed her, their treatment of her mother was something she had never been able to ignore.

She first truly noticed their distain and contempt when she was about six or seven years old. Tabby supposed that they had never hidden their feelings in front of her, but it was at this age that she was aware enough to know that it wasn't right.

Despite their attitude, her mum remained positive. She continued to take her to the big house outside the village once a week for dinner.

Now, as a teenager, Tabby had an evolving respect for her mother. She never appeared to let their prejudice affect her. She would simply shrug and smile and remain completely impassive in the face of their comments.

She was amazed that she had so much self-control. There had now been two occasions where Tabby couldn't hold back her temper and she had spoken, in their eyes, outside the boundaries of what they deemed lady like.

Each time, it had resulted in more unkind comments fired at her mum. So seeing that her outbursts were making it more challenging and causing her mother more pain, she had resigned to saying as little as possible. Her affection for her grandparents had morphed into tolerance, and she had grown to despise these visits each week.

Tabby knew that her refusal to attend would only make things worse for her mum. She didn't understand why her mum continued to take her there and why she hadn't simply cut contact. But then she supposed that there must be a reason.

"You're being very quiet…" Her mum was indicating at the turning into the drive. "You stopped humming, something on your mind?"

"Mmm."

"I'm here to listen if it will help Tabby." Her mum smiled at her and then turned in the entrance of the long drive.

"Just thinking mum, I'm fine really. Promise." She plastered a smile on her face as they meandered up to the front of the house.

The drive passed through a gated archway where the groundskeeper and his wife still lived. The gardens here were immaculate. Beautiful and there were so many places to hide and play. Yet Beech Manor had long ago stopped being a place of fun and adventure. The enormous trees that lined the drive, created menacing dancing shadows that she had grown to loathe. What she had once seen as magical with a touch of whimsy, was now intimidating and dark. Silver lining… this week's visit would soon be over, and it would be another week before they would be back again.

"Cheer up, I understand cook is making your favourite tonight! Roast…" Her mum chuckled to herself and then winked at her as the car rolled to a stop.

"Mum, it's always roast!" She stated, exasperated as she climbed from the car. Tabby took a moment to smooth the wrinkles from one of her three 'grandmother approved outfits'. She had once loved the frilly dresses her mum put her in for these dinners. She had liked to twirl and watch as the layers rose up in a perfect circle around her. She sighed. A few hours and it would be over. She plastered the fake smile over her features and crunched over the gravel to the expansive front door. "Love you mum." Tabby gave her a genuine and heartfelt smile before fixing her face unconsciously.

"Love you too little bug." Her mum squeezed her hand affectionately as the door was opened by an aging woman with short white hair that resembled a cloud. "Evening Aggy." The woman smiled lovingly at them and gestured for them to enter.

"Good evening, Miss Sarah, Miss Tabitha." She took their light jackets from them and expertly draped them over her arm. "Mr and Mrs Mirada are in the drawing room."

"Are they in good spirits this evening?" Her mother winked and Agatha merely battered her comment away and tilted her head down the corridor. "Here goes nothing!"

Tabby watched as her mother's back became straighter leading the way. She continued to fuss over the creases in her skirt not wanting to give any cause or ammunition.

The hall was dark and gloomy on such a light and airy evening. It felt cold and uninviting. The mahogany panelling was ornate and screamed 'money, money, money'. In contrast, the drawing room was light and airy, the floor to ceiling windows along one wall had their drapes artfully drawn back which enabled the warm sunlight to flood the room.

"Arrhh, here they are!" Grandfather was standing at the empty enormous fireplace. He was holding a tumbler full of amber liquid. He sneered at mum as she kissed his cheek. "Did you get lost?" He laughed deeply at his own attempt at humour. Tabby watched her mum's smile tightened but she didn't bite back at the first retort.

Her grandfather put down his glass and gave her a

one-armed hug awkwardly around her shoulder. Tabby smile expanded and retracted before she mirrored the action with her grandmother.

"Oh dear, Sarah." Her lips were pursed with disapproval. "This skirt really does need to be steam cleaned. This fabric is terrible for holding a crease." Mrs Mirada held both of Tabby's hands and gently pushed her back to arm's length so she could better critique her ensemble. "Perhaps we should take you shopping before school starts again next week?" She smiled up at Tabby and indicated for her to sit on the seat nearest to her whilst her grandfather handed her a small glass of cloudy lemonade. "Tabitha, you need a whole new wardrobe!" She fussed and simpered.

Her grandmother was off... her internal dialogue of young ladies needing the best of everything. The only difference was it was being declared loud and proud for all to hear. "Sarah, she must have more skirts. There will be so many functions to attend this autumn." She gave her the briefest once over, instantly taking a dislike to her mum's outfit. The clothing in question was smart, yet casual enough for the weather. Tabby had liked it as it brought out the colour in her mum's eyes.

"Thank you for the offer mother. We've already done her back-to-school shopping." The tone of voice was light yet firm enough to hopefully stop her grandmother from the huge shopping expedition that was probably forming in her head. "Perhaps a new skirt would be nice for the festive season though." She smiled at her. Tabby was amazed at her mother's ability to remain civil, sidestepping the barbs fired at her and come up with a solution to calm any brewing storm. But, as always, she would follow her lead.

"If you think that is best." Her grandmother's smile no-longer reached her eyes, nevertheless the matter was dropped, and her grandfather was talking about the state of the village green and how it was going to the dogs. She had nodded along with their comments and views of how bad everything was. The reality was that the village was up for yet another flowers in bloom award and was most likely going to win.

In no time at all, they were called through to the dining room for dinner. The candles were lit, and the drapes were drawn. Roast lamb this evening. It was delicious, as always. Tabby was determined to remember to thank the cook next time she saw her. She wondered what desert would be. Mrs Johnson knew her favourites.

"How is the shop doing?" Her grandfather's voice was deep and loud. He had the air of an old stern headmaster yet always appeared displeased with any change or growth for the future. Which Tabby supposed was something teachers embraced. "Mr Smithers says that his wife is always popping in." His look was disapproving. It was obvious to all that knew Mr Mirada. He saw his daughter's chosen profession as an insult to the family. Never mind the fact that she had managed to grow a successful business from nothing.

"Things are going well, thank you for asking father." Her mother was respectful and acted as though she never heard the dissatisfaction in his voice. "I have been meaning to ask."

All eyes snapped in my mum's direction. The air was instantly tense. Her mother never started conversations. She always reacted and responded, but was otherwise silent during these dinners. Tabitha stared at her mother in wonder. Was today the day… was she finally going to talk back and stand up for herself?

"You want money? The business isn't doing as well as you want us to believe…" He had thrown down his napkin, his emotions etched across his face. He stood up, his stature imposing, and Tabby felt herself shrink into her seat a fraction further.

Before her mother could utter a word, Tabby's grandmother had chimed in. "You need money?" There was a happiness in her voice which surprised her. "Edward! Please fetch the chequebook." At this point her grandfather waltzing from the table. A mask had slipped back across his face, successfully hiding all and any feelings.

"No!" Her mother had raised her voice above the gentle tone she always used whilst in this house. "No, father, I am not asking for money." She was wide-eyed yet a determination seemed to radiate from her in waves. "There is no need to fetch your chequebook."

"So, what is it you want from us?" Her grandparents chorused together.

"It's really the village that the favour would be for." Mum paused so that grandfather could make himself comfortable. He was perched holding his glasses and staring intently at her. "We, as in the village committee, were wondering if it would be possible to hold the village Christmas Faire here this year?" Tabby stared at her mother lost for words. Her whole life, she had never seen her mum ask them for anything. And here she was asking for something for the whole community. "The Christmas Faire was always held here when I was little, I remember. We were wondering if it was possible to restart the tradition. The Christmas Faire has been getting bigger year on year. It brings a lot of much needed funds into the village each year. There is a lot of potential to make Beech Manor profitable again whilst supporting the village. I am happy to manage the event so as to minimise disruption to the house and yourselves. I realise this is a lot to take in. I wanted to give you time to think it over. We will need to know before the end of next month so that we can make the necessary arrangements."

Once her mum had finished what she knew to be a well-rehearsed speech, she was met with silence. A silence that Tabby had the need to fill. She met her mother's eyes and knew instantly to stay as quiet as possible. All the time she marvelled at her and her strength. It amazed her, to see her mother had grown up in such a toxic house as this, yet she was so selfless and caring that she was certain that she must have found love and affection elsewhere. She wondered who had taken the time to give her mum a better start than her own blood relatives had done.

Chapter Eleven

Rhys

The return to Beechend had not gone how he had expected. Not that he had really had the time to think about it. He was certain that the hurt and pain would come, but it hadn't. He supposed this had meant that he hadn't truly been in love. Surely the heartbreak was meant to be devastating. Some all-consuming pain from which you feel you will never recover. Yet he had felt nothing more than discomfort and a side note of annoyance with himself. Perhaps he was in shock and the true emotions would surface down the line.

The thing was, since returning, Fiona had not really entered his thoughts, unless provoked, until now. In truth, all he thought of was Sadie. Her smile and her determined independence, which he was sure most people mistook for being stubborn. The way she would absentmindedly scoop back a wayward strand of hair, or the times she would bite her bottom lip as she thought hard about something only she knew.

The shrill ring of his work phone interrupted his

errant thoughts. "Morning Stan." He almost sang into the phone. Rhys's smile was determinedly plastered to his face as images of Sadie swam in his vision. "Yes, settled in thank you. The plans are still ready to go ahead. Um I'm ok." He paused listening to the concern being bombarded at him. It would probably annoy him if he wasn't really over the whole mess. He really was over her, in fact he was certain that he was ready to move on entirely.

The email responses took longer than he had expected, and it was almost noon before he left the cottage on the way to the new school site.

His company had been recruited to manage the building of the village primary school. The existing building that he remembered so well from his own childhood was no longer cost effective. The leaking roof now meant that three of the classrooms were temporarily in mobiles on the school fields. Not an ideal situation.

The second call of the day was to his personal phone. "Ewan, this is a nice surprise! How is London treating you now you are back?" His brother's booming laugh was like a warm hug.

"It's boiling and uncomfortable in the city this time of year. Wish I was back there with you, enjoying the cooler country air." Ewan was the life of the party in the city. Rhys doubted his brother really meant what he said deep down. He loved living in the capital. "The reason for my call. I was um, I was wondering if you had seen any of the villagers this last week?" Rhys stopped walking and moved to the inside of the path to let a person by in the opposite direction. "Rhys, are you there?"

"I'm here." The humour in his voice was unmistakable. "To which local are you referring?" The smirk crept over him and the idea of having a little fun at his big brothers annoyance was too big of an opportunity to pass up.

"Are you laughing at me?" Ewan boomed down the phone.

"I would never!" Rhys's mock disgust was short lived as he burst into uncontrollable laughter. "I haven't seen Mae if that is who you were asking about."

"Oh" Ewan's disappointment was palpable. "Well, I guess. Um." There was more silence down the phone.

Rhys waited for his brother to speak. "I can't wait to hear the rest of these sentences!" His smile broadened as he caught sight of Mae standing outside of Sadie's shop. "Look, you don't have to tell me. But I could see that you were taken with her." Ewan's grunt down the phone spurred him on. "I genuinely haven't seen her until now." The statement was met with a string of profanity. "Language big brother. She might hear you." He stood still, half hidden from her view so as not to attract her attention.

"We had a thing last weekend. I'm not sure if she wants to see me again. I don't like how we left things." Ewan sighed into the phone. "I just wanted to know that she was ok." His voice was almost a whisper. The gentle giant had caught feelings by the looks of things.

"All joking aside. I'll keep my ear to the ground for

you." He wondered when something could have happened between his big brother and Mae. But all thoughts and conversations were rudely interrupted by two women calling his name from across the street.

"Who is that?" It was Ewan's turn to sound amused.

"Um, two elderly ladies. One is waving her stick at me. Um, I didn't think I was likely to get lynched in Beechend, but I guess the odds are not in my favour!" Sarcasm dripped from his words as he turned to face the ladies who were now walking towards him, a lot faster than he would have presumed at their age. The taller one was still pointing and waving her stick in his direction. "Seriously, they don't look happy!"

"They must know you then!" Ewan laughed knowingly before he made his excuses and hung up.

"Some big brother you are!" Rhys cursed down the empty line and pocketed his phone. He could see that the second lady was a little behind the first and was using a walker to aid her in her endeavours.

"Mr Knight!" The voice appeared familiar, but he couldn't place the face. He knew they were likely to face opposition, but he had hoped that he would face it in the meeting next week, once he was better prepared. Not the main street through the village. He squared his shoulders and plastered his award-winning smile across his face. "Mr Knight! I've been meaning to speak with you. This whole business about the new school being build next to the church field. I just don't agree with it." And she was off, she scarcely drew breath as she rambled on about the proximity of the building site to the church and how it was going to disrupt the weekly ladies group on a Tuesday morning. Rhys nodded along and several times tried to respond and help alleviate her fears, but there was no let up. It was during the third go round that he suddenly remembered who the lady was. He had a vague memory of the Sunday school mistress. She had been a force to reckon with even then. Now, as a grown man, she was more terrifying.

During his second attempt to try and reason with her, he was saved by an angel that swooped down and plucked him from the fiery wreckage.

"Mrs Grimshaw, how lovely to see you out and about!" Sadie's face beamed at the older lady who had been drawn up short by the unwanted intrusion. "I had heard you had taken a bad tumble and that was why you were not able to help out with the summer fete this year." Sadie's smile left no one present, in denial. She knew that Mrs Grimshaw's excuse had been just that. And now the four people present all knew. Sadie Mirada was not someone to be trifled with. She was giving this woman a serious run for her money. Rhys wasn't sure if he should laugh, cheer or bow down at her feet.

"Well, I seem to have made a miraculous recovery, as you can see." Mrs Grimshaw's eyes narrowed as she silently dared Sadie to contradict her.

Not missing a beat, clearly knowing how to play the game Sadie responded with a combination of jovial wit and the stern intention of a Victorian school mistress. "Oh, it certainly is miraculous Mrs Grimshaw. I look forward to seeing you at the village meeting on Friday. I for one cannot wait to hear everything about the new school being built!" At this point she turned to Rhys, smirked briefly before returning her composure. "The village is certainly lucky to have someone managing the build that has a history in these parts and is sure to ensure that the end result is something we will all be proud of!" At the end of Sadie's speech, Mrs Grimshaw audibly huffed before forcing a smile, turning and walking towards the church at the end of the street.

"Wow!" Rhys exclaimed. "Just wow!" Sadie beamed at him and then the most glorious blush spread across her cheeks. "Thank you."

Sadie nodded "Don't mention it!" They continued to stand in silence for a moment, the pair of them watched Mrs Grimshaw's retreating back. "She's a softie really!" Sadie laughed at her own joke as Rhys raised an eyebrow sceptically. "Maybe not!"

Chapter Twelve

Tabby

The first day of the school year had arrived. Tabby had secretly been dreading this day and it was with a heavy heart that she left the cottage and made the short walk to the bus stop near the village green.

She was swift to put in her earphones and block out the world as she wallowed in the misery of no longer having her best friend with her. It wasn't like she had depended on her to get through school. She could stand on her own two feet just fine. It was that having a best friend made it more fun. It could be 'us against the world'. She sighed. Tabby would make the most of this year, her last year at school. She just needed to get through the first day!

In the distance, she watched as Mr Knight got into his car and headed out of the village. She wondered what his story was, if she would ever find out. He didn't wave as his car passed. But then she chastised herself for assuming he would.

Tabby allowed her mind to wander some more.

She thought about life would be like in the future. The throng of students grew up around her. She didn't make eye-contact. She didn't want to talk with any of them. They knew she was on her own. They knew she didn't really want to talk with them and that they would only talk about her behind her back. So why bother. She would focus on making it through today, then see what tomorrow would bring.

So immersed in her own thoughts, she didn't notice the taller boy hovering round the edge of the group. He was also alone. Also pretending to listen to music. His dark eyes followed her as she got onto the bus. He wore his tie loosely around his neck. His bag was torn and patched. His dark hair looked messy and partly hung across the right side of his face. He was neither smiling nor scowling. Just watching impassively. He stood on the bus as there were no seats. He held on to the rail and continued to stare. It was only when Tabby gave up her seat for an older lady that a small smile appeared on his face.

She hadn't seen any of it.

The morning had passed just as predicted. A few girls had briefly greeted her, but it was fleeting, and the rest of the time had been spent alone. She knew that she ought to make more of an effort. But what if she did. What if she made a new friend. What if that friend was great and they laughed together. What if that friend left? Where would she be then? It was all too much. Besides, it wasn't going to be long, and she would be out of here too.

She gave herself a mental prod and walked

towards the drama department. She had barely taken a dozen steps when she collided with someone, and her books and bag fell to the floor.

Tabby apologised and began scrabbling on the floor to retrieve her things.

"No, I'm sorry, It was my fault, I wasn't looking where I was going." The voice was male and deeper than most of the lads in her year. She glanced up and into the face of the unfamiliar voice. Instantly she felt a zing of excitement rush through her. "Are you ok? Here, let me get these." Her voice seemed to have deserted her as this dark knight continued to gather her possessions and hand them back to her. "Name's Alex, I'm new here." Tabby nodded as that was safer than using an unstable voice. "You don't seem to talk much." He smiled at her and she felt her face redden as she returned the smile and shrugged. "Maybe I can continue this conversation for a little longer?" Tabby glanced up at him from beneath her hair, she was trying to decide with he was being genuinely sincere or poking fun at her. He smiled again, though it was smaller and uncertain, it still seemed to light up his face. Clearing her throat, she reached out for the last of the books.

"Tabitha, but everyone calls me Tabby." She hugged the last book to her as if it was a lifeline.

"It was nice bumping into to you Tabby. Where were you heading?" Realisation dawned; she was going to be late...

"Oh, um, I have to go. I'm going to be late!" She smiled again and made to carry on towards the auditions. She noticed that he was keeping in step.

"Can I tag along? You're the first conversation I've had all day!" She didn't falter a step as she jovially replied.

"Depends, can you sing?" The replying snort was all the answer she needed. "It's auditions today for the winter music festival. It's been a bit of a thorn in my side since I started here four years ago." His faltering smile was infectious. "Alex you say?" He nodded. "They always need stagehands and crew to help out if you are interested. Where on earth had that come from? What had gotten into her. He fell into step with her as she led the way to the building on the far side of the campus.

Almost half an hour later, Tabby was very aware of Alex. It was like a sort of magnetism. She could feel his gaze on her as the auditions progressed. Usually, the thought of singing for an audience terrified her, but somehow her confidence seemed to have appeared like magic. Even during her performance, it was like the rest of the room had simply dissolved into nothing. She doubted it was her very best attempt, but she knew it was really close.

She found herself pondering, who is this guy? She came to the conclusion that it was only his first day. He would soon discover that she was a nobody and that there were far more superior people to spend his time with.

As the last person finished their audition piece, Tabby looked up into the stands. He was looking right at her. It wasn't creepy as such, but rather, curious having someone watching her every move. This time the blush filled her face as she turned her attention back to the drama director Miss Scott.

"Well done all of you! A great turn out this year. The postings will be on the board at the end of the week. Please remember to sign up for stage crew and decoration. Every little help is a big help in the theatre!" The sing-song voice trailed away, and everyone made to exit. This time when she glanced in Alex's direction he was surrounded. Jennifer was fawning over him and her cronies were following suit. She sighed and decided to make her way to her next class. "It was nice knowing you Alex." She whispered to herself as she left the building.

Chapter Thirteen

Sadie

By the end of the week, Sadie was restless and irritable. Each time the bell chimed signally a new customer in the shop, she would look up expectantly then chastise herself when the face didn't belong to Rhys. After their little - she wasn't sure what to call it - in the street the other day, Sadie had not been able to stop thinking about him. It was, in her mind, completely absurd and if truth be told the butterflies were not helping the situation.

She supposed that had been a silver lining to today being on the quiet side as it had given her nerves a break this afternoon.

The loud tinkle of the bell broke through the silence of the shop. Spoke too soon she thought as she looked up expectantly.

"Mum!" Tabitha waltzed in, a lad following close behind her looking somewhat uncertain and a little uncomfortable at finding himself in a 'ladies shop' despite her having plenty of men learning to knit in one of the groups. Though she supposed a teenage lad wouldn't really care about such things. "Mum!" Sadie stood up from cleaning and restacking the bottom shelf. "There you are. I'm just dropping my things off. We're going to get some chips; I'll be home a bit later." Tabby's announcement came out a bit garbled and a little faster than normal. Sadie nodded to show she had understood then turned to face the lad that was having to stoop behind her daughter to avoid hitting his head on one of the beams. Her first thought was of Darren, Tabby's father. He had been tall with the same dark floppy hair.

"That's fine, do you need any money for your tea?" She continued to eye him as she started looking for her purse.

"Nah, I have some left over from the weekend." Tabby smiled at her mother; her eyes widened for a fraction of a second. "Mum, this is Alex…" She waved in the boys direction.

"Hello Alex, how are you settling into the village?" He stepped forward and took her hand. Firm handshake, good sign.

"Miss Mirada." The females laughed and Sadie waved him off.

"Everyone calls my mum Sadie." Tabby continued to chuckle.

"We're getting to know the place, thanks for asking." He smiled and stopped shuffling his feet. Alex seemed like a nice lad.

"I'll be outside in a minute, just need to speak to my mum quickly." Tabby beamed at him and his face split in two. He nodded, made his goodbye and left the shop. After the bell had stopped jingling, she turned to Sadie. "Go on then…"

Sadie raised a brow. "He seems nice. You can bring him round again. Think he might be a keeper." She handed Tabby the five-pound note and winked at her.

"Thanks mum." She turned to leave but stopped just shy of the door. "You know mum, there is another good guy in this village that wasn't here last year." Tammy smirked. "I think he's a good guy." Sadie stopped short. How had her daughter become so smart? "See you later mum." Just like that she was out the door, the bell jingling in her wake.

Sadie was back on the floor, finishing the clean-up. 'Rhys is a good guy' was all that she was thinking. In that moment a decision was made. She gathered up the last of the stock and hastily placed it back on display before turning the closed sign and gathering the rest of her things.

"Evening All!" The voice of the vicar could be heard clearly throughout the hall. "My oh my, we do have a good turn out." His gentle gaze swept around the room. Then he smiled as though knowing a secret. "Well, it isn't me or The Lord himself that has brought you here. Nevertheless, it is wonderful to know that so many in Beechend really care about our community." There was some light twittering amongst a few residents at the back. "Mr Knight, I do believe all these fine folks are here to hear what you have to say!" With a sweeping arm gesture, he signalled for Rhys to step forward and take point on the meeting.

Sadie shuffled uncomfortably on the plastic seat as Rhys introduced himself to the many dozens of citizens in front of him.

"Firstly, I'd like to say, I am truly honoured to have been chosen to manage this development. As most of you probably remember, I was once a member of this community. I know the importance a school can have in a village like Beechend. And I hope you will see that we really do have all of your best interests at heart." He smiled out at them, but it didn't reach his eyes which Sadie found suspicious. He was standing tall in his expensive tailored suit. She sighed as the first of many hands shot into the air and the barrage of impatient questions were fired in his direction.

"You're just a suit, brought in, to sweet talk us!" The owner of the outburst had stood up, making him better to be seen and heard. Ironically, it was one of the newer residents on the little housing estate on the other end of the village. There had been a lot of unrest when planning permission was granted for the two fields on the edge of the village to be built on. "You know nothing about our lives out here!" The man looked to be in his early thirties, dressed in designer clothes. But, unfortunately he had managed to stir the crowd.

"I understand your concerns, but if you would be so kind as to take your seat. I will fill you in on the plans and will be happy to take questions at the end." Rhys' voice was calm and definitely in control.

"We don't want the new building. What is wrong with the old one?" The gentleman, who Sadie didn't know by name was just here to stir up trouble. She was sure of it.

As she made to rise from her own chair, several things happened at once. Sadie felt a weight on her shoulder and a gentle reassuring squeeze. Then the sound of chair legs scraping across the old wooden floor.

"Mr Edwards, isn't it?" Mae's voice was high and jovial. "Maybe you should take your seat." She smiled towards him, though all who knew her, would know not to push.

"This is a public meeting; I have a right to be heard as much as him." He pointed a manicured finger at Rhys who appeared to know when to stay quiet. "Several of us are happy with the quaint look of the school as it is. If we wanted a modern building, we would have stayed in the city!" He huffed and folded his arms like a petulant child, although the slight waver in his voice had already betrayed him.

"Well maybe, the safety of our children is more important than the building being aesthetically pleasing for city interlopers. Mr. Edwards." He looked shocked at being spoken to with so much contempt. "In Beechend, we listen to the meeting and ask questions in a polite and dignified manner. We will forgive your rudeness just this once, as you have only been here a short time." Her voice was gentle but to the point. She was most definitely on a roll. The Man, who was still standing made to speak again but she cut him off before he had the chance. "In fact, if we had behaved as you are now, I wonder if your home would have been built at all. Maybe, listen to what has to be said first. If you don't like it, you could always move back to the city!" Ouch. Mae's bark was brutal, but one hundred percent honest. The man who had initially caused a scene was now sat down next to a tight-lipped woman whom Sadie had assumed to be his wife, poor woman. He was scowling at Mae who had made a swift nod in Rhys' direction and promptly taken the seat next to her.

"Um, right then. On with the presentation. I will of course be happy to answer any and all questions at the end." He got back on track and delivered an outstanding and extremely well-rehearsed speech.

After a few minutes of people taking turns to ask questions about the development site, Sadie took her turn. "Mr Knight." She rose in her seat.

"Miss Mirada." His smile didn't falter and for that she was impressed.

"We are without a village hall or meeting place in this village. Because of this we use this hall. The school hall." Sadie paused, she wanted to get her point across.

"Yes, I am aware of this information. What is your question?" His tone of formality surprised her. But she gathered herself and dove on.

"This hall is not fit for purpose. We are constantly in conflict with the school over timings and despite everyone's best intentions, the school hall is no longer suitable for our growing village needs. Why has this not been addressed in the proposed building plans?" As she finished, she stood her ground and there were several murmurs of agreement around her.

"I was not under the impression that the design

did not fit the brief laid out initially. We are here to build a new school for the village of Beechend as the current building is quite frankly, too expensive to maintain." He stared straight at her when he said this. She almost felt herself waiver. "However, this development is about community. I will be more than happy to take suggestions back to the big boss and see what can't be done." The clapping started nearer the back, and it appeared that Rhys had won over the city interlopers. But Sadie was not entirely convinced that he would be able to pull it off. His smile was no longer meeting his eyes. Surely that was not a good sign.

After all the questions had been asked, the members of the community enjoyed the light refreshments and mingled amongst one another. The atmosphere was happier than when she had first entered the room.

She was almost halfway through her cup of tea when Rhys approached. He made a joke about it being safe. She had laughed half-heartedly but only because there were others around and she didn't want them to know.

"I will contact my boss first things about the ideas." The crowd around them nodded enthusiastically then one by one they slowly went on their merry way. When it was just the two of them in their little group, Rhys lowered his head so that only she could hear. "I was thinking, it might be a good idea for us to get together." He paused and her stomach did a little flip.

"You mean, us, together?" Sadie's voice squeaked slightly when she said together. Oh, the humiliation.

He rubbed his hand over his stubbled jaw. Then he momentarily looked confused, and realisation dawned.

"You know the villagers so well... and have a grasp on the needs on the new development... Between the two of us... I think we could make this work." She looked up at him and for the briefest moment she had thought he was talking about the two of them as in an 'us' an 'item'. Oh, she was living in a fantasy land. She was a grown woman; she was a mother. She did not get flustered over a man in a suit!

"I think that I should not presume to know everything about the village, and it's needs. Perhaps you should ask for representatives to come forward with their ideas." Her tone had been curt, and she hoped he didn't notice that she was upset. She abruptly handed him her cup and saucer. "I will ask around and gather some information if that is better for you." She didn't wait for him to verbalise a response and quickly turned on her heal and stalked out the hall.

Sadie didn't see the quizzical look given to her my Mae as she was so caught up in the process of getting out of there. She missed the look that passed between the knit and natter group and most importantly, Sadie failed to see the look of disappointment pass over Rhys' face.

Rhys

He stood still, staring at the doorway that Sadie had just walked through. Quite frankly he was a little bit taken aback. Who had that person been? Rhys was almost certain that it wasn't Sadie. He continued to think to himself as he briefly considered alien abduction and split personality disorders.

"Rhys!" The soft voice came from his right, and he turned to see Mae looking at him quizzically. "Where did she dash off to? I was going to see if she fancied a drink at the pub." Her voice was jovial and not a bit concerned. Clearly, she had not seen what he had seen.

On looking at him though, her features changed instantly. She had a curiosity that he was sure meant she knew everything about him. This realisation made him squirm slightly.

"I'm not really sure what just happened if truth be told." His brow furrowed, "I'm at a loss, but I think I have done or said something to upset her."

Mae's expression softened with a look of pity he really didn't think boded well for him. He didn't want her pity.

A clue would be nice though.

Chapter Fourteen

Sadie

On the following morning, Sadie was up with the sun. She had tossed and turned all night as she played the evening's events over and over in her mind. She was such a fool.

She had feelings for him, she couldn't deny that any longer. Just being in the room with him stirred up feelings she thought she had long since buried. Rhys hadn't liked her like that then, clearly he didn't see her that way now. Besides, she wasn't exactly a catch. Single mother with parent issues, who can't seem to control her outbursts around him.

Oh the rage at her own embarrassment just kept resurfacing. How could she have got this so wrong. To mistake his friendly banter and kind gestures as something more. She needed to get her head on straight.

By seven am the padding footfalls of her daughter could be heard coming down the stairs as Sadie opened the oven door to put in her third batch of cakes of the morning. "Mum?" She straightened and swept a loose whisp of hair from her face. "What are you doing? The shop doesn't open until ten!" Tabby looked at the disaster that was their kitchen. She may have used all the bowls that they possessed in an effort to get the cakes made. "Are you ok? Did something happen?" Curse her quizzical daughter and her ability to read her like a book.

"I'm a mess!" Covering her face in her hands she groaned. "I'm sorry if I woke you with making too much noise." Tabby swatted the comment away as if it was nothing. Sometimes she forgot that her little girl wasn't so little anymore.

"Why don't you go take a shower." She gently patted her hair and a small puff of flour surrounded her. They giggled. "I'll clean up in here and take the cake out when it's done." Sadie visibly relaxed, accepted defeat and made to head into the bathroom.

"Did I ever tell you how wonderful you are?" Tabby laughed serenely. "Because you are."

"Love you mum. Now go get ready!"

She was only out of the kitchen for twenty minutes, but when she returned the surfaces were ingredients free and Tabby was drying the last of the wooden spoons. "You are an angel!" She reached forward and hugged her tightly. Sadie wondered if there would be a time that Tabby wouldn't let her do this. She wished that they would always be this close before finally letting her go and pulling out a chair. She beckoned for Tabby to sit down and noticed she had made a fresh pot of tea and even started to construct the Victoria sponge for the craft class this afternoon.

"Do you want to talk about it?" Her voice was delicate, not in the slightest bit pushy. "Did something happen with Mr Knight?"

Sadie looked up and shook her head. "Nothing to worry about. Just village stuff with the new development. A lot of anxiety over the changes, that's all."

"Okay then, if, you are sure?" She poured out a cuppa for each of them then started added ridiculous amounts of sugar to hers, which always made her laugh. Her dad had been the same. Three sugars, bleh, the thought made her stomach turn. She marvelled at their similarities despite her never meeting Darren.

"Oh, I'll be fine. I want to hear all about Alex!" She gracefully accepted her own cup and took a sip. "He seems nice, quiet. Has he moved onto the new estate?" Tabby's cheeks went a little pink at the mention of his name.

"He doesn't have any friends so I'm showing him around." Tabby almost sounded defensive. "It won't be long before he is picked up by the popular lot and he forgets who I am." The revelation seemed to shock even Tabby. "I just mean, he'll be friends with them before you know it." She took a large gulp of her tea.

"I might have only spent the briefest of times with him, but I think that there is enough about him that even the most popular of popular people won't turn his head." Tabby's eyes lit up and Sadie could tell it had been weighing her down. At that moment the timer chimed on the oven and their magical mother-daughter moment had been broken. She took a last sip of tea before busying around with the cakes and getting ready to go to work. By the time she had finished, Tabby had slipped back upstairs to her room and the remaining tea in the pot was lukewarm at best.

Chapter Fifteen

Ewan

High up in a luxurious London apartment, Ewan was sat nursing a coffee cup that had long since gone cold. Since leaving Beechend he had felt adrift. He was one of those dinghies that come loose from their moorings and drift off into the unknown, until they are eventually destroyed on an outcrop of sharp rocks. That's what he was doing now. He was being rocked in all directions, and the city in which he lived, felt like the jagged rocks that would eventually be his undoing.

Ewan was now seriously beginning to question living in the city. He had started looking at estate agents online and was now looking out for somewhere large in the country, that he could sink his teeth into.

Of course, he had narrowed down his search considerably. He had only actually looked within a twenty-mile radius of Beechend. Something that he had repeatedly chastised himself for. It was ridiculous and one hundred percent out of character for him.

His work at the office had started to leave a bitter

taste in his mouth and in all honesty, he was starting to question the purpose of it all. The thrill of the job had diminished long ago, and he wondered if there was something else that could give his life more meaning.

He supposed that part of his feeling this way was to do with Mae and how they had left things.

Ewan thought about her constantly, one taste of his time with her was never going to be enough. He wondered about what she was doing and even started reading her column online each time it was published.

Her words jumped off the page and he itched to see her again.

Yet their time together had been so brief that he wondered if the whole experience hadn't just been a figment of his imagination.

What it came down to, was the fact that he had messed up. He wasn't exactly sure where it had gone wrong, nevertheless, he was certain that it was his fault. Perhaps kissing her had been the wrong thing, despite what she had said after.

The buzzer broke through his thoughts, and he realised that his food order had arrived.

Faced with the many fast-food bags on the kitchen side, he couldn't bring himself to eat. Maybe in a while, he thought.

Sometime later that afternoon, his phone pinged a message through from Rhys. It appeared; he too was having lady troubles. He had somehow managed to upset Sadie.

He asked him what had happened, but his response was vague, and he was none the wiser as to what had caused the rift.

In the end, after fetching his now cold chicken curry from the fridge, he messaged back that Rhys could say sorry with food! In his opinion, food could fix anything.

He laughed at his own musings. Did that mean that food could fix his problems? He doubted the magical powers of the Indian cuisine in front of him. Maybe something sweeter might work?

Chapter Sixteen

Rhys

The idea had not truly been his own. He had his brother to thank, but in the early hours, when he could not sleep, it had fully formed in his mind. Now he just wished his confidence from earlier would return. He knew that Sadie closed the shop at half-past four. If he got there about quarter-past the shop would probably be empty and he might be able to talk with her without a whole audience of crafting busy bodies.

So, here he was, standing on the high street outside the shop. Dread was coursing through his veins and his throat felt as though it had constricted as no amount of clearing his throat seemed to be easing it. A Victoria sponge was precariously balanced in his hands, all the while, he was trying to find the absent courage to walk in and face her.

When the door suddenly opened and the bell jingled in front of him, he almost dropped the cake. It was the lady who had been shouting at him just the other day. He stepped back instinctively he could not face her right now. "Mrs. Grimshaw!" He was shocked to be running into her and just a little bit intimidated to find himself in her presence. She pursed her lips giving off the air of someone deeply mistrusting of another. He wondered if that was her resting face as he had vague memories of it as a child.

"Mr. Knight." Her voice was reproachful and dripping with what he could only assume was disdain. "You seem to be loitering on the street again. I do hope that you have made the appropriate alterations to the school building plans. I must say, we were extremely disappointed." She stood still, staring him down. He smiled at her and tried his best to reassure her that the company had the village's best interests at heart. "I very much doubt that. But I hope some changes will be made! Good day to you." Before he had the chance to reply she had turned on her heel and began walking away. Not a limp to be seen. He stood gaping for a moment longer, Rhys was not at all sure of what just happened. But certain that she might come back for round two, he guessed he would be safer off the street.

Mentally, he gave himself a little shake and entered the shop. He held the cake high and silently gestured that it was for her the moment that he caught her eye. He was not sure he could fully trust his voice, as he felt sure it would wobble. Just the sight of her had him tied up in knots. There was a moment of hesitation and Sadie burst into fits of laughter.

He was a little taken aback, this was not going how he had imagined. Rhys could see that Sadie was trying to speak through the giggles and was pointing to the unit behind her.

At once he realised. On the dresser behind her were several half and quarters of cakes. She held out her hands and took the cake.

"It is a thoughtful gift! I thank you." Her face was a light with mischief. "Would you like a cuppa? The kettle just boiled." She wiggled her eyebrows at him and then continued to badger him until he caved. Albeit, he did not need much convincing.

An hour later, he was on his second cup and as many slices of cake. Together they had closed the shop and he had attempted to help with the end of day chores.

Somewhere along the way she had invited him round for dinner and he was now sat at the kitchen table surrounded by cakes whilst she busied herself preparing an evening meal. The conversation flowed and whatever had happened the other night, seemed to have been long since forgotten.

Rhys's anxiety had seemed to dissolve, and he felt much more relaxed now they were speaking. He wasn't certain, but he thought that her gaze had lingered on him several times throughout the afternoon. He couldn't help it. Several times he had caught himself staring at her. Her lips, eyes, the small of her back had been exposed as she had bent over to put the dinner in the oven. At that point he had felt the red-hot heat creep over his body. He had mentally chastised himself at once. They were friends, or at least he hoped they were.

Once Tabby had arrived and they had sat down

together and eaten, Rhys began to feel even more at home. The banter between the three of them felt natural and the weight he had been carrying around with him was easing as time went on.

"So, come on… How was the first week back at school?" Rhys questioned. Tabby appeared so light and carefree that he was surprised to see a moment that her face fell. She was quick to recover and, had he not been looking directly at her; it would have been missed. She was hesitating. Sensing that this was not a topic she wanted to broach, he tried his best to get her out of the situation he had created. "I would not want to be back there! The most challenging time of my life!" Rhys had kept his voice light and airy. Trying to make them laugh, which Tabby had done on cue.

"You didn't enjoy school?" Sadie's enquiry caught him off guard. The room grew more tense. Rhys always thought she had known how he had felt back then. The big brother was popular with both students and teachers. The girls just saw him as a friend, and he had always been on the edge of everything. "Rhys?" Her voice was soft, probing and he was beginning to wish he hadn't mentioned school.

"Does anyone really enjoy school?" He joked before taking a gulp of the beer in his hand. Sadie's features continued to show a mixture of concern and confusion. He wished the sofa he was sat on would open and swallow him whole. No such luck.

"Personally, I don't know how you survived without the internet. You went to school in the stone age!" Tabby threw out her comment with such a serious tone of voice that the tension burst instantly.

Both Rhys and Sadie exploded into simultaneous laughter that seemed to shake them to their core. "I'm serious!" Tabby protested.

"Oh honey. I can see that. It's just, if you have never had something, how can you miss it?" Sadie smiled encouragingly towards her daughter who had stopped to take in what had been said.

"Umm, I'm sorry mum. That is probably true about most things. But I don't think so for everything." Her voice had changed. Barely more than a whisper. "I think you can miss out on things in your life," Sadie had moved to the edge of her seat, eyes wide and no longer smiling but a deep look of concern etched on her face.

Rhys could feel the change, he was certain that he was encroaching on a family conversation. Before he could make his excuses to leave, he saw that Sadie had made to speak, but Tabby continued. "I think you can see others experiencing things, having things that you do not. I think that you can miss the idea of something." The room was now silent. Realisation dawned on Sadie's face a moment before Rhys realised that Tabby was in fact referring to the absence of her father.

The silence continued. But he realised, the sudden seriousness of the topic of conversation did not make him uncomfortable. This in itself was a surprise. He noticed that Sadie had reached out and was now covering Tabby's right hand with her own.

Sadie, it appeared, had no words.

Sadie

The pain was imprinted on her daughter's face. She wasn't sure how long the silence lasted. It was Rhys who finally broke it. It shocked her that someone else was in the room as she was so focused on Tabby.

"What would you like to know?" Rhys' voice, manly yet gentle was like a warm hug. The genuine soft smile on his lips was almost enchanting. The pair were then snuggled together on the sofa as Rhys spoke about Darren with such admiration.

"When did you first meet my dad?" Tabby's voice was a little scratchy. But if he noticed, he showed no recognition on his face.

"He was my brother's best friend. They were two peas in a pod!" There was such compassion in his voice as he continued to talk about the trouble they got into as children. "Considering I was a few years younger; your dad was pretty cool about me tagging along sometimes."

Sadie watched the two of them as Tabby continued to fire question after question at Rhys. He didn't miss a beat and it amazed her just how well he had known Darren.

Over the next hour, Rhys regaled them with tales of his childhood that even included Sadie. But for the most part the lead of the story was his brother and Darren. It was during this time that Sadie's frosty perspective of Tabby's father began to thaw a little. He hadn't been as bad as she remembered. She should have focused on the good times instead of allowing the hurt to eat away at her all these years.

So animated was Rhys' storytelling that on several occasions it was as though they had been back there, enjoying their miss spent youth. His eyes were alight with mischief, and it was at this point, around the time he started talking about their final year at sixth form, that Sadie decided it was getting late.

She thought she had seen a glimmer of disappointment pass across Rhys' face, but when she looked at him again his face showed no sign of annoyance and his eyes continued to twinkle as though nothing had changed. Sadie thought for a moment that it wasn't just Darren's positive attributes she had forced herself to forget... maybe she needed to rethink a lot of things.

"Thanks Rhys! You can come over any time!" Tabby chorused as she got up from her seat and walked towards the stairs. "I liked the way you talked about mum when she was younger, it's nice knowing that she used to have fun!" At this point Sadie and Rhys were stood mouths open as they watched her leave the room.

"I do have fun!" She called after her, but it appeared to have fallen on deaf ears.

"Thank you for dinner. I had a nice time." Sadie nodded along to Rhys as they walked into the small kitchen. "I enjoyed spending time with you both."

"I think you have been a huge hit with Tabby, she hung on your every word." He stopped suddenly and turned to face her as she reached out and opened the back door. Sadie wasn't even sure how it happened. It was both slow and unexpectedly fast, all at once.

Sadie was standing in the doorway her back resting on the frame as Rhys's tall stature took up the remaining space. Not a word passed between them. He continued to stare at her as if searching for hidden treasure. Her mouth had gone dry, and her legs no longer felt like they were her own.

As he leaned in further, he whispered, "I remember a lot from all those years ago, but I'd like to know more about the woman in front of me now." He was staring into her soul; she was sure of it. As he spoke her gaze dropped to his lips for mere moments. They barely moved as the words washed over her. "I want to kiss you." His words were a soft caress and she had barely looked up into his eyes, when they both reached out for each other. It was like coming home after the longest time away.

This just felt right, his hands had snaked around her back and gently pulled her towards him as she reached up and tickled the hair on the nape of his neck. The tingling started in her toes and travelled all over her body like being zapped with static electricity.

All reason and being seemed to have left her consciousness and she responded fervently and with a longing that she didn't believe she possessed. Too soon Rhys began to pull away, although he continued to lay small delicate kisses and gently rubbed his nose to hers.

Neither stepped away, preferring to linger in their cocooned embrace, in the doorway of her kitchen. She sighed, a long and sweet sound that she didn't quite recognise as her own. Rhys tilted his head down again, his eyes were molten as he gently continued his investigation as if nothing else mattered but her.

It was only when the sound of Tabby coming down the stairs reached them that they broke apart as though burned. Rhys's hair was tussled and his lips red.

"Mum, I was just thinking, maybe we can skip..." But Tabby stopped midsentence as she walked into the kitchen. "Oh, um, sorry!" She began to back way, the look of surprise quickly turning to a grin like a Cheshire cat.

"Busted," Rhys muttered, and Tabby stopped. She looked at Rhys and simply shrugged. "I should get going." Rhys was still smirking, his hand lingering in the small of her back, his fingers caressing a small exposed area of skin. The sensation was intoxicating and although bare to the night air, Sadie's skin felt like it was on fire.

"I don't have any qualms if that is what you are worried about. Just maybe keep the PDA to a minimum when I'm around!" The voice of Tabitha was full of an excitement that was being decidedly squashed. Sadie was sure of it. "Maybe Rhys can come with us to Beechend Hall on Sunday? It might make it more enjoyable!" With that Tabby grinned again and spun on her heel and left the room. Sadie was stunned and just a little bit confused by everything that had just happened in her kitchen.

"I'll see you tomorrow?" His question was interrupted by his kiss. He stroked her cheek and tucked a loose strand behind her ear. She nodded as he kissed her briefly again and then he was gone.

Chapter Seventeen

Sadie

Sadie took a deep breath, today was set to be a busy one. The trouble was, Sadie had been absolutely useless all morning. Her mind wandered easily, she found herself having long periods of daydreaming and when trying to run a business, it wasn't good to have your head in the clouds for long periods of time. Or in fact, any period of time.

Several tasks that were set to be completed had been started and then abandoned in preference of staring into space and reliving the moment that Rhys Knight had kissed her.

Luckily for Sadie the shop had been unexpectedly quiet all morning. But there was a knit and natter group due in later and because of the unusual quietness of the shop, she was expecting a rush either later on today or tomorrow. Only time would tell.

"Wow!" A voice loudly exclaimed over the noise of the bell. Sadie looked up and saw that Mae had arrived. "There is something different..." Mae waggled her finger in her directed then closed the shop door. Sadie shrugged and attempted to force her face to become emotionless.

She failed spectacularly. "Tell me everything!"

Only fifteen minutes later, they were sat on the sofa in the corner, halfway through a cup of tea as Sadie continued to recall the events of the previous night.

Her face, which had most definitely been what had let her down, was split into a coy smile that made her eyes dance.

"I must admit, this looks good on you." Mae was hugging her knees to her body. "Well, you've been honest with me. I think that it's only fair that I do the same..."

Sadie sat up straight and stared at her friend. Her smile faltered for the first time since the previous evening.

"Mae..." It looked like she was holding her breath.

"I met someone. Well, um, he and I." Mae was struggling for words. She couldn't seem to get a handle on how she really felt.

"OK, you don't sound too pleased about it. What's wrong, has he hurt you?"

Mae shook her head frantically; Sadie could feel the beginning sensation behind her eyes.

"He hasn't hurt me, but, given the chance, I feel..." Mae was stumbling over her words.

The woman who made a career out of giving advice, writing down that advice to thousands if not tens of thousands of readers, was struggling to get out what she was feeling.

Sadie looked at her and frowned. Her sympathy was probably the last thing Mae needed and she attempted to rein it in. "Mae… whatever happened, you don't have to tell me if you don't want to. But I know you, I'm here to listen when or even, if you are ready.

"It was me." Mae seemed to explode from the exertion of holding it in.

"Honey?"

"I did the hurting. At least I think I did." Mae's head drooped forward, defeated and rosy faced.

Realisation dawned. "Mae, you have a loving soul, I don't believe anything you said or did was done out of malice." She remained still and focused on her hands in her lap. Mae's silence seemed to spur her on. "But you have been a bit lacking on the man front." Sadie chuckled lightly. She supposed right, and instantly Mae's head flew up, just like she knew it would.

"Hark who's talking! I haven't seen many men in your hen house lately." They stared at each other for a moment, then the two women exploded into fits of laughter. There was no point in dwelling on that now.

After it was out of their system, they straightened up and Sadie asked her again what had happened with the mystery bloke. "We kissed." Mae paused and Sadie waited on tender hooks, "and it was… divine." A soft blush crept up her cheeks. "I don't know. It felt amazing. And then it didn't. It felt wrong…"

Sadie wasn't sure how to respond to that…

"I felt like I was cheating." Mae's last word

escaped at little more than a whisper.

There were no words. She simply put her arm around her friend and sat with her. Her own thoughts were not so silent.

Sadie had never been married. But neither had she been with anyone else since Darren had passed. She had gone out of her way to avoid the advances of the opposite sex. She hadn't felt that she had missed out on anything until something awoke in her less than twenty-four hours ago. Now, this passion, that came from she didn't know where, was coursing through her and she felt a deep-seated need to protect Mae.

She faltered just long enough to stop in her tracks. Did she feel guilt over kissing Rhys. In short, no. No, she didn't. Yet he had been a friend to them both. Was it a betrayal of Darren's memory? Now she was confused herself. She shook her head trying to banish the thoughts that were taking hold.

It was so easy to go down this rabbit hole and now she knew that her friend had gone there too.

"Mae, please believe me when I say… you were not cheating." Mae looked at her, imploring with her gaze. "Whilst you were kissing this guy, what did it feel like?" She waited for a response.

As the pink deepened to a dark rosy hue in her cheeks, "I felt like I had always known him. Like he was made just for me and me for him." Mae held her tongue. It appeared that she was having an internal battle.

"It sounds to me like the guilt appeared after the fact… When you describe being with someone as being made for each other. Do you think Michael wouldn't be pleased for you?"

Mae groaned and put her face in her hands. Then the door chimed and the first of the knitting ladies walked in. Not great timing.

As it turned out, they certainly were wise ladies. In a matter of seconds, they had caught on with the situation. Less than ten minutes later, once the last of the group had arrived, Sadie had been persuaded to close up for the rest of the day and the two were ensconced in the room with the knitting group. The latter had so far oohed and ahhed as they had taken it in turns to each regale their tales of life in the dating lane.

It was not lost on Sadie that Mae was yet to name the mystery kisser. That he had made her friends heart soar only made her more curious to uncover who he was. Taking her lead from her best friend, Sadie had also not mentioned Rhys' name, although she needn't have bothered in being so coy.

The knitting ladies were ruthless, and she was now wondering if they were spies as they revealed that they knew all about last night's visitor at her little cottage. Rhys, in their opinion was a 'fine young man' who was sure to make Sadie very happy.

Shock and aww ran through her as the ladies proceeded to out Mae's mystery kisser as non-other than Rhys's older brother.

She was speechless. Ewan had been back in the village, the village bongo drums had been working but she had not seen him herself, which was surprising. In fact, now that she thought about it. Sadie hadn't seen Ewan in a few months. He came to visit three or four times a year, he never stayed long, preferring to take them out for the day and lavish attention and love on Tabby. Something that filled Sadie with gratitude. A male role-model. A constant if not always here, she was certain that Tabby thought very highly of her Uncle Ewan.

This revelation was going to need some serious thinking time. Her best friend making out with Rhys' brother. This was surreal. Was she dreaming. Discreetly she pinched her inner arm and flinched. No, she was awake.

"Come on now girls, us knitters are living vicariously through you. Tell us more! Tall, dark and brooding..." Mrs Collins had married three times and was currently widowed. Wow, she was not backwards at coming forwards!

"Ooo, now Diane, leave the girls alone!" Chorused Mrs Brunt, who was sat to her right and was knitting away as the conversation continued. Sadie turned to her showing a grateful smile. "They know all about the birds and bees. What I want to know, is about the zing!" Mae and Sadie's mouths widened in shock. This wasn't real! Who were these ladies and where were the nice knitters that came in once a week.

"You two need to snap them up quick."

"We haven't seen a shotgun wedding in these parts for over forty years!" At the mention of this, the room became over-run with the twittering of ladies gossiping and laughing and it was several minutes before the noise came down to a level that was comfortable.

As the ladies continued to discuss the benefits of a

quick wedding before you begin to show, Sadie realised that she had completely lost control of the situation and was relieved that the shop was closed for the day and no other unsuspecting victims would witness the conversation that was unfolding in her crafty room.

A few minutes later, Mae regained the use of her voice. Smiling she began to put the ladies firmly but politely in their place. "It has been so kind of you all to help us with our man dramas." Sadie nodded along, smiling encouragingly. "To be honest, neither Sadie nor I are looking to marry right now, if ever." At this Mrs Collins began clucking again, about their youth and beauty being wasted on fools.

Near the end of the knit and natter session, Mrs Grimshaw, who until this point had remained uncharacteristically quiet, spoke up. "I remember both of the Mr Knights when they were still in the village school. I think that the younger of the two has always had a soft spot for Miss Mirada." She waved her knitting needles in Sadie's direction then continued. The revelation ringing in her ears. "They were both good boys. You two could do a lot worse than the Knight men." With that she put her knitting in her bag, snapped it closed and made to leave the room.

As she stood in the doorway she turned, "The real question is why they are still single in the first place." This point reignited the discussion between the ladies that remained. Whilst Mae simply shrugged and rolled her eyes as she began gathering the tea tray things.

Sadie had to give Mrs Grimshaw her props. The woman knew how to rile up a room. She was a true master.

Chapter Eighteen

Tabby

The last week had simply flown by. Tabby was now a member of the drama club and there was a real chance she could have a solo in the winter show.

School hadn't really changed all that much; except she was spending more and more free time with Alex. He was fun to be around and once he got going, he could talk for England.

The bell had rung for lunch almost five minutes earlier and Tabby was now waiting in their spot. She wasn't worried. The lesson probably overran.

Across the quad, a group of lads from the year below had gathered. They were lounging on the benches and generally being loud and obnoxious to anyone that passed. It was this that had prompted Tabby to move away and further out of sight. She hated confrontation and being on her own made her a prime target. Muttering under her breath, she began cursing Alex for being late. She had a bad feeling being near these guys. One of them was notorious for causing trouble.

"Hey!" The familiar voice sounded behind her making her jump. "Sorry I'm late, got kept back and given a load of extra work to catch up as I'm new and it was a different subject or something. Anyway, I'm here now, were you waiting long? Tabby?" She was still looking over at the group of lads. "Maybe we should find somewhere else to hang out today?" He tapped her on her shoulder and indicated they should go back the way he came. She shrugged and followed, a little relieved at the suggestion.

"I think they were looking for trouble." Tabby looked anxiously over her shoulder as another of the lads called out at a passer-by.

It was Alex's turn to shrug as he led the way back towards the main building and canteen.

"We'll just stay out of their way,"

"Great idea," Tabby replied, relief coursing through her.

"You were going to tell me about what happened the other night." Alex waggled his eyebrows causing her to laugh. "Come on don't leave me in suspense!" she smirked at him then began to recount the tale of walking in to find that her mum had been making out with Rhys.

To his credit he didn't laugh, in fact he didn't show much emotion at all.

"How do you feel about it?" he questioned.

Tabby shrugged in a non-committal sort of way. "As long as she's happy that's all that matters."

Alex appeared to take his time thinking this over before finally he agreed that she was probably right, but that it was a bit strange to have a parent acting like a teenager.

This made Tabby laugh before pointing out that it wasn't only teenagers that kissed. At this remark she noticed that his cheeks looked slightly pink. "I hope that adults get up to way more than just kissing." This comment seemed to cause Alex to go fully red in the face although Tabby, who was eating her lunch in between words, was oblivious. "Wouldn't you be depressed if you found out that only teenagers have fun."

Alex coughed, "Fun?" She was aware of the blush now and she liked teasing him. There was something about Alex that made her bold. Fearless. She came out of her shell when it was just him.

"Sex, Alex!" She exclaimed before laughing again. A little louder than she had meant to. This time she was the one the shade of a Tomato. Dropping her voice to a whisper, "It would be a sad existence if adults didn't have sex don't you think?"

"Oi!" The shouts and calls were coming from a group of lads across the hall.

Both Alex and Tabby looked up. It was the group of lads from the quad. Apparently, their private conversation had carried further than either of them had meant it to.

One of the taller lads had sidled up to Tabby, she instantly felt uncomfortable. He was too close for comfort and leering at her in a way that made her skin crawl.

She hated guys like this.

Thing was, when JJ was here, this didn't happen.

She was quickly realising just how much he had been protecting her all these years.

She knew that if she told them to back off, things could get bad quickly. She glanced at Alex to see that all emotion seemed to have been wiped from his face. There were now three more guys standing around him which meant they were pretty much surrounded.

Tabby started to gather her things and stuff them into her bag. Avoidance was the best strategy.

"Did I hear correctly…" He reached out and roughly tucked a strand of her hair behind her ear. She jerked away from him and went to swipe his hand away, but he was too quick, and he caught her wrist in his hand.

At this, Alex seemed to find his voice. "Guys, we don't want any trouble." He stood up and shouldered his bag as though making to leave. The grip on her wrist tightened painfully causing her to wince. She realised there were two more boys standing behind her. One of which was leaning over to her as though about to whisper in her ear.

"So, you're sleeping with Alex Williams!" The voice carried across the room and several others stopped their conversations to listen. The rest of the lads laughed, and after twisting and pulling she yanked her wrist free. "Who would have thought JJ's little sister was a slut!"

Her mouth opened in shock, in her head she screamed no! But no words came out. She stared at Alex expecting him to say something be he didn't. He just stood there. Two of the guys behind him clapped him on the back and asked if she was any good. She felt the familiar sensation behind her eyes and forced herself to hold it in as the group of lads jeered and continued to shout and gesture around her.

Finally, her voice surfaced, a feeble croak. "No."

They rounded on her again. The wider audience around the room was growing. This time the wrist grabber spoke. "No, you aren't any good? Oh baby, you just need some practice!" He grabbed her again and pulled her to him. The rest of the guys fell about laughing. She felt sick.

Somewhere deep inside her anger erupted. "No, I am not having sex with Alex Williams." She pushed at him with no success, "No I don't need to practise and if you ever touch me again, I'll call the police!" Finally free she backed away from him. The laughter fell from his face and turned into a nasty smirk. She stood her ground and noticed two girls were now standing beside her on either side. She didn't know their names and felt rather than saw that they were on her side.

"Break it up, break it up! Bell is about to go, get to class. Johnson, get your friends and get to class before you land yourself in another detention!" The teacher was one that Tabby had never had a class with before, but she knew of him and his attitude to the students.

She could feel herself shaking now. The group of lads dispersed, and a hand gently touched her arm. She jumped and dropped her bag before realising it was the girl on her left. "It's ok, they're leaving. Are you ok?" A few other girls had swooped round her like a protective glove. She just caught sight of the back of Alex's bag as he walked out the door.

"What's your name hun?" A second girl had picked

up her bag. She was crouched down in front of her and had a look of concern etched on her face. "JJ's little sister? Tabby, isn't it?" She had simply nodded; the sudden energy boost was leaving her, and she didn't see the purpose of trying to explain.

The bell sounded and Tabby jumped at the noise. "Jenny, can you let Mrs Dixon know what happened? I'm taking Tabby to the office." The other girl nodded as Tabby felt herself being guided towards the admin building.

Thirty minutes passed by in a blur of questions and answers. An older lady had made her a cup of sweet tea. The girl, who it turns out was in her year, had stayed with her through it all. It was only as they were being ushered into the head teacher's office that she learned the girl's name was Anna.

Luckily, she had witnessed enough that they were bringing the lad in. He was facing expulsion this time apparently. Tabby didn't care. She was so tired. She wanted her bed.

It was after her mum arrived that she began to think clearly again. She finally gave in to her tears. Her mum looked like she was ready to commit murder. By two fifteen, a police constable had arrived. Asked more questions from both Tabby and Anna and had taken photos of her wrist which was showing signs of bruising. The nurse looked her over and suggested it be checked as she couldn't be sure that it wasn't broken.

Anna was able to name every person in the group who had surrounded her including the guy who had grabbed her.

Mae was outside waiting in the car, not yet aware of what had happened.

By the time they had visited the nearest hospital, seen a nurse, and had x-rays before finding out it was simply bruised, it was almost six in the evening. Tabby and the rest of them were exhausted from the day's events.

It was only once she was home and finally in bed that she thought through what had happened. She questioned if her actions had made things worse or better. She thought about Alex walking away and his statue like behaviour. She was now angry about the whole thing. She was angry at the school, the teachers, and their stupid pacifying advice on how to deal with bullies.

Now as she was falling asleep, her phone buzzed into life. It was JJ, but it wasn't a text message. He was calling her.

She sat up and swiped the answer button, "Tabby, Tabby! Can you hear me?" He was shouting down the phone and there was a thumping sound of the base in the background. "Wait a minute, I'll go outside."

"Jacob it's late." She had slid back down under the covers.

"I only just got the messages from mum, are you ok? Did they hurt you?" There was a sense of foreboding and a panicked edge to his voice. She could also tell that he was drunk. "I'll sort them out Jelly belly, tell me who it was!"

"It's all over JJ, you don't need to worry." She yawned, "How much have you had to drink..."

"I do worry, I worry that someone is going to hurt

you. I worry that you are going to meet someone. I worry that you will fall for some guy who isn't worthy of you. You are so sweet and innocent. And I don't want the world to ruin that…" He was rambling and not really making much sense.

"Look it's late, I'm going back to sleep. Please go back to your dorm and sleep too." Her voice was barely above a whisper, and he mimicked the softness back to her.

"How about I stay on the phone with you until you fall asleep. I'm walking back to campus now anyway…" She giggled at his stupidity.

"Ok."

"Ok." He replied,

"Tell me a story to send me off to sleep…"

"Mmm, would you like a story about a princess locked in a tower, or one about the knight who battled the dragon." The seriousness of his voice made her face light up as she snuggled deeper under the covers.

She yawned again and struggled to keep her eyes open, "Princess of course," she murmured.

He talked of towers and turrets, of a dark spell that had been cast over the kingdom. He did all the voices, and she was certain that he was probably dancing down the street and waving his imaginary sword as he talked about the Prince who slayed the beast and approached the topmost tower. She drifted off on a fluffy cloud, the sound of his voice was a tonic to the most horrific day. She felt her body relaxing and before she was aware of it, sleep had taken her.

JJ carried on talking to her softly down the phone, wanting to make sure that she had sweet dreams after the day she had had. After several minutes of silence, he muttered "I'm so sorry I wasn't there to protect you princess," and then finally hung up.

Chapter Nineteen

Rhys

The voice of his boss telling him what he could and couldn't do was starting to aggravate him. They had been talking on the phone for over thirty minutes and the conversation was going nowhere.

All the plans had been finalised over the last three weeks. Rhys had been working tirelessly to get it ready for approval. The council had agreed the plans, and everything was ready to go. Then out of the blue, his boss had emailed him in the early hours demanding a meeting to discuss his changes and how it was going to impact them.

He couldn't see what the problem really was. And more importantly, he couldn't see a way to resolve the problem that his boss seemed to think was risking the company. The last three weeks had been spent making these alterations in order to best suit the villagers and the needs of the new school.

Hours upon hours had been spent traipsing from cottage to cottage. He had spoken with well over two thirds of the villagers to gain their ideas and opinions about what the new school would mean to the community as a whole. Their ideas had been inspiring and he realised in no time at all that Sadie had been right at about making presumptions on behalf of them. She knew that they were wise and creative. And that a solution to their problems was only going to come from giving the locals a voice.

Rhys had been surprised to discover that he had enjoyed the many chats of tea and cake. He felt relaxed in their company and once they saw that he genuinely wanted what was best for the village, they had become a lot more forthcoming in their thoughts about the future school building.

So after the effort of so many to really make a difference, the attitude of his boss, was making him think all sorts of things he really shouldn't be thinking.

"I don't care how long you have spent making these changes or who you had to grovel with to get them approved. Fix this mess. The original plan was going to make this company a lot of money!" Bingo! There it was the bottom line. Money! "You follow the original plans, or I will have you removed from the site and put in one of the other lackies from the pits. I sent you as I thought you were a team player. It was a bonus when I heard you were from the area. I thought you would sweet talk the locals! Your job is on the line! Fix it!" The line went dead, and Rhys was left open mouthed and shocked.

This was bad.

Sadie

Sadie had just returned home from work. Things had not really returned to normal. After her parents had heard about the events at school they had pushed and pushed until she had finally conceded to talk with Tabby about the situation.

It had been a sign of how bad it truly was that Tabitha had agreed to the suggestion without further discussion. And so, with less than a week to make the arrangements, Tabby had left the local comprehensive and started the private school in the nearby city suburbs.

It had only been five days, but she was relieved that Tabby would be home for the weekends at least. Life in the cottage without her was wrong in every which way.

Even Bruno seemed to have lost his zest for life. He spent most of his time laying on Tabby's abandoned bed. He head resting on his paws. He large eyes saying everything that she was feeling.

The cottage had been their home for only a few years. But, she had never lived alone before and that was exactly how it felt. Alone. She only hoped that Tabby had not experienced the same feelings whilst she had been away.

She had managed to make arrangements for a Friday afternoon at the shop. And she was hoping that Mae would be back from being at a meeting as she really needed to borrow the car.

Her parents had suggested that the chauffeur, Mr Smithers, collected Tabitha on a Friday, but she didn't want to admit full defeat yet. Smithers was lovely, and she knew that he would take great care of her little girl, but she wanted to collect her, herself. At least the first week.

She had got up extra early, stripped and remade the beds and generally tidied up. So now she was just left waiting. A nervous energy was coursing through her body. The cup of tea she made was undrunk and cold. She had just over an hour to kill before she needed to leave. Plenty of time. She was folding the clean washing when there was a soft knock on the back door. Had she been in the other room she wouldn't have heard it. Sadie knew it wouldn't be Mae as she would have just walked straight in.

"Rhys!" He was stooped in the doorway holding out a small and neatly wrapped bunch of flowers. The zing was there instantly, she reached out, but instead of taking the flowers, she held his shirt and pulled him to her. He moved the blooms out of the way and allowed her to pull him into the kitchen.

She was a frenzy and was fumbling with his buttons as his lips found hers. He made no attempt to hinder her progress, and she guided him to the foot of the steep stairs, the washing lay forgotten on the table.

Rhys

Sometime later they lay together in a tangle of sheets and limbs. Rhys's breathing was slow and deep, and Sadie stroked the side of his face gently waking him with a soft kiss.

At once he was awake and he grasped her and pulled her to him. The sound of laughter filled the room and Rhys was sure he had never felt this way before.

"As fun as this afternoon's endeavours have been Mr Knight!" He was now tickling her softly and listening to her squeal whilst she tried to get out of his reach.

"Endeavours! You make me sound like a tour guide who has been showing you around the Yorkshire countryside!" His comment was light and not one bit reproachful. But she stopped and straddled him, her face suddenly serious as she looked down at him.

"I for one loved your guidance!" She whispered seductively in his ear. She smiled at him before leaning in for another kiss. "I was going to ask, why the visit this afternoon?" He reached up and stroked the side of her face. He wasn't really sure how to broach the subject with her. This was not really the time or the place.

"Um, well, I need to talk with you, but you'll need to be leaving soon to collect Tabby. It can wait!" Rhys was certain she would support his decision but maybe he should think about it a bit more first.

Sadie lazily leant down for one more long a delicious kiss before they began getting ready. Once back in the kitchen, a message from Mae and several missed calls confirmed that she wouldn't be back in time for her to take the car. "No panic! I'll take you into the city. I'd like to see this fancy school anyway!" Rhys smiled at her and reached for his keys once he'd managed to tie his laces. The look on her face was not what he had expected. Her smile didn't quite reach her eyes and she wore a look of uncertainty that made his heart miss a beat. "Sadie?" She was hesitant to leave the house and seemed lost in some thought or memory that tormented her. "Come on," he called as he held the door for her. He knew, at some point she would tell him what she was thinking, but now wasn't the time to push her further. She seemed to snap out of her thoughts all at once, and plastered a smile over her face. She kissed him on his cheek and followed him out, locking up as she did.

Once in the car, they continued to twine their fingers as he drove out of the village and headed north. Rhys was sure that this is what domestic bliss was meant to feel like.

He was sure that Sadie was his perfect match, that she always had been. He had felt it when they were kids. He had been sure she had known his feelings, but maybe he had been wrong.

The drive to Smithton Prep School was uneventful. The pair had passed the time in companionable silence and Sadie had appeared to fully relax once they had reached the motorway.

On reaching the driveway to the front entrance, she had visibly tensed once more, he was surprised by her reaction but had squeezed her hand reassuringly, hoping that his gesture could pass over a little courage to fight whatever battle she was having today. She returned a weak smile. "Would you like me to come in with you or wait in the car?"

She appeared to deliberate for only a fraction of a minute before showing the gratitude and relief that she didn't have to enter the school alone.

"It's probably all in my head, but I felt like I was being judged and they were left wanting when I came to drop her off. I'm sure I'm being ridiculous, but I want Tabby to fit in and her having a single mum and no dad seems to be the opposite of the norm here." Sadie rambled on, her nerves clearly getting the better of her.

Rhys gently pulled her hand to his lips. "Well, I think safety in numbers sounds like a plan!" He smiled wickedly, told her to wait there and gracefully exited the car and then went round to hold open her door. "This is going to be fun." He announced to no one in particular. Together they made their way through the oversized stone arch and into the school.

Chapter Twenty

Tabby

As they pulled the car into Beechend, Tabby felt a type of comforting relief wash over her. "I can't believe you two!" She was laughing and shaking her head at the same time. She was chastising two adults as though they were children. "Please tell me again!" She squeaked.

She could see the smile on Rhys's face in the rear-view mirror. "Your mother and I went in the main entrance." Her mother groaned theatrically. As Rhys continued to recount the events of the afternoon. "The headmaster invited us into the office. He was rude and obnoxious. Only looking at me when he spoke and completely ignored your mum." Tabby nodded along. It had only been one school week but already the sense of entitlement was wearing her down.

"The whole school seems to have the same attitude. But the classes were good, and I've already joined the am-dram group." She sat back in her seat. It was a good sigh that she let out. She could put up with the hoity toity people if it meant she didn't have to go back to her old school. "Tell me the bit about you telling him off."

"That's a bit of an exaggeration." Rhys laughed. "Your mum was trying to get a word in edgewise. The guy kept talking over her. So, I asked him to stop for a minute as there were some questions that needed answering. I then signalled for your mum to speak. The Head teacher turned to me and said that any concerns I have about my daughter will be their top priority." She giggled. There was something about them thinking Rhys was her dad. She liked the sound of that. "I told them I wasn't your father; I was the taxi driver." Tabby rolled around laughing in her seat. Her mum groaned again. "The Head Teacher finally straightened up and addressed your mum directly."

"That wasn't exactly how I had envisioned this afternoon playing out when you said you would take me to collect Tabby." Her mother's words, although probably true and meant to show annoyance failed as she was struggling to contain laughter that was bubbling over.

Rhys shrugged as he pulled up outside the cottage. Before the engine had completely stopped, Tabby burst with the question she had been wanting to ask. "Are you free on Sunday Rhys?" He turned in his seat to face her, a quizzical look on his face. He glanced at her mum but then immediately turned to face her again.

"I am free, what do you have in mind?" The conversation continued at they gathered her things from the boot and went into the cottage.

"Well, we are going to my Grandparents for lunch on Sunday, I've never taken a guest before. But I'm certain it will be a lot more fun if you are there too!" Tabby smiled at him and wondered if she should have spoken with her mum first.

"You want me to come with you to Beechend Manor?" He was standing in the kitchen a bag in each hand. "Um…" Oops, perhaps she hadn't read the situation correctly. Maybe him and her mum were just friends and maybe he was just helping out. But he had come to collect her from school. She tried her best to hide the disappointment that was raging through her.

Tabby's mum stepped forward and took the bags from Rhys, placing them on the kitchen table next to a half-folded pile of washing. "Rhys, it'll be like old times." She winked at him. Her mum winked at him. What did that mean? He laughed and agreed to join them for lunch at the manor. Tabby squealed again and rushed forward to hug them both. Trapping the three of them in a warm embrace that made her heart soar.

This was going to be so much better than their normal trips to her Grandparents. They would be on their best behaviour if an 'outsider' was with them.

After thanking Rhys again for coming to collect her, she gathered her school bag and made her way out of the kitchen. She could hear her mum calling asking for her washing as she needed to get it on.

That evening, she took advantage of the quiet cottage to think about what it meant to have both her mum and Rhys collect her from school. When she had been little, she used to love the days that Uncle Mike would come and collect JJ and her from school. She imagined that it was what having a real dad felt like. She would live for those moments. The times that Uncle Ewan came and whisked them out to exotic places for the day, like the beach or the zoo. Those days had been the best, but she had known, even then, that Uncle Ewan was just mum's friend. This felt different.

She knew it was just a fantasy, but she felt like a princess returning home after being locked in a castle. Tabby let her imagination run away with her, imagining her mum and Rhys getting married, buying a bigger house and then having a little brother or sister.

That night she slept soundly for the first time since that fateful day at school.

Sadie

They were turning up the drive and there was no going back. So much had changed in such a short space of time that Sadie felt she had not had time to adjust or even catch her breath.

At the time Tabby first suggested this little get together; she had been high on life and recklessly agreed and even joined in with persuading Rhys to come with them. Now, less than forty-eight hours later, they were almost there, and the doubt had set in. Tabby's things for school were in the boot, as her parents offered to take her back to school this evening.

She had been replaying the times she could remember from her childhood. The Knights had been frequent guests at Beechend. They were from old money and her parents saw them as respectable members of society. Was that why she had ignored Rhys' attraction to her when they were teens? Had she sabotaged them as a way to get back at her controlling parents? Even though she had felt the attraction to him just the same as he did to her.

The thoughts had been swirling since the early hours of yesterday. Over and over until she had left the house and walked across the fields, watching the sun rise and finally feeling a little calmer.

"Here we are then ladies!" Rhys' voice was light-hearted and showed no signs of anxiety or doubt. Kissing her hand, he whispered. "I'm here, don't worry." He knew, crap. She didn't want him to know that she was worried about this. He squeezed her hand reassuringly. When had that become the norm? She could feel the anxiety building again. "Shall we leave your things in the car for now Tabby? I'll move them after lunch."

They were on the gravel and moving towards the front door. She felt his hand in the small of her back, strong and comforting. She took a breath and they entered.

"Rhys I must say, we had heard rumours you were back in the village. We didn't realise that you had been spending time with Sarah and Tabitha!" The booming voice of Sadie's father echoed around the room. "Has your brother been to visit at all. I hear good things about his work in the city!"

"Yes Sir." Rhys was sat a little taller and had fallen straight back into the society he was born into. "He is certainly a force to be reckoned with!" Sadie had remained quiet and aloof. The conversation was washing over her like she was a small shell on the sand. It didn't move her, but she could feel it, hear it, smell it.

"Tell us Rhys," her mother was fawning over him, she had brought him here like a lamb for slaughter. Tabby was tucking into her lunch and appeared to be content and listening. "Have you set a date for the wedding yet?" Sadie stopped, she felt as though there was no air in her lungs. She glanced up the table, first at her mother, then Rhys. "Only we heard about the engagement but haven't received any written correspondence as yet." What was her mother talking about. They weren't engaged, they were barely dating! Did a drink in the pub and him sneaking round to hers count as dating? Ok, maybe they were together, but they hadn't talked about marriage, at all. She definitely would remember a conversation about becoming someone's wife.

Her mother was rambling on about country weddings verses town, pros and cons, guest lists. Rhys was silent. Tabby was looking at her imploring for answers. She had none. Confused, she tried to form a sentence in her head. Her parents continued to discuss wedding venues as though nothing had changed. Then some of the words reached her ears. "Of course, men don't organise weddings, that will be your fiancée, did she find a good wedding planner?"

Sadie stared at Rhys, willing him to turn and look at her. His jaw was set. He was frozen in place. Realisation was coming thick and fast now. She had heard the rumours in the village about a ring. She had racked it up to idle gossip. Now she wasn't so sure. He never talked about his life in the city. But then she hadn't asked. She was so stupid. Of course he wasn't single. Look at him! The knit and natter ladies had said as much. How disappointed they would be to find out that they weren't the ones to unearth his secret.

She felt sick.

His eyes connected with hers, they had changed. Taken on a harsh appearance. It was fleeting before they melted, and his face softened. When he spoke to the group, he stayed looking at her as though she was the only one in the room. "I am not engaged. I have never been engaged. Rumours do have a habit of travelling round certain circles. One day I am sure I will be." She flushed at his words and her mouth went dry. Her father cleared his throat and Rhys turned back to face them. "When I do get engaged, I will be sure to notify you both myself."

He wasn't with someone else. She felt so much guilt at believing the lies so easily.

Tabby changed the subject and before long her grandparents were hearing all about her first week at her new school. Sadie heard none of it as Rhys continued to stare at her, a flicker of pain passed over his face. She wanted to reach out, comfort him and make the pain go away, but she remembered where she was, and sense returned to her. She wished that they were anywhere else but here.

"I got you some new outfits, they are in the wardrobe upstairs." Her mother's voice pierced her brain. "Sarah, they will be perfect for the upcoming social events. Did I tell you that I am a member of the parents committee, they made a special request as a grandmother and alum mother of a previous student."

"Mum, you went there?" The tone of voice was accusing and full of something she wasn't sure she liked. "Why didn't you tell me?" Her face showed hurt at not knowing.

"Oh, they both went to Smithton after they left the village school." Her mother seemed to be enjoying herself a little too much. "They were inseparable all the way to the age of what fifteen?"

"Mmm, Francis I think they were sixteen." Her father piped up. They were a double act now. Regaling her life that she had tried so hard to leave behind.

"Yes, they then went to the sixth form that you just left, as the education ended in the fifth year at Smithton back then." Her mother took another sip of wine and it was as though all inhibition had disappeared. "Your mother dropped him and started hanging with a different crowd!" She tutted loudly. "Such a disappointment." Was muttered under her breath.

Sadie felt herself deflate, there was no use arguing with them. She would never win.

"Excuse me Francine," Rhys was staring her mother down, she looked at him, plastering on a face that would fool the pope. "Did I just hear correctly?" His face seemed to be struggling to hold back the rage inside. He sighed and shook his head. "You are still playing this silly game?"

Her mother shook her head, whilst she attempted to catch Rhys' eye and stop this before it escalated. "I'm not really sure what you mean." Her voice was now high and squeaky.

"I saw the way you treated Sadie when we were kids, I couldn't do anything about it because I was a kid. I always assumed that you would have had a little bit more respect for your daughter now she was a woman." Rhys was still seated although he seemed to have grown and filled the room menacingly.

"You can't come in here and speak to my wife like..." Her father's words were cut short.

"Is this why you wanted me here Tabby? Did you think if there were others here, they wouldn't try to chip away at your mum?" The rest of the room was now silent, Sadie dared not move. She felt like they were all on the edge of a giant precipice. The slightest wrong move and they would all go over. "I'm sorry my presence here couldn't save you from that." He reached out and squeezed Tabby's hand. "It never could. I thank you for a lovely dinner, but I think it is best that we leave." He stood up and placed his napkin beside his half-eaten meal. Her father seemed to have lost his voice and all that was emitting from her mother were squeaks of derision.

"Ladies, gather your things, I'll be taking Tabby back to school this evening. Under the circumstances, I think it's best." Her father nodded his agreement and stood as a mark of respect. Both herself and Tabby said their goodbyes and followed Rhys from the dining room.

They were almost near the end of the long drive before she found her voice.

"Oh, my Lord! Did that really just happen?" Squeals of delight came from the back seat and all Rhys could do was clutch the steering wheel as they were steered home to the cottage.

Chapter Twenty-one

Ewan

The decision to come back to Beechend this weekend had been spur of the minute. Ewan had been back in London for almost two months. He had been so busy at the office, yet he had found himself trawling through listings of houses in any spare time he had. Yesterday afternoon he had found a listing that had taken his breath away. He had found himself calling the estate agents and booking a viewing and train tickets before he was fully aware of his actions.

Now, here he was, just before eight on a Saturday morning, waiting for the agency to pick him up. His hire car wasn't ready yet, so he would have to make do.

Ewan never made spur of the minute decisions like this. He wasn't sure what had gotten into him. He didn't even contact Rhys to let him know he was back.

There would be plenty of time for all that once he had taken care of business.

"Mr Knight, welcome! Change of plans, your car is

now available for you to take straight away. I hope this is to your liking." Ewan thanked the young man before taking the keys and loading his pitiful luggage into the boot.

He arrived at the first viewing a few minutes early. There was only really one house he wanted to look at, but the estate agent had persuaded him to view a total of three. It's all about conversion rates, if only they knew just how interested he was, they wouldn't have wasted theirs or his time on the other two residential properties.

Just over an hour later it was all over, Ewan had put in an offer on the house he wanted. But he had to wait for a response from the current owner. He had taken a risk and offered under the asking price, but it needed a lot of work doing to it and he was sure they would snap up the offer. All he could do now was wait. Wait and hope that his offer is accepted.

It was not even eleven in the morning; he was sat in his hire car outside his brother's cottage. Rhys wasn't answering and there was no sign of life. A different car was parked on the drive, a sort of four by four with smooth lines and an expensive looking dashboard.

After ten minutes of waiting, he gave up and opted to search on foot for him in the village. There were only so many places he could be as the car, which he assumed belonged to Rhys, was here.

Rhys

The church was empty, and Rhys let out the breath he had been holding in. He chose to sit in one of the pews to the right, taking care to fold his longer than average legs into the confined space.

He was there to seek advice; he had gone as far as he could and now a decision needed to be made. Things with Sadie were going well, and he was finding that he spent well over half of his evenings in her company. It was almost perfect. There were still things he hadn't told her, and he got the impression that she was holding back too.

Rhys was now battling with the thoughts of wanting to tell Sadie everything. The worry seemed to have settled over him as he fought with his inner demons.

He was happy with things as they were. But at the same time, he had the overwhelming urge to declare himself as hers and she as his and lock themselves in the cottage, never to be disturbed again.

The feeling that everything was about to go to hell hadn't left him since their meal at Sadie's parents. Rhys hadn't been invited back to the manor yet, which wasn't something he was going to lose sleep over, but Tabby had mentioned the week before that there were next to no comments fired at her mum the last two weeks. So maybe him losing his cool last month was a good thing. Only time would tell.

Yet being outed about his almost fiancé by Sadie's mother had given him the briefest taste of what it would feel like if he were to lose her.

A deep voice penetrated his thoughts, "Mr Knight?" He looked up and came face to face with the reverend. "Is everything alright?" He had a concerned face and indicated for them to move to the office to the side of the main building.

"It is much more comfortable in here, how can I help you?"

The room was small but well proportioned, Rhys wasted no time and got straight to the point. "That is quite something isn't it?" He nodded in agreement, "If I may, it seems to me that you have gone some way to rectify the situation. I believe that you have a kind soul Rhys. You have already looked at the paths that lay before you. You found one lacking and so searched for an alternative." Rhys listened and felt the tension leaving his body. "In short, you don't need an old man like me or anyone else telling you. Rhys you are fighting for what you believe in. There are risks, but all journeys have twists and turns. It will sort itself out in the end."

Rhys' reservations were lessening with each passing minute. "Courage of your convictions! Perhaps Miss Mirada is the perfect person to confide in?"

Finding his voice, "I am not quite ready to tell her everything yet, I want to, but I think I need to wait a little longer. But perhaps it is time to arrange another village meeting?"

"A wonderful idea, shall we say Friday?" The

reverend smiled knowingly.

"Um, I'll be picking Tabby up on Friday evening, is it possible to arrange for this Thursday? Is there enough time?" The reverend paused, then flipped open the black book on his desk and began writing.

"Consider it arranged, I shall ensure the flyers are here for the service tomorrow and put up on the notice board. Relax Rhys, it will all work out ok. Is there anything else I can help you with today?"

Rhys thanked him for his words of wisdom and agreed to attend the service the next day. Something that he had not done for many years.

After leaving the church yard, he made his way back up the lane when he noticed a young lad sat on the nearest bench. He was tall, a little scruffy and maybe fifteen or sixteen. It wasn't until he was about to pass the bench that he recognised him as the lad Tabby had been hanging with all those weeks earlier.

"Hi," he called out loudly. The lad looked at him as he removed the bud from one ear. "You're a friend of Tabby's, right?" The lads expression altered, and he shrugged. "I think I saw you with her in the village, a while back."

"Yeah, but she left. Haven't seen her." There was a rawness in the lads voice that he knew only too well. Bravado in the face of rejection. Not easy for anyone to deal with, but for a teenage boy... fate worse than death.

Rhys sat on the bench and faced the graveyard. "You know why she left the school?" The boy made no sound, so he turned to face him in time to see the last of a shrug. "She's still here, she comes home every weekend."

The lad seemed to take this information in and removed the other earbud, he supposed to better here him.

"What's your name?" He eyed Rhys suspiciously before answering.

"Alex." He murmured then hung his head. "She won't talk to me. I messed up."

For a moment, he wondered if he was one of the lads who hurt her, he saw red.

"I didn't protect her from those guys at school. That's why she left. I don't blame her." Rhys' shoulders dropped again, and he felt sorry for the lad. Granted, he wouldn't have let anyone touch Tabby, but he wasn't a teenager anymore. It was a whole other level of protection that he felt.

"Look, it happened, and it's been dealt with. Do you want to fix things with her?" Alex sat up straighter and looked at him. This time he found it harder to read his expression.

"Things aren't the same." He noticed the fading bruise on the top of his cheek as well as the semi-healed scrapes on his knuckles.

"You miss her." For a moment, it looked as though Alex was going to deny this, make an excuse and leave. But he didn't. In fact he just sat there silently waiting.

"Sounds to me like you know what you need to do," Rhys advised him, thinking of the guidance he had been given only moments ago. "You just need to have courage and do something about it."

Alex looked at him as if he was talking a foreign language.

"She'll be at the shop later, stop by, say your piece and make things right."

Rhys stood up to leave, "Hey, thanks." Alex called after him.

He stopped and turned back to face him. The growing smirk on Alex's face was half hidden from view. "For what it's worth, I think she misses you too."

Ewan

This was the last place he wanted to look, but really, what choice did he have? It was nearing midday and he did not relish the idea of going all the way back to London. He was still waiting to hear about the offer he had made. It was no good.

Stealing himself he stepped over the threshold of a quaint little shop opposite the village green. The soft bell tinkled somewhere near his head. It was busy for a Saturday morning, and he noticed there was a group of ladies in the corner chatting as though this was the place to be.

"I'll be right with you." sang a voice from somewhere out the back of the shop. He had a moment to make a decision, should he stay and face the music or high tail it out of there. He waited a second too long and it was decided. "Ewan?"

"Sadie." He stood waiting for her to say something. He seemed to be doing a lot of waiting around these days. Without warning, her face split and she beamed at him. He thought he caught a glimpse of a tear as she launched herself at him and held on for dear life. He scooped his arms around her and felt the familiar feeling of really being hugged by someone who cared. "I'm so sorry." He whispered into the hair pressed to his face. She squeezed him tighter before releasing him.

"You should be!" She chastised him playfully,

swatting him with one hand whilst the other tried to stem the tears. "You have missed so much." He noticed that she didn't ask why as though she knew already and the question was completely pointless. "Well, you're here now! That is all that matters. You'll get to see Tabby. She's missed her Uncle so much and, well, Oh my gosh I'm rambling." She hugged him to her again before telling him that he was coming for dinner. No excuses allowed.

The weight in his chest lifted a little and he realised how stupid he was to stay away.

She pointed him in the direction of Rhys's makeshift office near the church and reminded him to be at the cottage for seven. Threatening to hunt him down if he didn't turn up. After a fleeting third embrace he left the shop, remembering to duck the lintel at the last minute.

It was after the chimes of the bell had ceased that he saw her. Standing on the other side of the green, carrying a few bags from her car to the gate leading to her front door. She paused readjusting the bags and turned as if knowing he was there.

They each just stood and stared as though in a trance that neither could break out of. Her hair was longer, and the sun-kissed glow had ebbed away leaving much fairer delicate skin. He forced the briefest of nods and she raised the corners of her lips slightly in return before they both turned away and went about their business.

Chapter Twenty-two

Tabby

What a busy afternoon it was turning out to be! The last of the crafting group had just left meaning all she would now have to do was clean up, cash up and go home. It was a little early still, but she knew her mum wouldn't mind. They had had an amazing day and it had made up for the few quiet ones they had been having lately. Tabby's mum was full of beans. Apparently, Uncle Ewan had stopped by just before lunch. She was so disappointed not to see him, but she had been assured several times before her mum left for the day, that he was coming round for dinner.

Tabby pondered this notion for a moment. He wasn't really her Uncle but maybe one day he would be.

She was in the back washing the dishes when the bell sounded from the front of the shop. Was it her imagination? She was sure she had locked the door. But then, her hands had been carrying the tray. She was frozen, hands dripping soapy water onto the floor.

Tabby glanced at the backdoor that was mere feet from her. But it was just a courtyard beyond. No other way out. She glanced around her and settled on the kettle.

She couldn't hear anything coming from the shop. Maybe it had just been a gust of wind, that happened sometimes.

Lowering the kettle, she was prepared to use as a weapon she stepped into the main shop.

"Tabby," a voice sounded to her left.

Simultaneously, several things happened at once. She screamed, raising the kettle ready to strike. The voice yelled, there was an almighty crash and a whimper.

In all the chaos she thought she had seen Alex's face. Her mind was definitely playing tricks on her. There was a groan coming from the floor in front of the counter. "Tabby," The voice was pained and breathless. She reached out behind her and turned the light back on.

It was Alex!

She immediately went to him. "Oh, my Lord!" Several baskets of yarn were scattered over the floor and amongst the mess was Alex. He lay there as though gravely injured. "You idiot, what on earth were you doing sneaking into the shop in the dark?" She looked again at his pitiful state and burst into uncontrollable laughter.

Tabby held out her hand to help him up out of the mess. He tugged and she landed, not very gracefully in a heap on top of him. She squealed and he held onto her as they continued to laugh. When it was finally out of her system, she turned to face him. He at least had the decency to look ashamed. "I'm sorry."

"Well, you did give me a fright!" She lent her head and rested it on his shoulder.

"No, I mean, yes for that, but mainly I'm sorry that I didn't protect you. I didn't do anything to help you." Tabby was stunned. "I'm sorry." Alex had placed his arm around her, and she nuzzled into him as though trying to show him without words that she forgave him weeks ago.

They stayed this way for quite some time, neither speaking nor showing any indication that they wanted to move. He had rested his chin atop her head and she felt safe.

"Alex," She didn't want to break the spell that had been cast over them, but she knew that her mum would come looking for her if she didn't show up soon. "I forgave you a long time ago. I thought you didn't want to be around me. I should have come to find you after I left school, but I thought maybe you didn't want to be friends with me anymore."

They were face to face now, and he seemed to be searching hers as though looking for something. She bit her lip trying to hold in what she really wanted to say.

"Tabby, I don't want to be just friends." And before she had a chance to react he had pounced on her and covered her lips with his. Her first kiss, on the floor of her mum's shop. She didn't have a clue what she was doing, but followed his lead, it was different than she had expected it to be.

"What on earth is going on in here?" Did no-body

knock anymore she screamed in her head as they broke apart. Her mother wasn't alone. Just behind her an entourage of people had gathered, including JJ and Mae, her Uncle Ewan and Rhys.

The two of them scrambled apart and got to their feet. Tabby mumbled something about Alex falling as her face burned red hot. She held her hand over her mouth as if it would somehow hide the evidence. Alex was trying his best to hide the smirk that was fighting to appear. Her eyes widened at him warningly.

"Maybe you should go." JJ had stepped forward, a look on his face that meant business.

"I'll see you later?" Alex didn't need telling twice, but before he left leant down and popped a solitary kiss on her lips. Oh, when did he get so brave? This was not the Alex she remembered.

"Goodbye Alex," her mum called after him, clearly trying to hide her amusement. Meanwhile, both Rhys and Ewan looked ready to kill. "Oh, calm down!" Her mum told them. She turned to Uncle Ewan and poked him in the shoulder... "You did far worse at their age!"

"Good to see you're alive!" JJ glowered, pushing past the others. "I'll give you a hand closing up" He turned her around and started leading her back to the kitchen. There was something about the look in his eye that she had never noticed before, but she supposed that 'big brothers' didn't like to see their 'sisters' making out any more than 'uncles' did.

"Actually, Jacob." Mae seemed to be taking charge of matters, "I'll stay with Sadie, you go back to the cottage with Tabby and these two can go to the pub for a pint." Mae's face was taught in a straight line that was definitely not like her. But, oh the relief. She needed to get out of here. "The dinner is in the oven; we'll be back before it's ready. Set the table for us all please."

They about turned and she grabbed her coat and bag as they headed for the exit.

"Tabby, your friend can join us if he wants. There's more than enough food."

"Mum!" She exclaimed. Her face reddening once again as the giggles followed them out the door.

By the look of JJ's face, he didn't agree with her mother's sentiment.

Rhys

The air outside was a lot cooler and the two brothers moved quickly in the direction of the pub. Neither spoke or even looked at each other. The anger seemed to be radiating from them in ferocious waves.

Once they had been served, quicker than usual, they found a table in the corner away from the rest of the Saturday crowd.

"I don't like that kid!" Ewan declared to the drinks in front of them. "You saw the smirk."

Rhys had seen it, but the anger he was feeling wasn't for Alex, it was for himself. He had told the kid where Tabby would be, had encouraged him even. He was the one to blame and he wasn't really sure how or even when these parental feelings had come in to play. Sure he spent most of his time at the cottage, but Sadie and him were just dating, when had it turned into this.

"Rhys! Did you hear me!" Ewan was staring at him, frustration and rage in his eyes. In truth he hadn't as he'd been lost in his own sense of self-loathing. "That kid is bad news."

Rhys sighed, the common sense seemed to have returned. She was seventeen, they were kids and hadn't Sadie, Tabby's mother said, it was no worse than we had all done. "Alex isn't a bad kid." Rhys stated, defeated by his own reasoning.

"What!" Ewan slopped some of his drink onto the

table. "Am I the only one who saw what was going on?"

Rhys placed a heavy hand on his brother's shoulder. "They were making out. It isn't the end of the World. Besides…" He took a gulp before continuing. "Tabby is a great kid. She isn't stupid. I trust her and more importantly, her mother trusts her to make her own decisions." He could feel his brother still in the seat next to him. "We don't have to like it. But frankly, we don't have a say in what happens."

The brothers continued to drink and brood for several minutes. They were still and pensive as each reached the bottom of their respective glasses. When Rhys placed his glass down, a notion came to him. "Wait a minute! Why are you getting so bent out of shape anyway?" He turned to face his big brother. "I'm the one that's been here with the girls for the last three months. Why are you so upset?"

Ewan frowned and drained his glass. "The thing is, I was coming to visit them a few times a year since Tabby was born. Well I did until you moved back here. Then I stopped."

This was news to Rhys, he hadn't had a clue. "Right." Was all he had to say.

"Look, I really can't get into the details right now. Let's just say, even though I haven't always been here, I've kept in touch with Tabby and I've helped out. Besides, I'm her uncle."

So many questions were whizzing round his head he didn't really know what to think. It was clear that Ewan was not ready to talk about any of it. He knew better than to push for answers.

"Ok, when you're ready, I'm here to listen." He certainly wasn't content with the snippets that had been thrown his way, but knowing that he wasn't being forthcoming about everything, made him feel a little sheepish. Rhys would have to trust, that when the time was right, Ewan would open up to him. "Shall we get back. Sadie seemed excited to have everyone round tonight."

Ewan shrugged, he looked weary.

"Oh, before we get there, tell me quick. What's happening between you and Mae?" Rhys queried. "Think you've finally found the one!" Rhys regretted it the moment he'd said it. Glass houses, he thought to himself.

"We're friends, nothing more." It was clear from Ewan's tone that there was more to it. But the look that was being tossed his way was more than enough to tell him to keep his opinions to himself. The thing was, when it came to his big brother, he never could leave well enough alone.

"If that's what you believe." Rhys laughed as they walked up the garden path.

Ewan

In that moment, whilst his brother's smug face stared at him, a piercing sound broke the silence. His phone made the most annoying sound so that he was forced to answer it. "Expecting an important call?" Rhys had stopped with him just outside of the cottage.

For a spilt second, he was reluctant to answer it, they hadn't talked about why he was there. Not really.

"Um, yes." Ewan glanced at the screen and saw that it was the estate agents. Throwing caution to the wind he connected the call. "Hi, yes, this is Mr Knight." He continued to mutter agreements into the phone, all the while fully aware that his nosey brother stood trying to listen in. "Really? That's amazing. I was certain the response would be no after I didn't hear back right away. Thank you, yes. I'll look forward to your call on Monday. Have a great weekend!"

He couldn't help it, his face split in two.

"Ewan? Good news?"

Turning to face his younger brother as he popped his phone in his back pocket, he then patted him on the back. "We need to have a chat…"

Anyone passing by the little cottage, would have questioned what could possibly be going on as the two men stood huddled together near the low stone wall.

After telling him everything, Rhys stood silent as though he had been stunned and was completely immobile. Ewan stood patiently waiting; he had told his brother something that he thought he would be happy about. But he remained expressionless and then, a little annoyance seemed to creep over his face. "Don't you think that this is something that we should have discussed?" Rhys was pacing back and forth as though trying to expel excess energy surging through him. "How could you? You don't think that maybe it would be nice to know that my brother is… is, is." An echo of his words hung in the air. "Maybe I would have liked to buy it. Did that even occur to you?" Ewan was surprised by his brother's response. It was clear to everyone that Rhys wasn't really going to move back to the city. But after everything that had happened this summer, he didn't even think he would have wanted the house. Maybe his brother had every intention of staying in Beechend after the job was completed. He hadn't asked.

"I'm sorry I didn't consult you about this. I didn't think you would care this much." Ewan was torn. "I can pull out if you want and we can talk this through.

"You're right, we'll talk about this later." Although a little calmer, his voice was still harsh in tone and he knew that whatever Rhys had to say, he would accept it. He flipped his phone out of his pocket and scrolled through to find the number. "Um, don't pull out of the sale. If someone else was going to buy it, I'm glad it was you." Rhys was not easy to read, and he hesitated before popping his phone away again.

"Guys!" As one, they turned in the direction of the soft voice. "Are you coming in? Gosh, it is freezing out here!" Sadie turned on her heal and scurried back into the warmth of the kitchen.

All sign of discomfort had been wiped from Rhys's face as he motioned for Ewan to enter the house first. But as he walked into the warm glow of the kitchen, he couldn't shake the feeling that Rhys had a lot more that he wanted to say about his announcement. Based on his initial reaction, none of it was going to be good.

Chapter Twenty-three

Sadie

The following day Sadie was up at dawn. She was trying to enjoy the morning calm but after a few minutes of being pestered to take Bruno out, she caved in. Sadie found herself walking across one of the fields on the outskirts of the village. There was a mist hovering a few feet off the ground that seemed to swirl as she walked through it. Bruno seemed to have a newfound energy this morning as he bounded round, barking happily as a flock of disturbed blackbirds took to the skies.

The cascading water over the rocks in the stream seemed to be a lot louder than usual today. The water levels were much higher and she supposed this was due to the heavier rain they had had in the area of late.

Sadie would usually wade over to the other side of the stream and walk back along to the old bridge, but she thought better of it and headed along the southern edge instead that looped back round to the church in the distance.

Her mind wandered back to the events of the night before. She hadn't had a chance to talk with Tabby about Alex yet. She trusted her and so wasn't worried, however she felt the need to touch base as Tabby's education change meant she had very few opportunities to 'parent'.

Rhys and Ewan's reaction was almost comical. Fortunately, Alex had the sense not to take her at her word about the offer for him to join them. She liked that they cared so much and wasn't in the slightest put off by their protective behaviour. But something was going on with them. They had been so quiet when they returned from the pub. Then the pair of them had gone back to Rhys' almost as soon as dinner was finished with. It was very unusual. And a little unsettling.

Rhys had been practically living at the cottage and she had been a little surprised by his sudden departure. Mae had also been very quiet whilst Ewan had been there. She hadn't pried as the kids were there, but intuition was telling her that something was going on.

Sadie did not like being out of the loop, but she supposed that they would tell her if and when the need arose. She just hoped that everything was alright, or if it wasn't, she hoped that the Knight brothers would know that they could come to her about anything.

She called Bruno to heel. He was poking around a hedgerow and had clearly caught the scent of something juicy. He lolloped over and patiently waited as she reattached the lead. He was a loyal companion, and she was relieved to have him, with Tabby being away so much. He at least seemed to have gotten used to their new routine.

Together, they rounded the last bend that led to Church Lane, when suddenly Bruno stopped. His ears perked up and he growled. She couldn't remember the last time that had happened, if ever. Sadie stood by him and affectionately stroked the top of his head and tickled his ears in an attempt to calm him. The fog was denser here and she was struggling to see to the end of the lane. "What is it boy? Who's there?" She couldn't hear anything, but she trusted Bruno's instincts. Maybe it was a fox or maybe Betsy the goat had escaped again. He had never really been a fan. She pulled him back the way they had come. It was the longer way home, but why walk into the unknown.

As she turned, she smelt it. It was faint but there was no denying it. Burning, but like nothing she had smelt before. Electrical or maybe plastic. She wasn't sure.

Bruno was barking now and pulling back towards the lane.

In that moment, the smell seemed to intensify and she was amazed that she hadn't sensed it sooner. With a sinking sensation, she knew, it wasn't fog, but smoke that had been blocking her view. In her haste she hooked the lead over the nearest post before whipping out her phone. She called it in to the emergency services, giving the rough address as she wasn't sure where exactly the smoke was coming from. All the while, she could see tendrils reaching out along the surface of the path.

She had only stopped for a moment to make the call, but already her approach was now hindered by the thickening smoke that no longer swirled around delicately, but was more like a solid impenetrable barrier.

The lane that led to the Church was lined by small terraced cottages. It was in fact number seven that Tabitha and herself had lived after they left her parents. She loved this place and she knew it well. Using her scarf to cover her mouth, she ran from cottage to cottage in an effort to rouse everyone. Banging on doors and screaming at the top of her lungs. With each breath, she took in more of the acrid smoke. It burned and scorched and left her coughing even more.

With the cottages being all attached, they were therefore more at risk of also catching fire. She was a little over a quarter of the way up the lane when realisation dawned.

Rhys' car parked up ahead. Was it his cottage? Was he in danger? Panic filled her and as she neared the far end of the lane the heat grew ever more intense. Sadie could hear the people she had awoken coming out of their homes. Mrs Figg had exclaimed and announced to no one in particular that she would call in reinforcements. Sadie took this to mean the fire brigade but didn't stop to correct her. The more people who rang, the more likely help would arrive quickly.

All she felt coursing through her, was a need to get to the fire, to get to Rhys. Sadie felt it in her bones. It was as if she knew that the World couldn't stand for her to be happy. She wasn't allowed to find happiness.

She could see the home in question now. Was it Rhys' or next door? She was confused in the haze and panic. It was engulfed from the front, she could see no way in. The owner of the cottage had purchased a few of them along here and rented them out, which meant they all looked the same. No distinct differences between each of the facades. They were simply copies of each other.

Pushing down her fear, she ran at the door, banging and calling for anyone. She heard a cry like the sound of a wounded animal.

"Someone's inside!" She screamed. Reassessing, she could see the window upstairs had opened. Smoke was billowing out. "We need a ladder!" She couldn't see the face of the person and the flames were roaring louder in her ears making it difficult to tell if the voice crying out was male or female. Two lads ran forward with what looked like an old wooden frame ladder and leant it up to gain access. She was holding it steady all the while the choking and suffocating smoke threatened to engulf her.

What would have only been a few minutes felt like hours as she waited for the trapped person to be rescued. A slight figure was helped through the window. It wasn't Rhys. Relief coursed through her as the face of a woman she didn't recognise stepped gracefully from the bottom rung. Instantly, a person swooped in and helped the lady to safety.

"Sadie?" The voice was confused yet a comfort to her ears. Strong arms encircled her and pulled her back from the front of the cottage. "What are you doing here?" She threw her arms around him and held on for dear life. Rhys, was all she could think about.

"Rhys, is she alright?" Ewan was there too, but she didn't look up, she just continued to cling on as if he was a lifeline. She didn't hear him answer but he tightened his hold on her and guided her to the other side away from the flames.

All around her it was organised chaos. Several of the local farm hands had arrived with buckets and the villagers were approaching in droves. They were forming a line from the pond to the flaming building in an effort to put out the toxic fire or at least prevent it from spreading and causing even more damage.

"Sadie? Are you hurt?" She shook her head and through her booming coughs gestured that she needed to help the others. "No, there are enough helping." He rubbed her back as she continued to cough. Mrs Figg had brought her a glass of water and she obligingly took sips.

"Bruno!" She gasped pointing back to the other end of the lane. Ewan immediately took off to retrieve him and by the time he had returned with a frantic golden retriever, the emergency services had arrived and were trying their best to move the civilians back from the blaze.

After what felt like an eternity, the fire seemed to be under control. The paramedics had given her oxygen and monitored her before deeming her fit and if there were any concerns she was to go straight to A and E. Sadie hadn't heard the fate of the women she had helped to rescue. She had been taken in the first of three ambulances. She prayed that she would be ok.

Now they were back at the cottage. Rhys had been adamant that she delay opening the shop this morning and take the time to recover. Tabby had dutifully announced that she would open on her behalf, granted a little later than normal, but she would cover the morning to give her mum time to rest.

Rhys had seemed happy with the suggestion and had settled her on the sofa as though she was a glass bauble that might shatter at any moment. He had then extricated himself to the kitchen, made her a cup of tea and proceeded to bang around as though using every pot and pan she owned. The whole scene was laughable and in the end, she moved into the kitchen to join him as the suspense of not knowing what he was up to was killing her.

Rhys

The restless energy coursing through him was unbearable. He was making omelettes as he thought that would be nice and soft on Sadie's throat. Cheese omelettes, he corrected. Rhys had found after bringing her home to the cottage that he couldn't look her in the eye so he was keeping himself busy.

He could have lost her. That thought had almost destroyed him, his reaction to that thought scared him still further. What did these feelings mean?

Just six months ago, he had begun planning his proposal to Fiona. They lived together; he had believed his miserable existence was in fact love. It turns out he had known nothing. What he had in London had been a lie. Fi hadn't loved him. He wasn't even sure that she loved Cole, but that wasn't his burden anymore.

He could not imagine his life without Sadie or Tabby or even Beechend. Was that love? Maybe. It felt like it should be love. If it wasn't, it was a lot like it.

"Penny for your thoughts…" Sadie was sat at the kitchen table. He hadn't even seen her enter the room.

He felt flustered and caught out, "Just don't want to burn the eggs!" He flipped the food on to a plate and placed it in front of her before sitting down on the opposite side of the table. "Maybe let them cool down a bit first."

Sadie got up out of her seat and climbed into his

lap, she circled her arms around his neck and then leaned her body into his. Resting her head on his shoulder and feeling the length of her was intoxicating. He never wanted to let her go. She was safe here and she would always be protected in his arms.

He could feel the anger bubbling away inside of him as if searching for the surface to break free. He strived to push it back down but he was losing the battle. "What were you thinking?" His tone was harsher than he would have liked. "You could have been seriously hurt, you could have died!" He squeezed her tighter to him and stroked her hair. The lingering smell was encased in each strand and it made his throat constrict involuntarily.

Rhys pushed himself out from beneath her, he couldn't sit. The excess and nervous energy flooded his body once more. He paced the kitchen, back and forth. "You would have left behind all the people who care for you." His voice shook from the effort to keep calm. "Tabby with out a mother, Mae her best friend, me without..." His words trailed away.

"I thought you were in there!" Sadie's voice broke and the sobbing began.

He remained as he was for a moment, comprehending her words before scooping her into his arms and carrying her back through to the living room. He held her as she cried. He held her and waited until her tears were spent. His own fears had been overridden by her anguish at believing he had been hurt.

Once calmer, she told him what had happened on

her way back into the village. How each of the cottages had looked the same in the ever-increasing smoke. How she had been frantic to get to him. How she had struggled to call out and had a deep-seated need to get to him.

After the tale was told, he bent forward and softly pressed his lips to hers. There was a soft tang to her sweetness, but once they connected a fierceness surged through him and he felt Sadie cling to him as though he was the very air that she breathed. He knew because that was how he had felt. She was everything. This had to be love.

In that moment, there was only the two of them. All that mattered was right there on the old tatty sofa in the little cottage.

Chapter Twenty-four

Ewan

There had been a little smoke damage to the cottage and Ewan had made arrangements to stay an extra week in an effort to help out with the clean up. In all honesty, he had barely seen Rhys as he was back to stay at Sadie's most nights. He didn't mind as they were yet to really talk about his decision to buy a property here.

He hoped, with their relationship on the straight and narrow that Rhys would see that them both being here was the right decision.

Meanwhile, he had decided to make the most of his time back here. On the first evening after the fire, he had found himself bold and daring as he made his way over to Mae's home on the further side of the village green.

It was just after dusk and a solitary window was lit creating a soft glow of warm light over the shrubs out the front.

He had stepped up and rung the bell before he had

a chance to second guess his actions.

In no time at all the door had swung inwards with a slight creak that he found endearing. He was face to face with Mae as he had never seen her before.

Her hair was scraped back from her face with a few curls escaping and framing her face which was covered in what could only be described as a paper mask that he certainly didn't understand. She gave a squeal and closed the door on him.

"Um, Mae…" he started talking to her through the closed door.

"Mhum." She groaned in reply.

"Well, I've already seen you, so you might as well let me in!" He understood the method to his logic and he hoped that she did too.

He patiently waited a few minutes more, when slowly the door creaked open once more. Her hand emerged through the gap and a solitary finger beckoned him inside. Once over the threshold, she closed the door with a sharp snap. "I wasn't expecting anyone," she explained, waving her hand over the thin mask on her face.

"Well I think you look great in anything!" She looked to be raising her eyebrow, mocking him, but the overall effect was lost as this dislodged the mask which began to roll back over her face. She squealed again and tried to fix it.

She led him through to the sitting room which was pleasantly decorated and cosy. She sat down on the sofa and proceeded to smooth out the mask across her face. He sat down beside her and she immediately jumped up, making a fuss about putting the kettle on.

Ewan noticed that in fact, she had shot up the stairs. He laughed to himself, enjoying the fact that he clearly was having some sort of an effect on her after all.

She was gone for almost a full five minutes and when she returned, she was in blue jeans and an oversized jumper. She was no longer wearing the face mask and her eyes appeared to have a shine about them that he had never noticed before.

He stood abruptly and began babbling about it being late. He ached to reach out to her and take her in his arms but something was holding him back.

She looked taken aback by his sudden change, "It really doesn't matter, I've popped the kettle on and you are welcome to stay..." Her voice had trailed off and he found himself mesmerised by her full lips.

"Oh, I really should get going, sorry to have bothered you. I'll see you around."

Before she had the chance to respond, he was out the door and into the night air.

He wandered around the village for over an hour before returning to Rhys' rental cottage. He didn't know what was wrong with him. She had such a strange effect on him and he seemed to have lost the ability to function.

It was seven days since the fire, and he had taken back his car and was now waiting at the station for his train to arrive. Flashes of the previous six days appeared in front of his eyes as he recalled the times he had seen her.

Leaving the village in her car, walking into Sadie's

shop, chatting to the man who owned the goat and carrying her shopping into her cottage. He hadn't approached her or even smiled in her direction and she appeared to be oblivious of his presence. He felt like some creepy stalker and he wondered how much longer he was going to be like this.

He didn't really want to go back to the city. But there were so many things that he needed to do before the sale in Beechend was finalised. Ewan had taken part of his time away to be productive. He was already in the throes of setting up his freelance business that he was planning to run from the countryside.

For the first time since his parents passed, he felt like this was the right decision. He felt like he was coming home. Not just to Beechend, but to Mae and a life they could have together if they wanted.

Ewan continued to make a mental list of all the things he needed to arrange when out of the corner of his eye he saw a familiar face. He took a double take as this was not a face he ever expected to see here.

He stood, almost spilling the lukewarm coffee over himself in the process. "Fiona?"

She turned at the sound of her name and her face beamed at him. "Ewan!" she exclaimed, kissing him once on each cheek. "What a lovely surprise." He did not agree with her statement and waited for an explanation.

"Fiona," He sighed, not even attempting to hide his annoyance, "What are you doing here?" In fact he seemed to have accentuated his tone and his features had morphed into those of distaste and loathing.

"Oh, now Ew-an, there is no need to be like that!"

His frown deepened, he hated when she said his name like that. It made his skin crawl. "I'm here to see a friend. Aren't you going to congratulate me?" It was only then, as she moved her over-sized bag to one side that he saw her protruding stomach. She beamed some more and declared that the baby would be here in the spring.

Before he had the chance to utter a word, his train arrived and Fiona had kissed the air and waved her goodbyes as she tottered out of the station pulling her ridiculously expensive luggage behind her.

Rhys

Rhys was on cloud nine! Everything was working out great. He was taking Sadie into town this evening after the village meeting, hopefully to celebrate the new development breaking ground in a few weeks. They had managed to delay the meeting after everything that had happened in the last week.

His phone had died in the night as he had forgotten to put it on charge yet again. He felt bad that he hadn't taken Ewan to the station, but his brother had promised he would be back soon.

The night before, Ewan had made the announcement to them all, that he had made an offer on their old family home near the village and that it had been accepted. Sadie had been elated at the prospect. Rhys was slowly coming round to the idea of his brother owning their old home. Maybe it wasn't such a bad thing after all. Now he wished he had, had the chance to say as much before he left for the city.

He was making his way along the main street in the village, he needed to get back to his cottage and gather up everything needed to go ahead with the plans for the school.

Hopefully he could make it a quick work morning as he still wanted to stop by the florist and pick up a bouquet before their date this evening. He chuckled to himself at the thought of it. An actual date. He felt like a teenager and his palms grew damp with sweat.

Finally, a real date with Sadie Mirada. If his parents could see him now. He had never been very good at hiding his emotions from his family. All these years later, he had been grateful of that at least.

Mentally, he gave himself a shake. They were practically living together, did people living together go on dates? But he wanted her to feel like a princess this evening. He wanted her to know how he felt. He also wanted her to know everything, including somethings he'd rather no-one knew.

He turned the corner past the church and the cottage next to his that was blackened and in a very sorry state. Stopping short when he saw a car outside the front of his home that he did not recognise. He took out his keys and proceeded to unlock the door to enter when a voice rang out high pitched and squeaky. I managed to destroy any peace there might have been to his morning.

"Rhys, darling!"

He spun round to see Fiona standing in front of him. Her enormous sunglasses covering the majority of her face even though it was quite a grey and overcast sort of a day.

Rhys dropped the keys and hastened to retrieve them and get in the house as quickly as humanly possible. "Fiona, I don't know why you are here, or what you are playing at. I thought I made myself perfectly clear! I don't want to see you. You've had until the end of the year to sort out your living arrangements." He stopped again. She was stood with one hand holding her bag whilst the other lazily rubbed over her blossoming stomach.

"I think it is best if I come in. Unless you want the whole village to hear our business." Her smile was sickly sweet, and he wondered what he had ever seen in her. Rhys nodded curtly and stepped aside to allow her into the cottage.

She twittered around inside, picking things up and putting them down again as though examining their weight. He said nothing as he went through the motions of making two cups of tea. His body felt cold and as though it wasn't his own anymore.

Rhys placed the tea down on the coffee table and sat waiting for her to explain herself. She finally sat down opposite him.

"Is it Darjeeling? You know I only drink Darjeeling tea." Rhys raised one eyebrow but didn't reply immediately. He did know she only drank one type of tea, how could he forget.

"It's decaf as I'm guessing you don't want to harm your unborn child?" His tone was flat and he waited for her to react.

As he expected, her face contorted into a distasteful grimace that he had so often seen on her features. But then a triumphant smile erupted, and she declared. "Our baby, darling." She fluttered her fake eyelashes at him and continued to rub her belly for effect. His insides squirmed.

"Really?" His voice showed no tone of surprise at her announcement. Her smile faltered for a fraction of a second before she regained her composure. "How does Cole feel about this?" Rhys showed no sign that he was happy about her announcement and knew that there was going to be something, there was always something with Fiona. Some angle that she was trying to swindle out of someone. Something that she hoped to benefit from.

She swiftly covered her face in her hands and loud crying sounds filled the small room. For a fraction of a second he considered that the child could in deed be his.

He lent forward and offered a tissue from the box which she gratefully accepted. It wasn't lost on him that although she had been crying for several minutes, when she emerged from behind her hands, her makeup was immaculate and there was no evidence that a tear had been spilt.

"Cole left me; he broke up with me when he realised, I still loved you." She simpered and made out like she was drying her eyes. But he knew better. Rhys had seen enough of her behaviour to know that she had an ulterior motive in being here.

"Fiona, what do you want from me?" Rhys remained seated though his tone showed that he was beginning to lose control of his calm façade.

"It's a lot to take in, I understand. I'm staying at the bed and breakfast next to the pub when you are ready to talk." He groaned as the door closed behind her with a soft click. Rhys' happiness and good fortune seemed to be evaporating before his very eyes.

Ewan

When he finally walked into the apartment, his phone buzzed into life. Seventeen messages were waiting for him. All of them from Rhys.

The most recent message asked him to call as soon as he was home.

Before he had even removed his coat he slid his thumb across the screen and pressed through the call. "Rhys."

"Ewan, you're home. Did you get all my messages?" The rambling voice of his brother continued as he regaled him the tale of his life going up in smoke.

"So, she says it's yours?" Ewan's jaw was still tight from his encounter that morning. It was beginning to ache. Rhys confirmed by repeating what she said.

"I don't know what to do!" He sounded defeated and a little lost. "I just don't know what to do…"

Taking a deep breath, Ewan began to take charge of the situation. "Ok, first things first… do you think this baby is yours?" Rhys rambled on but ultimately stated that there was a possibility. "Ok, do you want to be in the child's life?"

"Yes, if the baby is mine. But Fiona, I can't go back to that."

"I understand." Ewan consoled. "Perhaps she will consent to staying in your apartment a little longer until matters can be sorted out."

Rhys sighed into the phone, Ewan didn't like to hear his brother this way, especially when he was so happy and his life was getting back on track. "So I need to go talk with her again?" There was a steeliness in Rhys's voice that Ewan was not familiar with.

"Yes, you need to talk. Offer the apartment and state that you want a DNA test as soon as it is possible. You and I both know it might not be yours."

Ewan was wishing he had stayed after seeing Fiona at the station, he didn't like to be so far away when his brother clearly needed his support.

"I'll get ready for the village meeting and head over there to tell her we will sort things out and she can go back to the apartment." Ewan nodded along as his brother hashed out the plan.

"Just keep your cool and wait this out. There is nothing more you can do." Ewan ended the call with a sense of dread. Perhaps he couldn't be in Beechend, but he was certain there was something he could do here to get to the bottom of this mess.

Chapter Twenty-five

Sadie

The shop had been so busy today. Tabby had helped this afternoon and she had been a godsend. The majority of customers were regulars from the local area but there had been a strange request from a pregnant woman this afternoon. She had wanted a baby blanket, cardigan and matching hat. Sadie had understood that this was not an altogether odd request being that she ran a craft shop and displayed many hand-knitted items. However, the woman in question had wanted them to be knitted for Monday morning. Sadie had politely pointed out that they didn't make items to order and the knitted projects she wanted making would take several weeks. She had apologised but the woman, whose voice was high pitched and unnaturally squeaky had declared that this place should be run out of business and that she would tell all her friends not to come here.

The woman hadn't purchased anything and although Sadie didn't like to judge a book by it's cover, she had doubted that the woman had any friends who would have purchased here anyway.

It was no loss really, but the woman's behaviour and attitude had stayed with her the remainder of the afternoon and by closing, she had felt incompetent and was certain the business would go under in the near future.

After regaling her tales of woe to a sympathetic ear, Tabby had proclaimed that the woman was crazy and she shouldn't be taking business advice or criticism from someone like that.

Yet again, her daughter's level headedness and calm persona had saved the day. It was good to know that she was raising such a well rounded human who could spot an idiot from a mile away.

By five pm Tabby was nestled in front of the TV for the evening and Sadie had primped herself ready for the evening ahead. She was running a little late as the meeting was due to begin at half past. She had grabbed her coat a begun the short walk to the school.

Rhys

"Thank you for agreeing to meet with me. I only have a short amount of time as I have an important business meeting that I need to get to." Rhys was dressed in a suit and tie, his favourite tie so that he was ready for his date with Sadie. He just knew that he wouldn't be able to relax until he had sorted things out with Fiona.

She laughed, "You're working on a Saturday evening?" She stroked a finger down his tie, but he stepped back. "Oh honey, you are going to need a better excuse than a business meeting. I know you, remember?" She was using her seductive smile on him and he was happy to discover it had absolutely no effect on him.

"Yes, I have a meeting. But first things first. You can stay in the apartment for a few more months until all of this mess is straightened out."

She recoiled as if he had struck her across the face. "Our unborn child is a miracle, not a 'mess'." Her voice was getting higher and higher. He glanced at his watch to see that he had a little less that thirty minutes to get to the school. He felt rushed and this wasn't going well.

"I'm sorry, that was cruel of me to say that. I only meant that I have a few stipulations of my own." She appeared to be listening at least. "You need to leave Beechend, go back to the flat and make arrangements for the DNA test to be carried out. I will contact you in the coming week and make plans to discuss this further."

"You don't believe me!" She looked outraged, which given the circumstances of accusing her baby of being another man's he would normally understand. However, this was a unique circumstance and quite frankly he didn't believe a word that came out of her mouth.

"Fiona, you were having an affair with a friend of mine for months, maybe even longer and you are surprised that I don't believe the baby is mine. You are a smart woman Fiona. Leave here and we will sort things out for you and the child." He smiled weakly and moved towards the door.

"Wait!" She had reached out and grabbed his shoulder. He shrugged her off.

"Whatever the outcome of the results, you must know, I am happy here, I won't ever be coming back to you Fiona. Baby or no baby. We are over." He opened the door to leave. "Take care of yourself and I'll be in touch soon."

Rhys was out of breath and a little anxious after his encounter. He hoped that she would do as he asked and leave. He had kept his cool although being around her had made him feel sick.

He walked into the hall to see that most of the villagers were there.

Fortunately, he had come in before and set up ready for the presentation of the new plans. He was hoping that this time things would go smoothly.

"Mr Knight!" The voice was scratchy and filled him

with dread. He had not banked on this yet. "You are late to a meeting that you yourself asked for. This reflects badly on the company."

His boss was standing in the way of the podium and was the absolute last person he wanted to see here.

"Sir, how nice of you to attend this meeting. I have already set up as you can see. It isn't due to begin for a further ten minutes."

The short man huffed and narrowed his eyes as he continued to glare at him.

"I hope the necessary changes have been made to the plans..."

Rhys assured him that the appropriate changes had been made and before long the Reverend was introducing him once more and he stepped forward onto the little stage. He caught a momentary glance of Sadie and all his worries seem to dissolve.

"Evening everyone, thank you so much for taking the time to see our new and improved plans for the new school." Rhys launched into what hadn't been rehearsed. He spoke from the heart about the journey he had been on over the months he had been back here.

"After listening to the needs of each of you and your collective desire to make a better community at Beechend. I came up with this..." He pointed the clicker at the laptop and the screen changed to show the drawing he had painstakingly spent many hours on. The school would have seven purpose-built classrooms tailored to the needs of each specific age. The hall would have space to seat the school children and staff for their morning assemblies and the multifunctional stage could be used for performances as well as displaying their many accolades.

Adjacent to the school and attached by a corridor, would be the state-of-the-art community centre, kitchen, hall, classrooms, as well as an office for confidential meetings. There were ten individual lock cupboards for different groups to keep their resources and maintain their stock without the risk of damage. There would be a designated creche room for baby and toddler groups or even for a nursery to be set up in the future if needed. All the areas were on the ground floor and so wheelchair and disabled access had been paramount.

He stopped to take a breath and hoped that this time, he had done his job right.

Sadie

The presentation was amazing, the graphics blew her away and she was surprised to see so many of her ideas that she had shared with him. The designated spaces for different community groups. The link to the school so that it could be used by them also. It was amazing. She was completely bowled over and glancing around she saw that the rest of the villagers loved it just as much as she did.

"Excuse me, Mr Knight. A word please!" A short skinny man had stood up in the front row without any show of manners or polite decorum. Sadie presumed he must be someone involved in the project. She couldn't hear what he was saying, but his facial features and arm gestures showed her all she needed to know.

Suddenly, the little man raised his voice over the chatter of the crowd. "This is not the plan we agreed on. You have really done it this time! I will make sure that you never work in the city again!"

There was a collective gasp and a few of the men in the back jeered at who she now believed to be Rhys's boss.

A third man stood up. He was in the row in front of her. He wore a smartish suit and tie and from where she was sitting she could clearly see the evidence of a council lanyard around his neck. He raised a hand and called out. "Sorry to interrupt." He was making his way carefully along the row and out towards the front.

Sadie guessed he would be in his fifties and from his warm smile, she wondered if he hadn't heard the exchange between Rhys and his boss.

"My name is Simon Checkers. I work for the council and have been assigned the job of approving the building of Beechend Village School." The twittering between people began again although as he continued it quietened almost instantly. "I have seen many plans for what we hope will be an efficient and effective community project." He turned to Rhys and smiled encouragingly.

"Mr Knight, I would like to offer you the contract to create this amazing feat of engineering." He reached out and grasped Rhys's hand shaking it firmly before he was rudely interrupted.

"Mr Checkers, unfortunately, Mr Knight will not be able to manage this site as he no longer works for Smith, Smith and Cline." The council representative waved away the smaller guy and turned to face Rhys.

"Mr Knight, we will be happy for you to take on the contract. Do you have the ability to take on a contract now that you are no longer tied to the city firm?"

Rhys grasped his hand once more and declared loud and clear. "I would be honoured Mr Checkers."

There was a raucous round of clapping and cheers as Rhys's ex-boss slunk his way out of the hall.

Chapter Twenty-six

Rhys

The couple were driving out of the village as soon as the meeting was wrapped up. Rhys's heart was racing and couldn't quite fathom all the things that had happened that day.

He realised that he hadn't bought the flowers and that maybe, his heart wasn't really into the idea of going out after all. Actually, he just wanted to unwind back at the cottage and destress after all that had happened.

Glancing down, he could not help but smile seeing his fingers entwined with Sadie's. She was humming along with the radio as they whizzed through the country lanes.

Gently, he pulled her hand up to his face and kissed the back of it. She returned the smile, and he was pleased to see the sign of a rosy blush on her cheeks. What on earth was he thinking? Of course he wanted to take her out, he had been thinking about this all week. She didn't care that he hadn't given her flowers. Besides, he could get her some tomorrow.

"Are you going to tell me where we're going?" she sang as she reached up and touched the side of his face.

"You know it's a surprise!" She laughed and the sound gave his body a jolt of familiarity. Her laugh had not changed. "Did I tell you I really like that dress…" He was serious but she battered the compliment away.

"You're going to like it even more later on this evening." She winked at him, actually winked.

Rhys realised in that moment how truly fortunate he was.

The remainder of the journey went by in companionable silence, yet they each maintained contact with the other, holding hands, momentary glances and a smile that seemed to say all they needed.

"Here we are!" Rhys declared, his face split in two. They were outside the best hotel in town, notorious for delectable food and wine. Sadie gasped as he got out the car and strutted round to open her door like James Bond. "I've always wanted to do that!" he chuckled as he took her hand to help her out of the car. The valet stepped forward, Rhys tossed the keys and the guy caught and nodded his head. "Knight, Rhys Knight!" She smiled up at him coy and sultry.

"Who does that make me?" She questioned wryly. It was his turn to wink and nothing more was said. They simply held hands and walked into the foyer.

Sadie

They were halfway through their main course, when Sadie mentioned the elephant in the room. She hadn't wanted to break the spell earlier, but it was too important, too monumental to not bring up what happened earlier on today.

"Rhys…" she chorused. He murmured to her as he took another bite of the ravioli. "We need to talk…" Instantly, his body seemed to stiffen. His foot that had been playing with hers under the table had stilled. She smiled at him reassuringly, "About what happened earlier…"

He resumed eating and she waited for him to respond. "What happened earlier?" The corners of his mouth lifted although the joy didn't reach his eyes.

Sadie sighed, a little put out by his change in demeanour. "The presentation, which was amazing by the way, your boss being there."

"Ex-boss," he corrected.

"Exactly, honey don't you want to talk about it. You just lost your job…"

"A job I hated for making me go against all the things that I value. And I already have a new job lined up!" She had stopped eating entirely now and was looking at him gobsmacked by his nonchalant attitude at being fired in front of the entire village.

"But…" Sadie was now lost for words.

"Darling, I have everything in hand, you don't

need to worry. Everything will work out, just you wait and see. Now, tell me about your day... Was the shop busy?" He reached over and speared a piece of asparagus and popped it into his mouth.

After taking the time to savour the flavour of garlic butter, he paused looking at Sadie. "Please, I just want to enjoy this evening." He took her free hand once more and brought it to his face. Instead of placing a kiss as he had earlier. He slowly turned it over so that her palm faced him. He placed butterfly kisses sweetly from her open palm slowly moving to her wrist. Instantly she felt the pull in her body and a zap of electricity. He smirked up at her knowing exactly what he was doing to her.

He gently placed her hand back on the table and resumed eating as though telling her to continue.

She talked about her day, the fact that they barely drew breath they were so busy. She told him about the knitting group fiasco and the fact that they hadn't arranged who would make the cakes this week. "Quite the scandal!" She concluded. "Oh, and this outsider came in the shop today. Hardly showing yet demanding I make her several baby pieces for Monday. She wasn't happy when I told her that it wasn't possible and that we don't provide that service." Sadie had been so engrossed in recounting the events of the day, that she hadn't noticed the subtle change in Rhys' breathing or the fact that the colour was rapidly draining from his face.

"Oh no, some people just can't take no for an answer." He replied, surprisingly no longer interested in the food in front of him. "Did the woman leave a name and address." She looked at him, now seeing the clammy complexion and the feel of his sweaty palms.

"No, she left, no name, no details." She really looked at him, sweat was beading near his hairline. "Rhys, are you alright?" She reached over and placed the back of her hand against his forehead. "You're cold and clammy. Are you sick?" There was a slight panic in her voice that she tried her best to cover up. Maybe it was something he had eaten. Maybe it was the realisation that he'd lost his job.

"Um, I'm not feeling all that great to be honest." She pursed her lips briefly before raising her hand delicately into the air. Within seconds a waiter arrived, and Sadie was making the necessary arrangements. Their food was being prepared for them to take away and the car was being brought round. Rhys's complexion had taken on a grey waxy quality and for Sadie, she just wanted to get him home as soon as possible.

Thankfully, they had taken his credit card details when he had booked and so they brought out the receipt with the perfectly boxed meals as well as their best wishes as Sadie unceremoniously manoeuvred him out the ornate entrance hall and into the passenger seat of the waiting car.

Unfortunately, her footwear was in no way suitable for driving and so she slipped them from her feet and placed them in the passenger footwell.

It turned out that Rhys' car that he had leased long term, was a delight to drive. The radio played softly as she left the town and headed home. She wondered absentmindedly what had made him unwell. Perhaps the stress from earlier had been too much. She hoped it wasn't the food. She herself hadn't felt right earlier on. Maybe it was something they had eaten at home.

Their return journey into Beechend was a drastic difference to earlier. She had glanced across at Rhys as he hadn't uttered a word since getting into the car. It seemed that he had fallen asleep, and she sighed. "Poor baby," she crooned.

She parked up in front of the cottage and decided it was best to change into some flat shoes before she attempted to 'man-handle' him into the house.

He was so cute when she had to wake him up. She could support him yes, but there was no chance of moving an unconscious man more than a foot taller than her.

Rhys had been groggy and grouchy in equal measure. He didn't seem to be in full control of his faculties, and he droned on about flowers and Darjeeling. She merely laughed softly at how adorable he was. Knowing he was unlikely to remember any of this the next day.

When she had finally got him to bed, he was sound asleep within seconds and she was left to attempt at removing his jacket and tie to make him more comfortable.

Once he was tucked up and she had managed to get herself ready and into bed, she allowed her mind to wander. She thought about the short time they had been together and the man he was compared to the child and teenager she had known all those years ago.

He was kind and compassionate, that had not changed. His zest for life seemed to be returning and she wondered what lay ahead for them. They hadn't talked about it. Maybe it was too soon to even think about it. But her mind had gone there now and it seemed content to remain circling the questions as they formed.

Should they be together? Did he want to be tied down to a single mother? Why *did* he come back to Beechend? Would he ever see her as his equal or would it be like her parents relationship? Did he want to get married? Round and round the questions swirled. She groaned and rolled over. Attempting to banish her wayward thoughts into oblivion.

It was going to be a long night.

Chapter Twenty-seven

Tabby

"Good morning sleepy head!" Tabby sang in a cheery voice. Her mother had just surfaced, and it was almost ten in the morning. Granted it was Sunday and the shop was covered for the day, but she couldn't remember the last time she had been up before her mum.

She had grunted a reply that there was no chance of deciphering and headed straight to the kettle. She was surprised to see her making a cup of coffee. "So, it was a good night then!" She shot her a look that told her that she was way off and that she wouldn't discuss this further. Tabby smiled and took a sip of her tea. "To be honest, I wasn't expecting you to be here." Her mum didn't speak but looked at her confused and clearly searching for an explanation. "Rhys told me that you were staying in town, in a fancy hotel."

There was a gasp and her mum hastily put down her cup, cursing the coffee that had slopped onto her hand. "No, you must be mistaken!" The voice was slightly panicked. "He would have said."

"Mum, he asked me to pack you an overnight bag. I thought it was romantic." She paused, realising that they must have argued or something if they hadn't stayed over. "What happened? Did you fall out or something?"

"No, nothing like that honey. Rhys isn't well. I drove us back, he slept the whole way." Tabby was a little alarmed to hear that the date night had been a bust and Rhys wasn't well. But after a while and another coffee, her mother seemed to perk up and told her there was nothing to worry about.

"Ok, as long as you're sure. I'm meeting Alex in a bit. We're taking Bruno out for a long walk so that he'll sleep this evening whilst you're out." Her mother's knowing smile spread across her face and she simply nodded and told her not to be too late back as the car was coming to collect them this time.

A short time later, Alex was with her walking along the lane and out of the village. He had entwined their fingers together as they walked, and Bruno was bounding along in front of them. "I hate that you aren't in school with me anymore!" She hadn't thought Alex was really the moaning type, but every time they were alone together, he would bring it up. She would shrug in response, and he would either give her a look that she hadn't yet managed to decipher or give her hand a squeeze, again causing her to be confused and unsure.

Tabby liked that he missed her at school and being away in the week made waiting for Sunday morning that much sweeter. He seemed to have shot up in the last few weeks and now he towered over her, which was a little intimidating.

He released her hand and draped his arm round her shoulders. She couldn't control the smile that slipped over her features as she snuggled closer to him whilst they walked. Something in her liked the way he claimed her as his.

She just wasn't really sure about him anymore. In the time that they hadn't spoken, he had made new friends at school. They were popular and obnoxious. The sorts of people they had once made fun of together. But now he was one of them. Scratch that, he was trying to be one of them.

This, in Tabby's opinion was far worse. He was constantly acting the big man, he would talk about the things they got up to and in one instance they had made two younger kids cry.

Tabby hoped that this was just a phase and he would return to being 'just Alex' soon.

After just under an hour of walking, the air around them was biting and they gave up and headed back to the warmth of the cottage for some hot chocolate and marshmallows. Tabby hoped that being around grown-ups would make Alex the best version of himself.

Sadie

Reeling, Sadie had returned to the bedroom ladened down with a tea tray, toast and jam just in case Rhys was up to having a bite to eat.

He was sat up when she entered the room. That was definitely a good sign. Rhys had more colour and grinned as she settled the tray down on the table. All thoughts of the hotel and his previous night's plans completely left her mind.

Once she was a little closer, he made to grab her, and she tumbled onto the bed and he embarked on a tickling attack that had her squealing. Yes, he was feeling better.

After Rhys had thoroughly made up for the previous evening, they got ready for the day ahead and appeared downstairs.

"Oh, hey guys!" Rhys was talking to someone as she entered the kitchen. Tabby had returned from her walk with Alex in toe, granted a little sooner than she had bargained. A rosy glow was still covering her cheeks as she entered the room. Slightly embarrassed at being caught out, she avoided her daughter's gaze and busied herself on doing the dishes.

Once the guys had emigrated to the lounge and put on some sporting event that was a 'must see', Tabby came up behind her and deposited her cups in the sink. "We just walked in when Rhys came down. It was far too cold out there this morning. I think it might snow!" Sadie mumbled her agreement and felt her shoulders relax.

"The car is due in an hour, your clean clothes are folded and placed on the end of your bed. Don't forget to pack them this time." Sadie half-heartedly scolded.

Tabby shrugged and walked towards the stairs, she stopped and turned. "Mum, do you think I made a mistake changing schools?"

Sadie was a little taken aback by this statement. She wished that her daughter was home more than she was, but did she want her back in a school that didn't keep them safe? No, she didn't. Did she wish there had been an in-between option? Yes.

"Alex mentions it every week. I'm grateful for all my Grandparents are doing. I know they are paying my tuition fees. But I wonder if I should have left." Tabby stared at her as if trying to interpret her silence.

"I'm sure it is difficult, being away from everyone in the week. Maybe after you finish your mock exams, we can look at other options for next year." Sadie felt like she was holding her breath. It was her turn to be trying to read the subtle nuances of her daughter's breathing.

Smiling, Tabby nodded. "Moving schools once in your final A 'level year is risky, twice would be education suicide!" She laughed at her own joke and headed back to the stairs to what Sadie hoped was going to include finishing her packing.

Tabby

Mr Smithers had been prompt to arrive and was parked in front of the cottage with more than five minutes to spare. Rhys had helped to load her measly possessions into the boot and before she knew it, the goodbyes had been said and she and her mum were whizzing out of the village towards the manor house on the hill.

She wished that Rhys could have come with them this afternoon, but he said that he had a lot to do now that he was his own boss!

Tabby wondered what this change would mean and if Rhys would be heading back to the city sooner rather than later. She pondered that this was maybe one of those topics that adults discussed but felt it not worthwhile letting younger generations in on the secret.

She wasn't bitter, but sometimes, she didn't like being left in the dark.

"Are you looking forward to returning to school Miss?" Smithers' kind smile was glancing up at her in the rear-view mirror as he split his attention with the road.

"Does anyone really enjoy school?" she sang back causing him to chuckle heartily.

"There will come a time, when you would give anything to be this age again." She was sure that he must be right, but for now, she would give anything to be done with school.

The conversation changed to the weather, Mrs Smithers' desire to weed the garden despite the frozen ground and whether or not the adults would be attending the quiz night this evening.

Tabby's focus started to drift and float around as though detached from the rest of the world. She was startled to realise that they had not only arrived at the house, but her mum was getting out of the car and calling for her to do the same.

The monotony of the weekly dinners at her grandparent's home was starting to grate on her even more. She supposed that this was also a big factor on her desires to move back to her old school. Then they could go back to once or twice a month here without the risk of emotional blackmail hanging over their heads.

"Good gracious Tabitha!" Her grandmother's face was pinched and showing an expression that was extremely displeased. "You cannot be eating with us wearing that! Go upstairs and change into one of the outfits I have ordered for you." She didn't argue as there seemed little point. She simply did as she was told.

On returning to the dining room, wearing an outfit that she absolutely detested, there was a heated discussion underway. Actually, discussion was stretching the truth to breaking point. She would say it definitely sounded like an argument.

"She is your daughter, and it is your responsibility that she toes the line!" Her grandfather's booming voice carried and in hearing his outwardly thoughts, there was no denying that today they were finding fault in her. Yet instead of saying whatever the problem was to her face, they sniped at her mother.

Tabby hadn't been seen yet and so she skulked silently back out of the room and waited out of sight as the argument continued to unfold. "I understand that you find her being out in public as something unfitting for a lady." Her mum's voice was calm and although in control, she sounded strained. Tabby felt a pang of guilt and racked her brain for what she might have done that they found so awful.

Her grandfather spoke, but it was muffled and she couldn't make out what he had said.

"Tabitha is a girl, still a child. I won't have these ridiculous expectations thrust on her like they were on me." There was no malice in her tone, although even Tabby had to admit that her mother's side seemed pretty concrete and surely was the end to the little spat.

"Really? You don't seem to mind us paying for your child's education at one of the most prestigious schools in the county." Her grandfather was on a roll. She definitely heard him that time. It felt good to know how he really felt.

She wasn't sure where the courage and confidence had materialised from, but Tabby found herself barging into the dining room where all three adults looked up in surprise that she was even in the building let alone the room. Her grandmother had the decency to look abashed at being caught out, but her grandfather's steely gaze was piercing and for the first time she saw the father her mother had been subjected to.

He seemed to remember himself and his features softened. "Tabitha, darling. You look so grown up in that dress. A proper little lady." His smile was approving and it made her blood boil.

"You don't really think that though do you Grandfather?" Tabby's words were out before she had time to check herself.

"Tabby, please." Her mother's voice was pleading. But she seemed like there was no going back.

"I am grateful for all that you have done for me, including you paying my tuition fees at Smithton."

Her grandmother interrupted and exclaimed that they were happy to do it and that she was doing so well there.

"I am not happy though." She interrupted, an yearning in her voice that she couldn't control.

"Tabby?" Her mother's hurt was a sure blow, but the truth needed to come out. "Honey, why didn't you say anything?"

"I hate it there. I hate being away from home so much. I even miss my old school. So the logical solution to all our problems is just that. I'll finish the remainder of the term and start back at my old school in the new year." She turned and faced her grandfather. "You don't have to worry about me being lady-like out in public anymore. I won't be able to be a disappointment anymore if I'm not there." He didn't speak but instead grunted his acknowledgement.

"Tabitha, you are being childish, really!" Her grandmother's disapproving tone cut through her. She went to retort back, but this time her mother cut her off.

"Enough!" the cry out made Tabby jump. "Enough, I might have taken you talking down to me all these years, but I won't stand for you speaking to my daughter like that." Her mother's face was red from rage. "How dare you?" She was up on her feet and gathering her bag from the side of the chair, something Tabby knew had been one of the many things to annoy her grandmother. "Tabby, get your things. We are leaving!"

"Mum?" her voice had been little more than a whisper, but she had responded with kindness in her eyes. "I'm sorry."

"It's ok darling, you did nothing wrong. You spoke your mind, don't ever apologise for being you."

Before they knew it, they were back outside in the chilly afternoon air that was biting with an unrelenting wind. They were standing next to her school bags. Her mother's hand held on to hers with a fierceness she had never before encountered.

She looked up into her mother's face. "I am so sorry that I didn't protect you from this better. You are far braver and aware of who you are than I ever was." She squeezed her hand again as though trying to portray her meaning.

"Mum, if I am brave, it is because you taught me to be brave. If I know myself it is because you taught me to be me and to trust myself above all else. I love you." The embraced and held on as though their lives depended on it.

Chapter Twenty-eight

Sadie

Sadie rested her head back as they made the turn into the village. She could finally feel her body beginning to relax. Tabby's face was pale and tear streaked. She was yet to make a sound or even look in her direction. Sadie would reassure her once they were back in the cottage. It was not her fault and she wondered whether she had done irreplicable damage by subjecting her daughter to them for all these years.

They had never out rightly said a word against Tabby before. There had been many comments of course, but she had always taken the hit as there were designed to wound herself and not their grand-child.

She wondered if allowing Tabby into their lives more, accepting their offer of paying for school, had been the catalyst.

Sadie reached out a hand the short distance to her daughter and squeezed her smaller hand reassuringly. She hoped that she would understand their unspoken truth. She felt rather than saw the returning squeeze and she felt her heart grow lighter as she felt the beginning twinge of tears threatening.

"Miss Mirada, we're here." Before she had looked up, the older man who she looked up to more like a father than her own was out of the car and swiftly unpacking the luggage.

Tabby gathered her things and set off through the gate and into their home.

"Sadie," The use of her name prompted her to turn. His face was lined for sure, but kind and a comforting reminder that he cared about them. "Whatever happened up at the house, I'm happy to go and collect Miss Tabitha every Friday from school. Your father won't need to find out." His warm smile broadened and he embraced her in a hug which took her by surprise. He held on to her and she was reminded of spearmint and the faint aroma of pipe tobacco.

Sadie hugged him back and realised that she didn't want to let go. This felt like home, not the place she had just left. "In fact, you can always come round for dinners like you used to, I know that Betty would like that. We know you're busy though so she doesn't like to ask." He patted her roughly on the back and walked purposely back to the drivers side of the car.

"Matthew!" She followed him and he wound down the window to hear her better. "We'd love to come round. I'm sorry we've not been to see you both, I'll ring in the week and make arrangements." He squeezed her hand, "Give my love to Betty." He nodded and drove away leaving her standing in the road. She waved and waited to watch him round the bend. A mixture of comfort and guilt raced through her body keeping her frozen to the spot. She should have reached out to them more. When she was a child, she had spent most of her free time down at the gables cottage or her own kitchen if Betty had been there. How selfish of her to think that they hadn't cared for her as much as she had for them. Maybe today's wake up call was what she had needed.

"Sadie!" The shrill voice rang out and brought her out of her daydreaming haze. "What are you doing standing in the street girl?" Her tone was instantly admonishing, and her facial expression confirmed the same.

"Mrs Grimshaw! Goodness, you made me jump." Sadie approached with a look she hoped was warm but doubted that she had managed to pull it off effectively. "How are you this evening?" She waved her hand as though trying to bat her away like an annoying fly. This action had the desired effect of winding her up.

She took a deep breath and attempted to calm herself whilst she waited for the frail looking woman in front of her to get out whatever she needed to. Sadie knew from experience that Mrs Grimshaw was a notorious gossip. There could be no other reason that she would stop her so unexpectedly, especially as the weather could only be described as bitter. The wind whipped around her bare legs, and she began to shiver. Now that she had noticed the cold, there was no way of ignoring it again.

"Ooo, I have to tell you!" She began and she leant in closer, the better to impart her wisdom she was sure. "This woman is most definitely in the family way. Jenny saw her crossing the village green yesterday morning and Anita saw her entering the Bed and Breakfast." Mrs Grimshaw rabbited on for what felt like an eternity about who had seen the mysterious woman.

"I think she came into the shop yesterday. I don't seem to understand what is so significant Mrs Grimshaw?" Sadie was quickly losing her patient and the numbness in her fingers was beginning to inch up her arms. She inwardly groaned at her inability to extricate herself from these gossipy situations. "I really need to be getting in, would you like me to walk you home? I can grab my coat..." She made to leave but was grabbed on the arm by a hand that had a far stronger grip than she would have imagined in a woman of her age.

"No, that's what I needed you to know. You see, this woman has been seen twice with your man!" There was no other description for Mrs Grimshaw's face, she looked grim and clearly had no joy in sharing the news. Sadie wasn't sure if it was the cold or the day's events, but her brain didn't seem to be working all that well. The old lady, who was still holding her by the arm, began rubbing it up and down in an affectionate sort of way. "Yesterday morning, she was seen waiting in front of his cottage. Then he was seen leaving her room where she is staying in the village."

She paused, giving Sadie's brain, time to catch up, which began working frantically to put all the pieces together. "I was told, just this morning, then I saw her again this afternoon walking round by the church. I knew I needed to tell you. You deserve to know." Mrs Grimshaw was rambling again and Sadie knew. Rhys's behaviour yesterday had been out of character. The woman was pregnant. She knew Rhys. Was the baby his?

"Thank you Mrs Grimshaw, I met the woman you are describing, you have nothing to worry about." She plastered the smile on her face, she knew not to lay it on too think or she would never be believed. "She's a family friend, visiting... I'm sure she's meant to be here a few more days yet. Um perhaps even be staying the rest of the week. I must get in, lots to do! Have a wonderful evening Mrs Grimshaw!" She had walked past and up the path, firmly putting a close on the conversation.

Rhys

Rhys waiting patiently to hear from Sadie later on this afternoon. He knew that she was at her parents this afternoon and they had made plans for him to come and get her and bring her home to his for the evening. It was only just afternoon when his phone beeped with a message. He thought maybe Ewan or even one of his friends from the city. But he was surprised to see that it was Sadie. Just two words. 'I'm home' appeared on his screen. This surprised him and he instantly wondered what had happened to cause the change in plans. Before he could finish typing his reply, another message turned up. 'Come round.'

He didn't need telling twice, he grabbed his jacket and keys and high-tailed it round there. He didn't even think about it, just couldn't wait to see her.

But when he walked through the door and into the kitchen, he knew instantly, something was wrong. Tabby's bags were piled up in the corner, even though there was no sign of her. He called out and was greeted by a frosty face that normally beamed at him.

She didn't speak, just stood and stared at him with eyes that showed no warmth. It gave him the impression that she didn't see him. "Sadie?" He whispered but made no attempt to approach her. His mind flashed and in that instant he knew. She must have found out about Fiona being here. But he didn't know how that was possible. He had never even mentioned her name, of that he was certain. Rhys knew that she had been into the shop, and they had met, but he didn't think anything more was said that would have showed his part in the whole fiasco. "Sadie, we need to talk. I can explain everything." At once her features seemed to dissolve into nothing but pain. Still she said nothing. "She turned up on my doorstep yesterday. Fiona means nothing to me. You, you are the one I want to be with. It has always been you."

He reached out a hand to her and she flinched away from him. "Don't." she murmured, her voice was high and coarse as though her throat was scratched. "She's the reason you're here. You ran away!"

Withdrawing his hand he felt trapped like a deer in headlights. It was the truth. He had run back to Beechend. Giving one solitary nod, he looked up to see a tear rolling down her face. This broke him. He had hurt her.

"You should go back to the city. You should go back to Fiona and your child. You should be a family, besides, there is nothing for you here." Despite her facial expression, her voice was now strong and composed. There was a stony determination that seemed to have washed over her.

"No, I won't be returning to the city!" A fire seemed to have erupted within him. "You have been waiting for an excuse to fall into your lap. You have been wanting to push me away from the very beginning!" Her hand had covered her mouth but did little to hide the sound of her gasp or the wild eyes that had widened at his words. "Sadie, if you do this you are going to end up alone, with no-one."

She had stepped back as though he had struck her. "I think you should leave." They both heard the sound of Tabby coming down the stairs. "I think you have said all you needed to!"

At her final words his whole body seemed to deflate as if all the energy had left his body and soul. "Sadie…" he whispered to her, pleading as his mind raced for something, anything that he could do to fix this moment. "I thought…" but he had no words.

"Mum." Tabby was standing staring at the two of them, she looked confused. "Mae is on her way over; she is going to take me to school." Sadie nodded and without another glance, she turned and walked back into the lounge. The resounding click of the door was the final nail in the coffin that was their relationship. "Rhys. I think you should go after her…"

Suddenly he felt weary, as though the last two days had been months. "Tabby, whatever is happening between your mother and I… You need to know, I'm here, whatever you need." He pulled her into a hug and she clung to him. "I'm sorry." He whispered into her hair as it tickled his face.

"Please, fix it. Just fix it." Her round eyes were brimming with unshed tears as he backed away from her and neared the back door. "Rhys, she needs you." Her voice was breaking, "I need you."

He shook his head, the last of his resolve leading him out the door. "She doesn't want me." And with that, he closed the door and left the cottage. No longer whole, he was a broken and wounded imitation of a man.

Chapter Twenty-nine

Tabby

"So, tell me again, I want to make sure that I really understood this right..." Alex's facial expression told her that he understood perfectly well. But she decided to indulge his demands.

"I'm coming back to school in the new year." He cheered and punched the air above his head. She chuckled at his behaviour, and they continued to walk hand in hand as she regaled the events of the previous weekend.

The wave of guilt washed over her as she pictured her mum's miserable face when she came down for breakfast. How could she be happy when her mum was so sad.

Tabby had used her downtime to devise a plan of getting everything back to how it should be. She just needed a little help getting it all underway.

"When the new term begins, I think you'll be back in all the same classes... We haven't had any other new people in our year and so there is still space." Alex was rambling and Tabby was ashamed that she hadn't really heard a word, simply nodding and smiling every so often. Although, it felt good to see him happy for once, the feelings she had experienced earlier on seemed to have dwindled. She didn't look at him the same way anymore.

Suddenly, he had stopped walking. This caused her arm to stretch out as she didn't immediately stop with him. He tugged her to him, whilst he repositioned his free hand round her back. Alex was growing confident with that move which seemed to only annoy her more today.

She rested her forehead against his briefly before he leaned in and kissed her.

"Something is the matter with you today." He murmured between kisses. "You are sad and I want to make you happy." He was looking down at her, staring into her eyes as though hoping to find the answer to his questions there. "Kiss me Tabby…" She stayed still and silent, not wanting to cause an argument, but at the same time, his demands were beginning to nettle her.

He rubbed his nose on hers in an Eskimo kiss. She couldn't control her reaction and grinned at him sheepishly. Seeing that it had the desired effect, he swooped back down and covered her lips with his own.

It was different this time, more urgent and less about being tender. He had pulled her body up against his and she was torn between suddenly craving more and struggling with the urge to suck in more air.

She broke the kiss and placed a hand on his chest

to push him back. "Slow down." She gazed meekly at him. He briefly pecked her on the cheek, muttering the word females and difficult under his breath. Tabby decided this was not the hill to die on and so chose not to acknowledge his hushed words.

Guiltily he shrugged and expressed regret for letting his hormones rule his actions and they continued on their way. Hand holding and Alex talking about their plans for the afternoon. Tabby remained mute and pensive, wondering if today was just a one off or if this was becoming a bit of a pattern between them.

Sadie

Less than a week since that horrendous Sunday afternoon and Sadie was yet to speak with Mae about what had happened. In fact, apart from her daughter, she had not really conversed with anyone. She had kept chatting to a minimum in the shop as she pretended to be busy and had spent the rest of her time alone in the cottage in an effort to not bump into Rhys or his girlfriend.

This had not stopped her from hearing the gossip in the village. The damage had already been done before it had even reached her ears last weekend. The village was awash with little old ladies dashing about with nothing better to do. She just hoped that everything would die down soon enough.

As soon as she closed the shop on Saturday evening, she gathered her things and after bundling up against the elements, she had hightailed it round to Mae's at the far end of the green.

Fortunately, the lights were on and the door was opened in record time. "Sadie!" she had hurried over the threshold and closed the door firmly behind her. She had snow covering her hair and she could already feel the sting from the biting wind on her cheeks. "What on earth." Mae helped her to remove her layers and offered her a cup of tea to help her fight off the chill.

After a few minutes, they were huddled on the sofa

with their respective beverages and Sadie had caught her up with the whole sorry business.

"So the woman is still here?" Mae was outraged on her behalf. "Do you want me to go deal with her, because I will if you want me to." Mae was sat up straight and putting down her cup as if going to head out the door and into the storm right this very moment.

Granted her reaction did make her smile for the first time since this all began, but nevertheless, it wasn't a wise idea. "Mae, of course not!" She exclaimed, placing a hand on her arm. "Besides, she's pregnant." The bitterness in her voice couldn't be any more obvious.

"And he said that the baby was his?" Mae was back to recounting her last conversation with Rhys.

"Yes, um, no, no he didn't." Sadie faltered over her words. In her waking hours she had become so righteous about her actions being better than Rhys', but now she thought about it. He never said the baby was his. She had assumed because that is what the gossipers had proclaimed.

"Well, what did he say?" Mae questioned. Sadie could feel the panic rising as she strained to remember their interaction word for word, but struggled to recall anything but the look of utmost pain etched on his face. She shrugged as putting it into words seemed impossible. "Did he admit that they were together? Is he going back to her?"

"He said that he wanted to be with me, I told him to go back to Fiona and the baby, go back to the city." Sadie recited her words like a parrot. They calmed her. She felt that she was right.

"Oh honey, why?" Mae's question stunned her. She couldn't see a reason that Mae wouldn't fully understand and agree with her. "He wants to be with you and you sent him packing into the arms of another woman." She drew breath and gave time for her words to sink in. "He loves you..."

"No! He doesn't, he can't love me, he never said." The pitiful look on Mae's face made her gut clench painfully. "Fathers should be with their children. He was going to abandon his unborn child to be with me. I can't be a part of that. I can't be with someone who would do that." Sadie's voice trailed away, and she sat motionless on the sofa. In all honesty, she felt numb. She was certain the pain would come, but she wasn't ready to face it just yet.

Did he love her? There had been moments over the last few months that she had thought that he did, but now, she didn't know anything. "Oh Sadie, he isn't Darren." Mae's sympathetic voice was only just audible, yet it had felt like a knife in the heart. "I don't think he was going to leave you." She reached a hand towards her, but Sadie was already on her feet, pacing the room as she had at home.

"He has to leave. That woman can't go through what I did. What Tabitha has gone through..." as her voice trailed away, she sank to the floor and began to sob. Her whole body ached as her chest heaved. Mae was there in a flash, embracing her and holding her as she finally fell apart.

Chapter Thirty

Rhys

The car was taking a battering from the wind as he pulled into the long drive leading up to Tabby's school. Mae had called that afternoon and asked if he could collect her at 5pm. He was surprised by the call, but it had instantly turned to hope that maybe this would be his chance to set things straight.

Rhys hadn't spoken with Sadie in almost two weeks. He had glimpsed her briefly as she walked home from the shop, but it was late, and he hadn't approached her. Ewan had told him to give her space and time to cool off. But after nearly a fortnight he was starting to feel desperate.

He cursed Fiona once again under his breath. This had become a regular thing as she had managed to completely destroy everything by pulling the rug out from under him for the second time this year.

After he'd parked the car to the side of the main entrance, he hopped out and went in search of Tabitha. She was waiting for him just inside the foyer, sheltering from the worst of the weather.

She spun round to face him when he called her name, a mixture of shock and elation spread across her features, and she launched herself into his arms. "Rhys!" She squealed. "Oh wow. I'm so pleased that you are here!" It was like music to his ears. A rare ego boost that he didn't know he needed after he had been firmly placed into the pariah category in the village.

A woman behind the front desk, who reminded him very strongly of Mrs Grimshaw, tutted loudly and looked at them disapprovingly over the rim of her glasses. Stifling a laugh, he waved over at her and announced that he would be collecting Tabby Mirada today, did he need to sign her out?

The woman's lips were pursed together giving the overall effect of an extremely angry librarian who had caught someone talking loudly and simultaneously burning books.

Sometime later, they were back in his car, the heating was on full blast and Tabby was talking his ear off. He had attempted several times to reply but she had so much to impart that he was resigned to nodding and agreeing to all she had to say.

"So, everything is sorted now then." Her voice was high and cheery. She sounded as though Christmas had come early. "You and mum, you've made up." He indicated left to leave at the next exit. "I'm so pleased, I was starting to worry that you would never sort things out. What happened anyway? Mum wouldn't tell me and I've been so busy I haven't been around to hear the gossip." His heart sank.

"Tabby." She finally stopped and he could see that

her features had frozen. "Darling, your mum and I aren't together. It's not her fault. It's mine." Rhys went quiet and focused on driving the car.

"Is there anything that you can do to fix it?" Tabby was pleading, he could hear the desperation in her voice and it just about broke his heart all over again.

"I'm giving your mum some space at the moment, but I'm not going anywhere, see." He waved his hands at her one at a time, barely prompting the smallest of smiles. She seemed to be absorbing what he was telling her and she sagged a little in her seat.

"But you clearly love each other, everybody thinks so!" He didn't know what to say to that. They hadn't said 'I love you' or even close to it. But he cared about her, a lot. He cared about both of them. It was tearing him apart that he was sitting on the edge of their lives but not being able to share it with them. "Adults are stupid!"

"Sometimes adults don't have all the answers, they make mistakes and don't always know how to fix things." Rhys' voice had stayed soft and he hoped he was being gentle with Tabitha's feelings. As if she was accepting defeat, she turned her head away from him and stared out of the window.

They stayed in companionable silence the rest of the journey back. Once they were driving into Beechend, he asked if she needed a lift back to school on Sunday. She said that it was already sorted.

"Hey, only one more week of school and then it's Christmas!" His tone was too cheerful and she forced on a fake smile that didn't meet her eyes. "If you need anything."

"I know," she interrupted, "It just isn't the same." Once the car had stopped she gave him a swift hug and thanked him for collecting her.

Tabitha turned to leave but stopped before she opened the door. She turned back to face him and he noticed her cheeks were a little pink. "Rhys, I do need to talk with someone about something. But if you're busy that is ok, maybe another time…" She was rushing her words and made to leave the car again.

"Tabby, I am never too busy. If I can help, I will." He waited for her to speak again. Whilst waiting a sense of dread seemed to seep into his very pores. He knew this couldn't be good.

"How do you know if someone is the one?" Her face was a deeper shade of red now and he squirmed uncomfortably.

"Well, I'd have thought you would have talked with your mum about this…" She shrugged and told him she didn't want to pester her with her problems. "Well then, I guess for me it's a feeling, deep down, you just know. They make you a better version of yourself."

"You mean that they make you change?" She looked genuinely intrigued by this notion and he was certain that wasn't really what he had meant.

"Yes and no, your core self stays the same, but you worry less, feel lighter, happier." She pondered this for a moment and he waited for her to respond.

"Did you love mum when you were little?" That was like being hit by a car and he blustered through a response. "Honestly though, did you have the feelings then that you do now?" It was his turn to stop and think about the question. It didn't take him long to answer her.

"Yes. Yes I did feel the same. I felt very protective over your mum when we were little. Then when we were about your age, my feelings changed and I didn't look at her the same way anymore."

"Do you think that your feelings back then were less valid than they are now?" He shook his head then rubbed his chin at the direction the conversation was taking. He wasn't sure if he was heading for disaster. "I mean, love as an adult and love as a teenager, it's all the same isn't it."

"I'm not sure it is. I'm older, wiser and I can take responsibility for my actions better now than when I was your age." Instantly he began to back peddle and the look of indignation on her face. "I was a teenage boy, same as all boys. It doesn't mean I didn't care, but my hormones were undeniably ruling the head."

Rhys sighed then it came to him as if he had always known. "I'm glad that your mother and I were friends when we were younger and it never became anything more. She wouldn't have you now and that would be a terrible shame for the world we live in. Besides, we had all those years to build our relationship into something meaningful." He patted her shoulder awkwardly.

"Something worth waiting for you mean?"

Finally feeling back on solid ground and out of the waters he had been treacherously wading through. "Oh definitely. When you are older and more in tune with how you really feel, everything is much more special."

Tabby smiled at him, "Worth fighting for..." she looked at him pointedly and he realised the double meaning of the whole conversation. She pecked him lightly on the cheek and scurried from the car before he had a chance to respond.

She hurried into the cottage, where he knew Sadie would be waiting to greet her. He felt awful, and for the first time since returning to Beechend he thought about returning to the city as an absolute end of days solution for the mess he was in.

Sadie

Tabby barrelled through the kitchen door like she was high on life. After putting down her bags she threw her arms around her and squeezed tightly. "Well hello to you too!" She returned the hug and held on a bit longer than was normally tolerated, she would take the affection whilst it was offered.

"Only one week left!" She exclaimed happily and then she began unpacking her dirty washing straight into the machine. Tabitha didn't ask her about her week, maybe she had sensed that it hadn't been great. Maybe she needed to take control back and find her feet again. She had been moping around here for a while now. Maybe she needed to get on with life again.

"That's great honey, are you looking forward to getting back to your old school?" She shrugged and said something about missing out on the school concert, but there was always the auditions for the summer show. "Did Mae head straight home after dropping you off?" She was adding the detergent and turning the machine on now.

"Oh, no, she couldn't get away from her meeting in time so Rhys picked me up." There was no malice just a case of stating the facts. But just the mention of his name seemed to cut through her and she felt the feebly mended wounds burst open.

"Oh, that was good of him." Sadie replied, the words getting caught in her throat.

Before she could ask, images had instantly flooded her mind at the mention of Rhys' name, Tabby was up and walking towards the stairs. "I'm going to get changed, shall we have fish and chips for tea?" She had mumbled her reply then slouched down into the chair. Head in her hands, she wondered yet again if she had done the right thing. Her heart certainly didn't think so.

The thought of him having a baby with someone else had hurt far more than she liked. But the part that had really pushed her over the edge was how easily willing he was to leave the mother alone to deal with the situation. He was ready to cast her aside, the same way Darren had wanted to do with her and Tabby.

She had been that woman. She still was that woman. How could he leave her to fend for herself and their child. Sadie had never before thought that Rhys was capable of that. Which brought her to her final thought that swirled around her brain in the wee hours of the morning. If he had been willing and honest about the situation, offered support to Fiona and still shown that he wanted a relationship with Sadie. Would she have accepted that. The possibility of continuing their fling, knowing he had another child out in the world without their father.

Oh, but she missed him. So much that she ached for him. She wondered what he was doing and if he was missing her too.

Sadie was conflicted and hoped that if that ever was a possibility, that she would have the grace and courage of her own convictions to do what she believed to be right.

Chapter Thirty-one

Sadie

The following morning, less than an hour after opening the shop and almost exactly to the minute, two weeks after she first came in, Fiona waltzed into the shop.

There was a small cluster of ladies in the corner choosing yarns for a project they were planning together and Sadie hoped that Fiona was only here to ask about the baby things again.

"Good morning, how can I help you?" Sadie plastered on a smile that she hoped looked genuine and came out from behind the counter. "You popped in the other week, I do have the name of a lady who may be able to make your things before your due date... I'm sorry I didn't ask when you are expecting..." She was surprised by the ease her mind managed to recall facts whilst facing off with the woman that had ruined her relationship with Rhys. No, Rhys ruined the relationship or did she ruin it. Her mind really was all over the place. She reached behind the counter and pulled out a card for a woman who lived a few villages over. She crocheted mostly and made the most beautiful baby pieces. She was sure she could accommodate Fiona's needs.

"Thank you," she smiled serenely at her and snatched the card as though it was made of gold. "I'm not due until the end of June." Fiona was glancing around the room as though she was casing the place for a robbery.

"Oh, well then I'm sure there is plenty of time for baby things to be made..." Sadie was interrupted by Fiona waving her hand at her dismissively.

"I'm not here about that!" Her voice was exasperated. "I'm here because a member of your staff is breaking up my family!" Fiona was moving around the isles now, and Sadie was certain that she was knocking things off on purpose. "A girl in the B and B told me this morning that my Rhys is seeing some slut that works at the craft shop!"

The women in the corner were now eyeing Fiona and herself suspiciously. They had put the yarn down and were no longer trying to hide the fact that they were listening what, in their eyes, was good gossip.

"So where is the home-wrecker? Is she out the back? Or upstairs perhaps?" She looked to be on the verge of tears.

"Fiona..." Sadie was standing with her arms folded across her chest. This wasn't going to be pretty.

"How do you... You? You are the one my Rhys ran off with?" Her laugh was high and cruel. "What on earth he sees in you..." She laughed again and Sadie could feel her face flush red hot.

"We aren't together…" Her voice came out timid and so unlike her that she was sure someone else must have spoken.

"Don't give me that! You are, he won't come home because of you. You have cast some sort of a spell over him. He's leaving me and our child for an old shop woman with frizzy hair!"

"Now I think you've said enough!" One of the woman browsing yarn had stepped forward. She couldn't remember her name, but knew she had been to one of her classes.

"You're just after his money! Found out he's worth over a million and decided to keep him for yourself!"

"I don't know anything about any money…" Sadie was trying to argue back and defend herself against these blatant lies.

"A likely story, you won't win. I won't let you!" She tore up the card into confetti like pieces and threw them up into the air.

"Well I never, such a terrible way to behave." The second woman in the corner was tutting her disapproval and Sadie felt shame wash over her.

"You won't be seeing Rhys again. We're going back to the city, and we're going to be getting married!" With this last announcement, she spun on her heel, wrenched open the door and marched out. The tinkling of the bell having the last word.

Silent tears slid down her face as the realisation of Rhys leaving hit her like a sledgehammer in the chest. He was doing what she had told him to do. He had made the decision to be with Fiona and their child. It was the honourable choice. No one would ever speak badly of a man stepping up and looking after his child.

Yet, the thought of him leaving Beechend and never having the chance to put things right between them made her chest constrict.

"Sadie, are you alright love?" The first of the three ladies was rubbing up and down her arm, concern etched on her face. "She was a nasty piece of work, clearly not from round here. You are best off out of that mess!" The other ladies chorused their agreement before they made their purchases and left the shop.

Once they were gone, she turned the sign to closed, locked the door, shut off the lights and slumped down in the corner to let her emotions run free in the dim December light.

Rhys

Rhys had just got off the phone from the best brother anyone could ever have. He had the answer that he had been searching for and now he could finally confront the woman that was intent on ruining his life.

Without thinking he stepped outside, only to have an icy blast of air force him back inside to search for more appropriate clothing and footwear.

On his second attempt he marched straight to the end of the lane and veered right towards the centre of the village. He wasn't sure where she would be, but a good guess is that she might still be at the bed and breakfast. It wasn't yet ten and he knew she didn't like to rise early at the weekend.

Rhys was surprised to see her walking along the street towards him. He didn't want to have this conversation out in the street for all to see, but at this point he was so furious he wasn't in full control of himself.

"Fiona!" It had come out far louder than he had intended. Contempt dripping from each syllable. She smiled at him as though he was the best thing since sliced bread. But he knew her game and he wasn't in the mood to play. "This is over, Fi. I know everything!"

Her face faltered and a nasty scowl replaced the smile that had been on her face only moments earlier. "Darling I miss you and you know that we were meant to be!"

"Cut the crap!" He sniped at her. She gasped and stepped back, finally realising how truly angry he was. Rhys had never hit a woman and would never hit a woman, but he would get her back on that train if it was the last thing he did.

Instantly her face transformed and she seemed to deflate. "Who ratted me out?"

He sneered at her and was surprised by the true hatred that he was firing at her.

"You and I need to talk!" She whimpered and looked around to see that she had no audience to capitalise on. "We'll go back to the B and B, you will be packing anyway and I'm going to book you a taxi to the train station." He marched past her and headed across the green and around the pond to the building she had called home for the last fortnight.

"You can't tell me what I can and can't do!" she called out to him.

He stopped so suddenly, she almost bumped into him. "You are right, I can't make anyone do anything. But I can call Woking and Co." She gasped, the company that she worked for was a low blow and he doubted she would do anything to jeopardise her career. "Would you like to lead the way…" He gestured for her to walk ahead of him which she did so without a word.

Once they were inside her room, Fiona sat down and removed the ridiculous heals that she had been wearing.

"The only reason you are here is because you found out about my inheritance." He spat out the last word as though the thought of it made his skin crawl. "How did you find out about it?" He was pacing back and forth in front of her as she began to speak.

"Cole, mentioned it. Said that I must really love him as I was able to walk away from you and all that money!" Rhys rolled his eyes and shook his head at the absurdity of the woman in front of him. "I was livid! We lived together, I thought you loved me, yet you never told me you had inherited a small fortune!" Her features, which he had once thought breath-taking, were now twisted and ugly. She truly was a horrible person. "So are you going to pay me off then, me and our unborn child!"

"Stop lying," he shouted as he slammed his hand down onto the dresser in the corner. "The baby isn't mine!"

Fiona's face fell and all the fight seemed to leave her body. The last piece she held over him, her last bargaining tool was worthless. "No, the baby isn't yours." Her voice was softer now and she absentmindedly rubbed her hand over her abdomen. "How did you know?"

Rhys seemed to sag with the relief that he was right and that everything could go back to normal. "My brother has been investigating. He found out your due date. The numbers didn't seem to add up. So there was no way that this baby could possibly be mine."

She nodded and told him the father was Cole, but that things weren't so rosy with him and that she thought she and baby would be happier with him.

He released a bark of laughter. "Nice try Fiona, it

was about the money. Just admit it…"

"Fine, yes, it was about the money!"

"Well you are out of luck! I will only get my inheritance once I am married." Her mouth dropped open at the revelation. "So there is no money!"

"Wow, then why didn't you marry me, or the shop girl to get your money?" She shook her head, completely shocked that he could have got his hands on the money years ago but that he hadn't.

"Shop girl?" Sadie, she had been to see her… "What have you said to Sadie?" Rhys bellowed. Fiona at least had the decency to look ashamed of her actions.

"It was my attempt to get you back to the city. I thought if I split you two up…" This woman really was Satan.

"She ended things with me as soon as she found out about you and the baby, the lie…"

"Wow, I misjudged her." She murmured as folded her clothes into her case. "Turns out, she might be better than all of us!" She laughed uncomfortably.

"She is, she sacrificed her own happiness for you and your baby."

Fiona took barely any time to pack up the rest of her possessions and thankfully the taxi was waiting for her when he carried her bags out.

"You understand why I did what I did…" Fiona looked as though she actually cared what he thought.

"Whether I understand or not is completely irrelevant. I won't be seeing or hearing from you again Fiona. I hope you and Cole can be happy together." She reached out to hug him goodbye but then seemed to think better of it and simply nodded her goodbye and got into the car. "Best of luck,"

Rhys watched as the taxi circled round the green and headed out past the church and away from him forever.

As soon as the car was out of sight, he walked in the opposite direction and straight into the florists.

The woman behind the counter was arranging flowers in a vase and trimming some of the stems. She looked up and beamed at him. "Back again!" She was going to like him a lot. Rhys had the idea that he was about to become her most valued customer.

Chapter Thirty-two

Tabby

Tabby had hated seeing the haunted look on her mother's face yesterday. She knew that it was because of something that happened with Rhys, but she was yet to unearth the truth.

She had spent the morning up in her room getting the last of her homework finished for next week and also looking up the reading list for the next term as she knew she must be behind on projects and would certainly need to use the Christmas holiday's to catch up if she was going to pass her exams at the end of the school year.

At about half ten, her phone had beeped with a text from Alex. He was downstairs and wanted to know if she was finished doing her work.

Her heart wavered at the thought and headed down the stairs two at a time and threw open the back door. He was standing huddled in the porch with an awkward grin on his face.

Not waiting to be invited in, he loomed over her,

immediately his lips found hers and he led her backwards until she bumped hard against the kitchen counter. He slammed the door shut and then lifted her up onto the worktop and continued to devour her as though he hadn't seen her in years instead of the six days it had essentially been.

The question of him being the one passed through her mind as a small groan escaped her. This small sound seemed to cause him to double his efforts and their kissing became wilder as he groped for her top.

Instantly out of her comfort zone, she broke contact, wrenching her body from his grasp, she came up for air as he continued to pepper light kisses along her jaw and down her neck. She felt hot and knew that they could easily take this further. But a thought popped in her mind and she faltered. She wanted her first time to be special. This was something, but she wasn't sure just yet. She wasn't sure if he really was her someone special.

Alex's mouth had found hers once more and he was beginning to work on the buttons of her shirt, grazing the skin beneath. "Stop, please, stop." It was an abrupt red light and his hand stilled, the button came loose and the fabric gapped from the strain of her heavy breathing. He kissed her gently and swept the hair from her face.

He smirked at her, staring like she was some prize to be won. "I just don't want to wait anymore" He looked at her with an intention that he was going to have her, a laugh escaped her lips, but it had been a hollow sound, not at all like her normal laughter.

"I'm not sure I'm ready yet." Tabby lent down and

kissed him briefly and refastened the rogue button. He stepped back to give her room to hop back down, entwining his fingers with hers. She looked up into his face and smiled weakly. His face seemed to have changed from the guy she first met only a few months earlier.

With a suddenness that caught her off guard. He scooped her up into his arms, she reached up and cupped the back of his neck with her free hand so as not to fall. She clung on to him and squealed, "Alex!" Tabby wasn't even sure how they had ended up on the sofa, but there they were, making out and his hands were roaming over her body as though she was a treasure map that he needed to decipher.

Before, when they spent time together, she had enjoyed it. The attention, the exploration, the feeling of excitement. But now she felt nothing. "You aren't going to tease me any more." His words speared her brain and she froze.

He reached down for her again, and his tongue was in her mouth, probing and taking and she felt his hands all over her body. He continued to grope and feel his way beneath her shirt. She was made of stone. She didn't participate, she merely watched from her prison of fear.

She wasn't sure this was how she had envisioned this happening. But she was pretty sure that she had expected to feel something, anything other than a rising sense of dread.

Alex's fingers had made light work of her shirt buttons she had refastened, and she felt the cool air over her skin. He gathered her hands in one of his own and raised them over her head as he slid over her, their lips never breaking contact.

The weight of him was unsettling and she felt a twinge of panic as he reached between them and popped the top button of her jeans. He stopped and stared at her, grinning before his teeth grazed along the line of her jaw. She simply stared at him; words seemed to have lost all meaning.

She wanted to speak, she wanted to stop him, she wanted this to stop.

"What is your problem? I thought you wanted this?" He wasn't shouting as such, but his tone caused Tabby's eyes to widen in shock. Did he expect them to do it here on her mum's sofa? Panic seemed to consume her now, and she re-doubled her efforts to twist her wrists free of his grasp.

He was beginning to frighten her. "Alex," she whispered, hoping that he would let her go and they could pretend this never happened. "Please stop..."

His hold tightened and she felt the tears start to prickle her eyes.

She was rigid and paralysed in fear. "Please stop."

A far away sound began to leech into her brain, and she became aware that he had released her hands. They were simply laying above her head as though detached from the rest of her body. "Tabby, god, your phone's ringing." The annoyance in his voice would have been comical at any other time.

She was still laying back on the couch, still fully clothed with him hovering over her. He looked angry and frustrated at the interruption. "If you aren't going to answer the phone, then maybe we should go upstairs…" He got to his feet and pulled her up to standing. Her legs were unsteady, and she felt like her limbs were jelly.

She felt sick to her stomach as he kissed her neck and pulled her up against his body.

Looking down over his shoulder, she saw the screen of her phone flash one name over and over again, Jacob.

Her body tensed. Alex stopped and looked down at her. "Don't you want to do this for me?" It wasn't so much as a question but more of an attempt to mould her into doing what he wanted. "To show me how you feel about me, about us…"

"No," she whispered, "No." He made no reaction to her words, and she doubted they ever left her head. She tried again and again to speak her truth as the tears cascaded over her face. "No."

The phone had stopped and he had stepped back, finally hearing her. She slumped down onto the sofa, her head in her hands. "No." She repeated again, shaky but louder than before.

He stood over her ranting some horrible truths. "If we aren't having sex then what are we?" He spat out at her.

She was trembling now. "I'm not ready." She whimpered, finally looking up at him.

"Well, I am, and if we aren't going to do it, then we're over!" He was shrugging on his jacket and waiting for her to respond.

Her mouth fell open wide, "Then we're over." She replied in a shaky breath.

She looked up at him, her full attention on him

and all thoughts of his kindness when they first met was gone. Tabby saw him as he had been for weeks. Manipulating her to be a certain way. Criticising little things to make her second-guess herself and who she was.

Had he heard her say stop? She thought that she'd said it, over and over. If the phone hadn't interrupted him, would he have… Her stomach somersaulted with revulsion.

"Oh, by the way… on my way over here, I saw Rhys with another woman. They walked into Rosie's Bed and Breakfast together. I think he's with someone else. So you're perfect little family is anything but…" With that he walked out. Leaving his jacket draped on the chair.

Tabby simply curled up into a ball and cried.

She wasn't sure how long it was before JJ found her. His voice had been soft and concerned. She had recoiled when he reached out a hand to her shoulder.

"Tabby, what happened?"

On realising who it was she reached for him and sobbed even harder. She couldn't tell him, she couldn't tell anyone.

Ewan

He was only going to be back for the weekend, there was some paperwork that needed signing for the house and he liked the idea of checking in on his brother with all the changes going on.

Whilst he had been on the train first thing, he had received a text from Tabby. She said that she needed his help today. Something about it being urgent and could he come round at mid-day.

He felt a strong sense of responsibility to help her in any way he could and had confirmed that he would be there with cake at mid-day.

It was now five to and he had just pulled up outside of the cottage. Balancing a tray of cakes in one hand and holding a bag of doughnuts in the other, he struggled to lock the car prior to heading up the path.

The door opened before he had even had the chance to attempt at knocking. He almost dropped all the food when he realised who had opened the door for him.

Mae was smiling up at him and offered to relieve him of the box and stepped aside so that he could enter. The look on her face developed meaning as he saw what was going on inside.

A full on argument was underway in the middle of the kitchen. JJ was there, as was Alex. It was clear that these two did not see eye to eye. There didn't seem to be punches being thrown, but the tension in the air, suggested otherwise.

Tabby was standing between them trying to force them apart. Alex had hold of her wrist in a vice like grip and JJ was grabbing at his shirt a look of pure loathing as he was trying to free Tabby.

He waltzed straight between the pair and waved the bag of hot sugary doughnuts. "Come on gents, let's call a truce and eat first hey?" Alex turned to him and grunted an acknowledgement, releasing Tabby at once. JJ moved in front of her as if to guard her from a monster.

Ewan wasn't sure what was going on here, but he was glad he had arrived when he did.

Tabby came and hugged him as Alex left without a word.

A short while later, once most of the doughnut bag was empty and he was on his second cup of tea, it was he who was raising his voice.

"I am telling you, I know my brother and he is not with the woman you described. He loves your mum Tabby, I'm certain of it!" She beamed at him, then glanced at the others as though daring them to contradict him.

"So, Tabby, you've gathered us all here because..." Mae took charge and prodded the discussion with question after question.

The plan it turned out was good. He was sure that if each of them played their parts, then Rhys and Sadie would be able to reconcile their differences.

Ewan didn't see the need of telling the younger two about what was really going on between the two they were striving to match-make. But he had caught

Mae's eye more than once which had given him the impression that she knew more than she was letting on too.

Then after another half an hour, JJ said that he was going to get going. He had his first shift at the pub that evening and he wanted time to get ready.

He noticed that JJ held Tabby just a fraction of a second longer than was expected. But he knew how close they were and perhaps they had argued too.

Eventually, when it was just the three of them, Ewan offered to do the dishes but Tabby jumped up and said that she would sort it all and they were free to leave when they were ready.

Knowing that they were being dismissed, Mae and Ewan gathered their coats and made to leave.

Once out in the cold air, they huddled together for warmth. "Are you staying at Rhys's this weekend?"

"I'm staying at the B and B, just the one night. But I'm going to visit the house I'm buying first. Would you, would you like to come with me?"

Her face looked torn and he quickly back-peddled. "You have plans, it's ok. Another time maybe?"

"Yes, another time would be great. Thank you for the offer though." She stepped out of the porch and headed down the path ahead of him.

"You aren't staying at Rhys's then?" He shook his head and she seemed to take time in digesting this information. "I'll be at the pub later, maybe see you in there for a drink?" She waved and turned. She was halfway across the green by the time he had gotten into his car. He watched her disappear through the gate before he eventually started the car and drove off.

Chapter Thirty-three

Sadie

After pulling herself together, Sadie had reopened the shop for the last few hours of the day.

A couple of her regulars had popped in but it was relatively quiet she was pleased to see.

Just before she was scheduled to close, a bouquet of flowers walked in to the shop. Or rather a florist carrying the biggest bouquet of flowers she had ever seen.

"Hi," the woman croaked before gingerly placing them on the counter. "You're Sadie, right?" She nodded staring at the flowers that were all shades of pink. "These are from someone who really cares a lot about you. I have never made an arrangement so big before." She laughed and then stopped short. "I think I know you."

Sadie shook her head, "You've opened the new florist on the corner! I'm sorry I haven't had the chance to pop by and say hello yet. It's our busy season at the moment... Christmas!"

"No, that's ok." She smiled at her as if remembering something extremely important. "I think you were the person that helped get me out of the fire."

"Oh my goodness, that was you! I'm so glad to see that you are alright." Sadie came round and hugged her. The woman was a little taken aback, but Sadie waved her concerns away. "It's been a really awful day. So thank you, you have made it so much better." She spun around to pick up the flowers, when a cold sensation spread through her body. Instantaneously she felt clammy and the flowers slip from her grasp. She didn't see the vase smash as everything had gone black.

When she came to, there was a cold wet dishcloth on her forehead, and she was lying on the floor. "Don't try to sit up. Just stay where you are and take your time." The woman's face came into focus, and she tried to sit up but again the weird feeling came over her. She ached all over and her mouth felt like sandpaper.

"Did you have lunch and breakfast today?" The woman was kind and clearly knew what she was doing. She nodded a response, but on reflection, she had only had one slice of toast and some crackers all day. She just hadn't felt hungry. Which, she realised was not like her at all.

"I didn't get to ask your name before I collapsed." This time the woman batted her worries away.

"Harriet. But let's not worry about introductions right now. If I support you, do you think you can sit up?"

After a few minutes and a small glass of juice, Sadie was sitting up and her colour had returned. As she had been the last delivery of the day, Harriet had offered to walk her home for her own peace of mind.

It was just as well Sadie had been helped by such a good Samaritan. As she stepped over the threshold of the cottage, the feeling came over her again. This time she had remained conscious although very weak and the room didn't stop swaying.

"Would you like me to call a doctor for you?" Harriet's face swam in and out of focus.

"Mum! Oh my god, what happened?" She felt Tabby touch her arm, but she didn't feel up to moving her head or speaking. "Hi, um, what happened to her?"

Harriet explained her funny turn and that there was no sign of a head injury, but that maybe it would be a good idea to call someone.

Mae arrived in what felt like no time at all. Sadie had been moved to the couch and was not aware of Harriet leaving, but she had been assured that she mentioned popping by tomorrow to check on her.

Now that the dizziness had completely passed, she felt foolish and a little more than embarrassed by what had happened in front of a virtual stranger no less.

"Maybe you should contact Rhys?" Tabby sounded far away still as the ringing in her ears hadn't entirely subsided.

"No! I'm fine." Sadie declared to the room in general. And as though proving her point she made to get up from her seat.

"Stay where you are." Mae ordered. "Don't panic, I won't be contacting Rhys." Her eye's flashed at Tabby who bashfully left the room.

She came and sat with her and asked her how she was feeling now. "A little tired and a bit shaky, nothing a good night's sleep wouldn't cure." Inwardly she cursed that someone had been with her. If she had been alone, there would have been no need for all this fuss. "It's probably just stress. We've been so busy and there is so much going on…" Her voice trailed off at the sight of Mae's face. Kind and caring, but also showing an expression that told her she wasn't believing a word of it.

"How long has this been going on…" Mae questioned accusingly. Sadie's mouth formed an O before she went to speak. "The truth Sadie, I'll know if you aren't telling me the truth!"

She sighed deeply and lent her head back. "It's been a few weeks that I've been feeling off, but that is the first time I fainted, I promise."

Mae seemed to accept this and nodded, "Ok then, we'll sort you an appointment at the Doctors first thing Monday morning."

Sadie was about to protest what she felt was an extreme exaggeration, when Mae hit the message home. "How will you care for Tabby if you aren't caring for yourself?" She had to concede, that with everything going on, she hadn't been making her health a priority. She hadn't been eating properly, but she supposed that was the result from losing Rhys. She couldn't really blame the dizzy spells on him too. Shame, she thought, it felt good making him out to be the devil. It felt like she had been justified in her actions.

Rhys

Meanwhile, a short distance away, at the other end of the village, Rhys was up and finishing off some paperwork for Monday morning. Things had sort of snowballed and he was due with his final presentation this week.

If his plan of winning Sadie back was going to work, then he had to ensure that he secured the school build contract with his newly formed company. Being a one-man band had some perks he was sure, but the main downfall was most definitely having to manage everything himself.

He certainly wasn't regretting it though. Rhys was certain that setting up his own building design firm in Beechend was the right move.

Whilst in the middle of packing the designs away the doorbell rang. He glanced at the clock. He hadn't been expecting anyone and it was just after seven. Not late by anyone's standards but not the norm in this sleepy village.

As he got to his feet, a thought entered his brain. Maybe it was Sadie, she had received his flowers and couldn't be apart from him a moment longer! Hastening to open the door he didn't even notice that the shadow of the figure was far too large to be her.

"Ewan!"

His brother looked haggard and stepped over the threshold before he'd had a chance to invite him in.

"Um what are you doing here? I didn't know you were coming back this weekend."

"I'm staying at the B and B for the night, I know you're busy with the final proposal so didn't want to be an inconvenience to you." He battered his brother's worries away as they were so minute, and he would always be happy to see him. "I'm not here about that. The thing is, I was at the pub, Mae had just arrived, and I was buying her a drink when she got a call from Tabitha." At the mention of her name, his blood ran cold. Something was wrong. Why else would Ewan have come round here.

Rhys didn't give his brother a chance to finish what he had come to say. He had already grabbed his coat from the wrack and marched out of the door.

He practically ran to the end of the lane and through the adjoining streets to get to the village green.

He wasn't fully aware of his brother's ramblings behind him, his only focus was on getting to the cottage.

The soft glow of light through the windows did very little to calm his raging heart as he barged past the gate and pounded on the door.

Mae answered.

He didn't give her much more than a glance before he barged into the kitchen and called out for Sadie and Tabby.

He didn't notice that Ewan had followed him into the kitchen and was now apologising profusely to Mae for the intrusion.

He called out again as he stepped towards the

doorway leading into the small lounge at the front of the cottage.

Tabby materialised as if fairy magic had made her appear.

Quickly, looking her over, he saw that for all intense and purposes she looked unscathed. He pulled her into a hug and was surprised when she hugged him back as though her very existence depended on it.

Still cradling her to him he turned back to Mae and his brother. "Will someone please tell me what on earth is going on?"

"Oh, I'd like to know that too!" Came a soft voice from inside the lounge.

After releasing Tabby, he popped his head around the door, suddenly sheepish and feeling that this was not how he had envisioned seeing her again.

Instantly goosebumps raised up and down his arms and the hair on the back of his neck felt like it was standing to attention. "Sadie..." He rushed into the room and towards her, when she raised a hand in front of her, he stopped short.

"Why is he here?" She demanded, the action of raising her voice seemed to drain what little colour she had.

"What is wrong?" He demanded, going to her side regardless of the look she was throwing in his direction.

"That's my fault I'm afraid, I went round to tell him you weren't well, and he didn't get the full message." Ewan's presence in the room seemed to make it contract.

"I thought there was something wrong with

Tabby." He interjected, "Are you ok? I can take you to the hospital!" Rhys felt cold all over at the thought of Sadie being unwell. She was pale with a soft sheen of perspiration on her forehead.

"She's fine, if she isn't better I'll call the doctor." Mae glanced up at Ewan and gave him a look that he didn't quite catch. "I think it is best if you go, she doesn't want you here."

"Come on Rhys, let's go ok!" Ewan had walked the rest of the way into the room and had to crouch between the beams.

He wasn't sure what was for the best. He hated that she was sick and that he couldn't be the one to care for her.

Reluctantly her got to his feet, only now realising that he was only wearing socks.

"Whatever is going on between us, I want you to know that I care about you, and I'll do whatever it takes to get you back." The corners of his lips lifted slightly, and he turned to walk away.

"I don't want you back." Were the parting words that floated to him like a whisper on the breeze. He strode through the kitchen and out of the cottage.

Chapter Thirty-four

Tabby

When she had left for school the following evening it was with a very heavy heart. Her mum had looked a lot better and was up and moving around, but Tabby had known something wasn't one hundred percent right.

Mae had offered to stay with her and so Jacob was driving her back to school for the last time. They had barely left the village when he had started on her. Clearly he had an axe to grind and he was going to say his piece.

"Are you going to tell me what yesterday was all about?" His voice was stern and accusing. But she didn't reply. Embarrassment washed over her and her face reddened. "I walk in to find you alone, in the foetal position on the sofa, distraught. What am I supposed to think?"

"I don't want to talk about it JJ." Tabby whispered. The continued through the lanes heading for the motorway. She was relieved that he had appeared to drop it all together and she felt her body finally beginning to relax.

"Jelly Belly…" His voice was gentle.

"Mmm?"

"I saw you, when he came back to the cottage." Her eyes flew open and stared straight ahead. "He did something to hurt you…"

His words hung in the air, mocking her.

Tabby's eyes began to fill and the car pulled into a nearby layby almost entirely hidden by the snow covered hedgerow.

"Look, I know that this is none of my business. I know that you aren't my little Jelly Belly anymore. But if I can do or say anything to make this better I will." His voice had been level and in complete control of his emotions.

She risked a glance in his direction and saw that he had turned to face her and had removed his seatbelt. "We aren't together anymore." She had surprised herself at how even her own voice was despite the tears. "Alex isn't the guy I thought he was."

"So he did hurt you…" his voice trailed away as he gripped on to the steering wheel for support. "Did he…"

"No."

He nodded his understanding.

"I see the bruises…" JJ traced a finger down the sleeve of her jacket and slowly hooked it and eased it up to reveal the marks that had blossomed over night. She shrugged her sleeve free and shook it back down to cover the evidence. "I know he did that. I saw it on your face yesterday."

They sat in silence staring out at the darkening sky before them.

"It's all over now, it's ok. You don't have to go 'big brother' about it." She forced a laugh that he did not reciprocate.

"Tabitha, it is never ok for someone to hurt you. No one has the right." He hung his head. "My feelings are anything but…"

Her eyes widened at his words. She dared not speak or move. Had she heard him right?

"Forget I said anything." He reached over his shoulder and began to refasten his belt before restarting the car and carrying on with the journey. "Come on, I've got to get you there by five."

The rest of the journey she felt super aware of everything he did. The way he held the wheel, his grip on the gear stick as he finally entered the motorway. The lazy way he tapped along to the music.

By the time they pulled into the drive up to the school she thought she was going to explode. The tyres crunched over the gravel. Tabby started to unbuckle her belt to leave. Jacob placed a hand over hers and she stilled instantly. A tingle of electricity shot up her arm at his touch.

She looked up and found he was a lot closer. His eyes were wide and she noticed the flecks of amber around the pupils that gave them the look of liquid gold. Tabby didn't move, she didn't dare to breath.

He was leaning in over the gear stick towards her. His eyes seeming only to see her.

She found herself mirroring his actions and his focus flickered down to her lips.

Just as they were about to collide he stopped and she dropped her gaze, retreating back into her seat. Her cheeks were reddening, she could feel the warmth radiating across her body. The shame she felt at the feelings she was having.

JJ's finger grazed across her cheek as if caressing her, following the line of her jaw and slowly but with a determination that she knew only he possessed, he lifted her chin until their eyes met in a blaze of fire.

She was the one who broke the gap between them. The tension had built to a point that she thought she might expire from trying to hold her emotions in.

When his lips met hers, it didn't feel wrong. It was different, like they had always meant to be. There was a faint taste of peppermint from the mints he had eaten earlier. Despite the look in his eyes, Jacob was in no rush. It felt like a full minute of their lips touching before he even attempted to move.

Their first kiss had been tender and she knew that this was not going to be their last.

Once they had broken apart, JJ had grinned like a Cheshire cat. "Um," she said, for all words seemed to be insufficient in expressing how she currently felt. "I thought you were dating Debbie at the pub…" Her words hung in the air and she cringed at the thought of being the other woman in some sordid love triangle.

He placed a solitary finger over her lips that silenced her. Then leaned in for their second kiss.

JJ's hand had snaked around her waist and attempted to pull her towards him. They were more frantic this time. The belt buckle was released and Tabby clambered over until she was practically on top of him. He tickled her and she giggled.

So many questions were racing through her head that she really couldn't think straight.

Their third kiss happened whilst they were standing on the gravelled drive. Her luggage was at their feet when he had gently pulled her to him.

Her hands had rested on his shoulders and his around her waist.

This had been her favourite kiss of her life so far. He had taken her breath away.

When they had finally broken apart, he had told her he would see her Friday night. Before pecking a soft kiss on the tip of her nose. "Have a nice week Jelly belly!" He winked at her and her heart soared.

It was only after she had stood in the cold watching and waving as he had driven back down the drive and out of sight, that reality dawned on her. She had just kissed Jacob. Her brother, ok, not her brother. Definitely, not her brother. But JJ, had kissed her, and more than once. But really kissed her. She wanted to do it again.

What did this mean? Were they going to date? Did he love her? Was he breaking up with Debbie?

One thing was for certain, she was head of heals.

Sadie

By late Sunday evening Sadie knew what was wrong with her. She had suspected the previous week and the week before that, but now she was certain.

All that remained was for her to make the decision of what to do and who to tell.

Once Tabby had left with JJ, Mae had sat her down for a heart to heart.

"Ok, tell me I am over-stepping, but I think we both know what is going on with you." They were back in the kitchen, sipping tea and munching on a ginger biscuit. "How late are you?"

Mae was never one to be shy in coming forwards.

"Five weeks tomorrow." She groaned.

"Five weeks! Have you tested?"

"I did after I missed my first period, but it was negative." Mae looked exasperated.

"Ok, do you have any more tests in the bathroom?" She nodded. "Well drink up! I want to know if I'm having another niece or a nephew." The delight was etched over her face. Whereas all she felt was despair at getting into this mess with a guy that was getting married to someone else. "It will be ok Sadie."

Upon finishing their tea, she made the trek up the narrow stairs and into the bathroom. They waited the allotted time and their in front of them as they perched together on the side of the bath, were the lines that confirmed her fate.

Tabby was going to have a little brother or sister.

The tension in such a small room was unbearable, Mae always had a knack for making her laugh, but in this situation, Sadie was certain there was nothing to be said. "So, who's the father?"

The pair of them erupted into fits of laughter and suddenly, the whole mess didn't feel as dire as it had only moments before.

"He loves, you, you know" Sadie shrugged her response. "He does, just look at how he reacted yesterday. If that isn't love I don't know what is." She placed her arm around Sadie's shoulders and gave a reassuring squeeze.

"When you're ready, you'll talk to him and all of this will sort itself out."

Sadie nodded, although she couldn't think this could be further from the truth. Tears leaked from her eyes as she thought about the situation she would be bringing this baby into.

An absent father who got another woman pregnant. A teenage sister. Toxic grandparents. And her, she certainly didn't have her life together. But then she thought about Tabby and realised, maybe, she hadn't done such a bad job after all.

Chapter Thirty-five

Sadie

This week seemed to have flown by. She had stopped the Doctors first thing Monday morning and they had in deed confirmed the test to be accurate. She hadn't seen Rhys all week but he had been in her thoughts.

In all honesty, his flower delivery set up had worked how she was sure he had wanted it to.

Each afternoon, at varying times, Harriet had popped round with a bouquet equal in size and beauty to the first. It was now Friday lunch time and already she was looking forward to her 'surprise' gift of the day. It wasn't just a chance to chat with her new friend, either. She found that she loved reading the hand-written cards that came with the blooms each day.

He hadn't written that he loved her, but it was there between the lines.

She had softened to the idea after her second appointment. They had given her a preliminary due date and she was shocked that the baby was due at the end of June.

It hadn't taken her long to recall Fiona's announcement that she was due then. The thought that Rhys had gone to the city and been with another woman, not only didn't compute, but just wasn't even possible. At the time they conceived the baby growing inside her, Rhys was practically living at the cottage with her. He didn't go to the city and therefore had not fathered Fiona's baby.

She had wanted to speak with him the moment she had realised, but the thoughts of all the horrible things she had said came rushing back to her and she lost her nerve.

So she was resigned to going about her business, secretly hoping that he would come and see her and she would have the courage of her convictions to fess up and admit she was wrong.

Sadie knew at some point she would have to tell him about their child. But she didn't want him back because he felt obligated. She wanted him to want her.

The irony of the situation was not lost on her as she felt a pang of sorrow for Darren and how long she had loathed him for. She wondered about his death and what might have become of them if he'd not been out that night. Would they have stayed together? Would they have gotten married and had more children? Would he have grown to resent her?

Her dreams had become so vivid that sleep seemed to have lost its restfulness altogether.

"Hey baby Mumma!" Sadie's head snapped up to see Mae waltzing in. Fortunately, the ladies group was upstairs and out of earshot and no-one else was in the main shop. Mae smiled and offered her a small brown paper bag. It contained an apple turnover and she groaned in desperation as her hunger pangs took over.

She was ashamed to say that she had devoured several of these over the last few days. The tangy apple filling was just what she wanted.

"So, I've been thinking…" Sadie looked up from licking her fingers. "We should have a girls night out tonight!"

Sadie was shaking her head, "No, Tabby's home tonight for good and I was thinking of having a chat with her… You know, about you know what…"

Mae was now shaking her head. "Nar, far too early, besides…" She dropped her voice to a whisper, "Don't you think the baby daddy should know first?" This Sadie could not argue with, but she still was looking forward to having Tabby home. "Besides, JJ and Tabby are going to the cinema later and I think they're planning on pigging out and eating junk food. You know, chilling out and being kids."

It seemed like she had no excuse left. She would be facing another evening alone at home. "I suppose an early evening out won't be such a bad idea."

Mae cheered a little too much, but she supposed that they didn't have too many nights out left. So, she simply asked her what time she should be round at hers.

"Oh, I've got some errands to run this afternoon, it might run over so I'll come straight to the pub, shall we say half six?" Sadie nodded as she discovered the second apple turnover in the bag. She grinned as she took a bite.

"Smithers is collecting Tabby this evening, should I let him know to drop her off at yours instead then?" Mae shrugged and said she would contact him as she was talking to his wife later about another stall application for the winter festival between Christmas and New year.

Mae made her excuses and left shortly after, a decided spring in her step, Sadie was left pondering what her best friend was up to.

Rhys

Rhys is in the nearest town for his big meeting with the council reps to approve the designs and to set things in motion to break ground in the New Year.

The meeting had been postponed twice this week for various reasons on their end and Rhys was starting to grow concerned that really they were just giving him the brush off.

"This is great Mr Knight!" the representative had been bowled over with the plans he had presented and loved the ideas for creating a community hub for the whole village and not just a the school building.

"The relevant paperwork will be sent to your office, just get your secretary to send everything back once you've read it through and signed!" The man reached out a firmly shook his hand, patting him on the back and chuckling. "With designs like these you will go far in this department, I know of a few more projects in the pipeline, they haven't got the green light yet, but they sure will in the new year. You are going to be a very busy man!"

By the time he reached his car it was gone four pm and darkness had descended. There was a flurry of snowflakes swirling through the air, but luckily they hadn't begun to settle on the ground.

As the engine roared to life a call came through on the speaker system. "Ewan! I only just landed the contract!" Rhys's voice could not hide the joy he was feeling. "They said that there is the possibility of more in the district too." He could hear his brother cheering down the phone.

"So where are you? We need to celebrate! I'm already in Beechend, we'll head out for a few tonight." Rhys pondered for a minute. He didn't really feel like going out and celebrating, what he really wanted to do was tell Sadie, have her fall into his arms whilst he did all manner of things to make her scream his name. "Rhys? You're breaking up, I can't hear you."

"The thing is, I've got the contract being sent over and I really need to take the time to read it through before I get it back to them." It was a feeble excuse, but he didn't want to celebrate without Sadie.

"I'm not taking no for an answer! Look, you are probably shattered after a long week. Read the contract through tomorrow instead. We'll go out early, shall we say, six thirty at the pub. A few drinks to celebrate and you can go back to your place like a hermit!" His brother laughed and told him he'd see him in a few hours then hung up.

Rhys knew that his brother was probably right, but they were now nearing three weeks since the fight and still there was no sign of forgiveness from Sadie. He was starting to feel desperate.

He wondered whether the bouquets of flowers had been too much. He knew that today's bunch would have arrived by now and he hoped that she had been reading the cards.

Chapter Thirty-six

Tabby

By the time Smithers had loaded the last of her things into the boot of the car, the snow was falling in thick flakes and was without a doubt starting to settle on the grass and gravel in the grounds.

"Not to worry Miss Tabitha, the roads have been gritted and we'll be back in Beechend before you know it!" She had pecked him on the cheek and made to sit in the front seat, but he had shaken his head and held open the door for the back of the town car.

She had shaken her head and joked with him, that after today it wouldn't matter what any of these preppy people thought of her.

He had been insistent and wouldn't budge on the matter. So Tabby had nestled down in the back and flipped out her phone to find several messages waiting for her. Another three from Alex, saying that she was a tease and she should thank her lucky stars that he had given her the time today. She deleted them and then proceeded to block his number.

Maybe she had led him on, but he turned out to be

not the guy she thought he was.

There was only one message from JJ, telling her to be safe and that he'd already got the pizza and a movie ready. She grinned and wondered for the hundredth time this week what their mother's were going to say when they found out about them.

The remaining messages were from her mum, Mae and Ewan.

Her mum said that she was going out with Mae for a few drinks. Told her to have fun and that she would see her home at ten thirty. She smiled, knowing that the first part of her plan had come to fruition.

Mae confirmed that her mum would be in the pub at half past six.

Ewan, who was quickly becoming one amazing ally, had confirmed that Rhys would also be at the pub for six thirty.

This was it. The plan was in play and there was nothing more she or any of them could really do now.

She just had time to glance back at the school as they rounded the end of the drive. It really was a magnificent building, but as it turned out. It wasn't the place she needed to be.

Rhys

Rhys was pleased to see that he was leaving town ahead of the rush hour traffic. The snow was much thicker the further north he drove and by the time he reached the motorway he was surprised to see that the snow was beginning to settle on the grass verge and in the recovery lane.

He slowed down accordingly and began to let his mind wander back to Sadie. He should have called her this week. He had wanted to call her but there had been so much malice in her voice that he wasn't sure he could cope hearing it again.

The things they had said to each other kept rolling around in his brain, tormenting him. He didn't think he had really done anything wrong per se, but he could have handled the Fiona situation a lot better than he did. It turns out trying to protect those you care about by keeping secrets… not a smart move!

The truth was, all he wanted to say to Sadie was that he loved her.

That he loved everything about her, always had and always would.

Tabby

Tabby pinged a message to her mum, letting her know that they were on the motorway and she would be going straight to Mae's. She added that they were going to stay in because of the weather and then added some kisses for good measure.

Outside the window the snow was coming down faster and faster and it was becoming increasingly difficult to see clearly.

From what she could make out, the snow was definitely settling on the road as what looked like tyre tracks were gradually deepening in the lane to their far left.

Without any warning the car lurched to the left and then immediately to the right. The seat belt had kept her in place but the motion had knocked the phone from her grasp. As the car swerved again they narrowly missing another car travelling in the lane next to them.

Tabby was gripping the seat and called out to Matthew who looked to be grabbing his arm in pain. "Matthew!" She called out again, but he was now slumped over the steering wheel.

She looked up and through the windscreen to see swirling white passing so quickly that it was making her dizzy. She screamed as they collided with the central barrier and spun.

From the moment of the first impact it was as

though time was moving extremely slowly. The flakes became clearer and the car spun round and round finally coming to rest facing a glaring beam of white light.

Rhys

Through the haze of white snow he saw break lights starting to appear as a dark coloured car swerved across three lanes of traffic and back again. He honked his horn hoping to get the drivers attention as he slowed.

It was a miracle that they hadn't hit anyone. He supposed they had hit some black ice and were struggling to regain control of the car.

It suddenly lurched again this time heading straight towards the central reservation. It clipped two cars when it spun out and he narrowly avoided them. He turned on his hazard lights hoping that the vehicles approaching behind would see and slow down.

Finally the car came to a rest facing the wrong way. It looked a bit battered, but it was still in one piece. He had managed to come to a safe stop in the far left hand lane, the furthest from the collision, when he heard the screech of breaks and tyres squealing as they fought to find purchase in the icy road's surface.

The lorry shot past his driver's window and ploughed into the car that had originally swerved. It rolled over and the car became completely hidden from view.

He swore under his breath, and grabbed his phone, punching in 999 as he checked it was safe to exit the car. They were at marker nineteen, northbound, several cars involved, unquestionably one was serious.

Rhys stopped at the first car that had been clipped and spun out of control clipping two more in the process. The woman in the front seat was screaming for her children in the back. They too were crying. He helped them from the car which showed only minimal signs of damage. He steered her and the two young ones up the grass verge where another woman took over who had also witnessed the crash.

He told her he was going back to check the other cars.

By now, the road looked like utter carnage. Several other drivers had emerged unscathed and were helping those less fortunate.

Rhys ran round the front side of the lorry that had caused the most damage. The black town car had rolled over, he wasn't sure how many times. But it was now pined between the barrier and the lorry's overturned trailer. The car was resting on it's roof and the wheels were continuing to spin as though still under power.

It was only when he saw the motionless hand with sparkling painted nails dangling that a feeling of sheer dread and panic coursed through him.

He ran the remaining few metres and lowered himself to the ground nearest the smashed window.

Tabitha was suspended upside down, held in place by a combination of her seatbelt and the twisted metal that had pierced and speared the car.

She wasn't moving, her eyes were closed as blood

trickled down the side of her face. He felt the panic rising like bile in his throat, burning all the way through him as he screamed her name.

Chapter Thirty-seven

Tabby

The darkness has swallowed her whole. No warmth, no sense of smell, no sound, only darkness. Darkness, and pain.

"Tabby! Tabby, sweetheart, I'm here, Tabby!" A voice was reaching through the dense black fog and pulling her back to the light. It was muffled as though the person was covered in a thick winter duvet.

As the voice and light become clearer, so did the pain.

"Tabby, darling. It's going to be alright." The voice was strained but familiar. "I'm here, it's going to be alright." Rhys. Rhys was here, but where was here?

As the building pain reaches its peak a groan of pain left her and her eyes flashed open.

"Rhys," She cried, whimpering sobs as she took in the sight before her. She was alone. She was in the car. There was pain all over her body and her vision was blurred. "Rhys." It was a whisper this time as she wasn't sure that she wasn't hallucinating the first time. "Mum," she called out more panicked and desperate.

There was a crunching sound to her left side and a hand appeared through the broken window. It began knocking the remaining glass from the frame and then it was followed by another hand, arms and then the top of a head slid through the narrow gap and she wasn't alone anymore. "It's ok sweety, I'm here." Rhys struggled to get further into the wreckage and instead stretched out a hand and his fingers grazed hers.

The pain across her chest appeared to be growing in intensity and the worse it got the harder it was for her to catch her breath.

"I'm going to get you out." His fingers left hers momentarily and she groped for them in the darkness she only found air.

"Please don't leave me," she croaked but he had already left. She could hear his voice coming from the other side of the car and she realised that he was trying to wrench the door open to reach her better.

Each attempt caused pain to rip through her and she screamed out, once, twice, three times. She wondered if the screaming is only in her head, when the darkness enveloped her once more.

When the voice of Rhys broke into her consciousness, he was back in the car. Her body felt different than before. Her injuries seemed to be melting away and although she could feel him holding onto her hand, the sensation tingled like he wasn't truly there any more. She struggled to gain meaning from his words. But the sound of his voice calmed her and she felt her body begin to lose pain, inch by inch.

"She's waiting for you." Tabby told him, "You shouldn't be late."

He spoke but the noise that reached her was just garbled and the ringing in her ears had grown to such a sound, that even as the sirens grew in intensity, they seemed so very far away.

This was the moment she realised that she was going to die.

"Tell her I love her." She garbled "Your turn now." The pain was almost completely gone now. "No hurt no more."

Rhys

The sirens were a deafening roar now, but the car inside had gone still. "Tabby, Tabby, wake up sweetheart. They're going to get you out now. Tabby!" He squeezed her fingers but there was no response.

"Tabitha!"

The firemen pulled on his foot, he released his hold on her as he was extricated from the car.

"Sir, are you ok? Are you hurt?" The fireman nearest to him was checking him over.

"I'm fine, it's not me, it's Tabby, my little girl. I couldn't get her out. She was awake but she stopped talking." His chest heaved from the weight of holding back a choke of sobs.

He watched helplessly as a member of the crew assessed the situation and sent in someone to administer fluids and oxygen.

"Tabby!" He called out again.

A woman had come and to stand with him, draping a warm blanket over his shoulders. "Can you give me some details about your daughter?" He looked up but chose not to waste time in correcting the mistake. "Her name is Tabby, how old is she?"

"Tabitha Mirada, she's going to be eighteen in a few months."

"Ooo, teenager, they bounce back so quickly, she'll be back to blasting her music before you know it." Her smile was weak and not at all encouraging.

Rhys glanced around at the emergency services surrounding the scene. He heard them announce that the driver was dead. "It looked like a heart attack. Not the devil, it was an accident and could have happened to anyone." The paramedic stated. He nodded although wasn't really taking it all in.

Then he heard a scream of pain and relief flooded his body once more. "Tabby!" he called out, the paramedic and another fire fighter were holding on to him, probably concerned that he would get in the way. "It's ok honey, they'll have you out soon."

That's when he noticed that he was shaking. "Be brave and they'll have you out soon, I'm right here."

She whimpered again and cried out for her mum. The realisation that the person she needs most doesn't even know about the accident yet seemed to wake him from the haze he had toppled into.

He pulled his phone from his inside pocket and found her number and hit the dial button. It rang and rang for what felt like an eternity before the line clicked. "Sadie!"

"Hello, you have reached Sadie's phone, I can't answer right now, but leave me a message and I will get back to you." There were the beeps and he was speaking, he was telling her there had been an accident. Tabby was alive but they were working on getting her free. He said he would stay with her and keep her safe until she could get to her. Then he told the answer phone that he loved her and that he would ring again when he had more news." The machine beeped and the call disconnected.

Rhys stood in the middle of a motorway wreckage

as emergency personnel did their best to save the sweetest, most caring little girl he would ever know.

Chapter Thirty-eight

Sadie

The pub was relatively quiet for a Friday night, she was sat in the corner nearest the log fire, cradling a lime soda. It was almost ten to seven and Mae was still nowhere to be seen. She was late, and she had been the one to want to go out in the first place. She inwardly cursed her best friend's name, knowing that she would forgive her the moment she arrived.

Sadie pulled open her book and continued to read. She never got time to just sit and read next to the roaring fire. Mmm, peace she thought to herself as she took another sip. Life was always on the go. She turned the page and continued to read.

Why do the women in these books have their lives together? It isn't reality! Life isn't like this she pondered as she continued to read about the heroine's amazing life and how wonderful it all way.

Pausing to take another sip of her drink, she looked up as the pub door burst open and Mae ran in. She looked like she'd seen a ghost, she was so pale.

She called out from the doorway the moment their gaze connected. "It's Tabby!"

Ewan

In the car, Ewan was waiting with the engine running. His heart was beating a mile a minute. JJ was seated in the back of the car, his face buried in his hands and his body silently shaking.

The phone rang less than seven minutes ago. They had been in Mae's kitchen as planned, waiting for Tabby to arrive back. They were all a little on edge wondering if this scheme of theirs was going to actually work or not.

It had been Rhys on the line. He had been expecting him to call and tell him he was a git for fixing up the get together with Sadie. He had been expecting Rhys to tell him he was a git, but that he loved him anyway. He was expecting him to say that Sadie and him were together and that everything was alright.

But Rhys hadn't said any of those things. His voice had been hoarse and full of unshed emotion. He had seemed far away and it was a Rhys he never hoped to encounter again.

Suddenly, his voice had cracked and the panic had seeped in. Tabby had been in a car accident on the way back to Beechend. It was serious and he couldn't get hold of Sadie.

The car in which she had been travelling had collided with several other vehicles before being ploughed into by an articulated lorry.

She had been trapped and the fire crews were now working on getting her out. He didn't give the details of her injuries, the tone of his voice was enough for them to know the seriousness of the situation.

Rhys needed to get hold of Sadie but she wasn't answering her bloody phone, he had then changed direction and announced that they were cutting the car roof to get her out. The sounds of metal on metal reverberated down the phone.

His brother had then sobbed and Ewan had felt his heart break at the thought of them losing that precious little girl.

"She's out!" He had yelled.

After getting over the initial shock of what was happening, Ewan had taken charge. He had reassured Rhys that she was strong and that she would come through anything. He had found out which hospital they were being taken to and assured Rhys he would find Sadie and get her there.

All in just seven short minutes, he had rallied the troops and gotten them round to the pub where Sadie was waiting for Rhys, although she would never know it.

Sadie

The world was moving in slow motion and there was a constant buzzing sound in her ear which made the voices around her distorted.

In these crazy times, there were three things of which she was certain.

One; Tabby was involved in a serious car accident.

Two; her baby was hurt and being taken to hospital.

Three; she would move heaven and earth to get to her.

Time is a funny business, when you are short of time and wish for it to last longer, it will inevitably whizz past in the blink of an eye. On the other side, when you want to be somewhere or achieve something quickly, time seems to slow down to a snail's pace. Time makes a mockery of us all.

Sadie was sat in the front seat of Ewan's car as he drove like a man possessed towards the only hospital within fifty miles.

She could hear Mae talking behind her, but she couldn't register the words or their meanings. All she could think was how bad was it? Was she hurt? Was she conscious? Was she still with us?

She seemed to snap back to her senses.

"Rhys has been trying to get hold of you, where is your phone?" Mae's voice seemed to be getting clearer and the buzzing was subsiding. "Sadie, honey?" Mae asked her a second or was it the third time.

She snapped, "Why is Rhys trying to get hold of me?" She then turned to Ewan, "How much further?"

"Just one more exit and then we turn off to the hospital." Ewan replied.

The people in the car became collectively silent as they rounded the bend and saw a mass of blue flashing lights on the opposite side. There were several vehicles involved. Two cars looked as though they had been opened like a tin of beans. A sound escaped her throat and it was like none she had ever made before. She was a wounded animal and all at once she began to howl.

Chapter Thirty-nine

Rhys

After reaching the hospital just a few minutes earlier, they had wheeled Tabby through the double doors whilst a woman in blue had stayed with him and fired question after question at him. Some he answered without hesitation. Others he didn't know where to begin. Does she have any allergies? They may take her to surgery has she had a general anaesthetic before?

He had answered as honestly as he could, before asking the one question that had whirled through his head since first realising she was in that car. "Will she be alright?"

"The team are with her, they are going to do everything they can to save your daughter. Please take a seat and someone will be along as soon as they can to update you on the situation." The efficient nurse had reattached her pen to the top of the clipboard and briefly smiled before walking briskly away.

Meanwhile, as he sat in the plastic chair, the word

daughter swirled in his brain. Inside he beamed with pride that anyone would think Tabby was his and then dread flowed through him that he might never get to make things right and that the family he wanted to be a part of might be slipping away from him.

He sat with his head in his hands and waited. He waited for the nurse to reappear. He waited for the news that Tabby was going to be making a full recovery. He waited for the tears to subside. He waited for the realisation of what had happened to wash over him. He waited for a sweet oblivion to take him away from the reality he was finding himself in. He waited for Sadie to come to him, to forgive him and for their unconventional attempt at a family to fix itself. He waited for himself to once again be whole.

He was waiting to wake up from this nightmare.

Sadie

The sterile smell of the hospital flooded her senses as they entered accident and emergency. Her daughter was somewhere in this building. Her little girl needed her.

"Excuse me," Mae had cornered a nurse, "We're the family of Tabby Mirada. Can you take us to her please."

The nurse looked stern and not to be trifled with. "All visitors need to go sign in at the main desk." She pointed in the direction we had just come from, the queue was something alright. It was snaking round and back out into the cold night air.

"Excuse me," Mae retorted, "That is fine, I will get us all signed in, but can you please take her mother to her…" the nurse looked as though she was about to protest, but seemed to think better of it. "Thank you." Mae squeezed her tight and told her she'd be with her soon.

Sadie followed the nurse silently along the corridor and through two sets of double doors. "Your husband is waiting over here. This is all I can do for you at the moment. They'll be out to get you when there is more news." Sadie had given one swift nod and turned to see Rhys rising from the chair.

He was dishevelled and there was a long gash across his face. There were splatters of blood across his shirt and hands. The sight of him brought everything to the surface. Her baby girl, her angel, what horrors had she been through in the last hour.

Rhys walked to her and enveloped her into his arms without so much as a word. His body was consumed and he shook with the fear that they both felt. She knew he loved them, he loved them both. "I'm sorry I couldn't get her out, I tried, but I couldn't reach her." He cried into her shoulder and for the first time, she became the rock that she had supposed him to be.

"You were there with her; she recognised you were there and that she wasn't alone."

He straightened up and bobbed his head, his bloodshot eyes boring into her own.

"She's made of strong stuff, she'll be ok." The tears slid down her face as she willed herself to believe the words she was saying.

They sat together clutching hands in the silence of their anguish and uncertainty.

Time again was not on their side. The others had made it in before anyone had returned with news of her daughter. All of them were on the brink of the precipice tumbling them down into despair when an unknown doctor emerged through the last set of double doors. He was dressed in blue scrubs and he approached them with a sombre expression that could only mean bad news. A whimper escaped her lips and Rhys's grip tightened on hers, giving her the strength that she had given to him.

"Mr and Mrs Mirada?" They all looked up with confused expressions. "Tabitha's parents?"

Rhys indicated Sadie and announced that this is

her mother. But Sadie overrode him, "Yes, we're her parents."

The doctor nodded his acknowledgement and explained her injuries. They were keeping her on a ventilator for the time being. She wasn't out of the woods yet, but she was stable, and they would be able to see her soon.

Rhys stepped forward and shook the doctors hand, thanking him profusely for all that he had done. Ewan and the others said they would go in search of coffee and give them some time.

The pair returned to their silent vigil and neither spoke of the declaration Sadie had just made. It was as though words were not necessary.

Rhys

Later that night, Ewan had taken the others home to Beechend whilst Rhys and Sadie were sat in a side room watching Tabby sleep.

She was extremely lucky to still be with us. She had several minor injuries then some broken bones and her right lung had collapsed. There had been a concern over the head injury she had sustained but the doctors were optimistic.

Rhys was sat in the winged chair furthest from the bed. He was watching over the two most important people in his life. Sadie was half asleep her head resting on the bed next to her daughter's hand which she was holding in her own. An hour earlier he had covered her with a blanket and taken to sitting and watching over the pair of them as they slept.

They were yet to talk about the two of them and what was going to happen in the future between them, but after almost losing Sadie to a fire and Tabby to a car accident, he knew that there were no words that could stop him for being with them and caring for them, keeping them safe.

Being there in that place he felt a peace wash over him. He knew in that moment that they were meant to be and that it was time to be completely honest with her. Because he wasn't afraid anymore.

Chapter Forty

Sadie

The following morning, Tabitha had the ventilator removed and was breathing on her own once more. Their consultant had warned that she would need further surgeries in the near future but that she was out of immediate danger. All that they were waiting for was for her to wake from the sedatives she had been given.

Sadie had been sleeping in the armchair to the right of the hospital bed, but for some time now, she had merely been staring across at Tabitha willing her to wake up and smile up at her.

There came a light knock at the door and Rhys entered carrying two cups of tea. He didn't make a sound as he placed them on to the table and sat silently in the spare chair.

Tabby had a cast on both her leg and wrist. Stitches covered by a bandage on her upper arm, minor cuts and bruises. A large number of wires seemed to be connecting her to several monitors.

After a while, Sadie moved and stretched. She lent forward over Tabby and whispered to her and waited for a response, there was none, but it was still early and they said it could take a few more hours for her to fully wake up.

I've got you some tea, but you should try and sleep, you didn't get much last night.

Sadie nodded but didn't speak as he handed her the feeble plastic cup.

She placed it down beside her and immediately turned to him and launched into a barrage of praise and thankfulness at him being there for Tabby and how she didn't deserve someone as kind and unwavering as him.

He was gracious and accepting but stated that there was no thanks necessary. Rhys was relieved that she was going to be alright and that he had been able to be there for her when she needed him.

"I am grateful regardless and I will always be in your debt." The corners of her mouth lifted in a half-smile and she turned back to watch over Tabby.

Rhys then began his own speech. He said that he was so sorry for everything that happened between them. How he should have been honest with her when Fiona had first turned up. But that he had panicked and didn't want to risk what they had. He knew he handled the situation poorly and she hoped one day she would forgive him.

"I know the baby isn't yours Rhys."

He looked up in surprise, "How did you find out?"

She smirked at him over the rim of her cup, "Call it woman's intuition." She declared.

"When you announced that you wanted nothing to do with Fiona and your unborn child it set me off. I was Fiona. Unwed and carrying a baby."

Sadie had moved over to his side of the room to be nearer to him. She didn't know why she hadn't already told him, but now seemed as good a time as any. "Darren and I argued the night of his accident. He was leaving us, well me I suppose." Her features were strained. "I only ever told Mae what happened. He walked out and showed no intention of ever coming back."

Rhys was out of his seat and pulling her into his arms, "I can see how my behaviour would have upset you. If the baby had been mine, I wouldn't have walked away from it. It was something I said in the heat of the moment." She placed her hand to his cheek and he closed his eyes for a moment, absorbing the feel of her skin on his.

"I never spoke about it because I didn't want to warp Tabitha's existence of her father. There was no use in her knowing that he walked out that night and who's to say he wouldn't have come back with his tail between his legs." They laughed gently at the thought, knowing that Darren was unlikely to have done that as it wasn't in his nature.

"The thought of Darren began to eat away at me until I began to despise him. He walked out on me just a few months before our daughter was born and neither he nor I got the chance to fix things."

Rhys was gently stroking her back, calm smooth circles as she continued to talk. "When I thought you were doing the same thing as Darren, something inside me snapped. I couldn't be with someone who could do that."

"All I want is to be with you and Tabby. Maybe one day, our family might grow, or maybe it won't." Sadie blushed and buried her face in his chest as he continued to talk. "Whatever happens, the two of you, you are my family." She looked up into his face as he lent down and captured her lips with his. Her hand slid round his broad shoulders and up into his hair. He tasted like heaven and she was certain that when the time was right and she told him about their growing family he would be ecstatic. But now wasn't the time. Soon, very soon.

He deepened the kiss and she moaned at the thought of what he would do to her next time they were alone.

The door behind them opened and they sprang apart like a pair of horny teenagers caught doing something they shouldn't.

A nurse walked in with a gigantic bouquet of flowers and declared that they were left at the front desk for Tabby but that they weren't permitted to be in the rooms any more. "Rhys did you send flowers again?" She laughed taking the card that the nurse handed to her. They were from her parents. "Thank you so much, do you have a cause they can be donated to?" The nurse nodded and thanked them before leaving with the extravagant blooms. Sadie handed Rhys the card who scowled but did not voice his opinions.

"Mum!" A small squeak was issued from the bed and the pair of them surround her in an instant. She was still groggy, but the medication seemed to be keeping most of the pain at bay. "Did I just hear right…"

Sadie and Rhys looked up at each other concerned that she had heard more than they would have liked.

"Are you planning on giving me a brother or sister?" Her face widened into a smile before she winced.

"Only if you are ok with that!" Rhys replied.

"I would like a little brother, but a sister wouldn't be too bad either…"

They each took a hand and gave a gentle squeeze, "I'll see what I can do," Sadie declared before reaching down and kissing her cheek.

Rhys

Later on that evening, once Tabby had fallen back into a deep sleep, Rhys had decided it was now or never to come clean; to finally tell Sadie about his inheritance.

They had headed down to the canteen, which was now closed for service. They purchased a vending machine cuppa each and found a secluded corner in which they wouldn't be disturbed.

"This must be serious," Sadie joked as he held open the door for her to walk through. He chuckled but knew that the anxiety on his face must have shown. "Whatever you have to tell me, you should know, I'm not going anywhere!" Her face shone with love and adoration, and he felt that warm fuzzy glow spreading through his chest.

"Well, as you know, my parents passed several years ago." She nodded, remembering their deaths being announced in the local paper. "We sold the house off as a way to access part of our inheritance." He took a sip of his scolding tea and winced. "The thing was, neither Ewan nor I were happy with selling the house. But it was the only inheritance that didn't have a clause attached. We owned the house outright and without the rest of our inheritance, neither of us really had the income to maintain it. So long story short, we were forced into selling our family home."

She squeezed his hand affectionately but remained

silent in order for him to continue. "We were both smart with the money and invested wisely, some investments paid off very well and this is why Ewan is now in a position to buy back the house."

Sadie nodded again, "That all seems to make sense to me. I don't understand what has got you so out of sorts. But whatever it is, we're happy at the cottage and we've no need for anything else." She reached forward and kissed him. "Go on, I'll try not to interrupt again." She winked at him and blew him a kiss.

"The rest of our inheritance is over ten million pounds between us." He let that sink in for a moment, waiting for her initial reaction.

Her mouth dropped open and she audibly gasped. He reached forward and took her cup from her hand to avoid her scalding herself.

"That's why she called me a gold-digger." He looked at her in surprise. "Fiona accosted me before she left, called me a gold-digging home-wrecker." She laughed and shook her head. "That's the real reason she came here isn't it, she found out about your inheritance?"

"I'm so sorry. Yes, she did, and she thought she'd have a go at trying to get a chunk of it for herself."

"But you didn't pay her off?"

"No, but I had suspected that there might be a reason for her turning up out of the blue, so Ewan did some digging, he unearthed her real plan and I sent her packing."

"Ok, so there is some clause then, something stopping you from accessing the money…"

"Yes there is, and let me just say, I don't want or need this money. But the thought of being able to provide for our kids' futures, it would definitely be the icing on the cake so to speak." She kissed him again and he could see that the suspense was really starting to get to her. "In order to access the rest of the money I need to be married."

The look on her face was one of complete confusion. "I don't understand, why is that such a bad thing? Do you not want to get married someday?" She was pouting and he could see that she wasn't really sure what he was trying to say.

"Of course, I do, and I am going to marry you one day." She blushed and he could see the glisten in her eyes. "But you have to understand what an inheritance like this did to me. I felt obligated to my parents. And then I felt like there was no one I trusted to not just be after the money. So, my brother and I decided not to tell anyone. If it happened, then so be it, but we wouldn't let the fortune rule our lives."

She kissed him and waited patiently for him to continue. "When the dies so unexpectedly, Ewan and I were living a life of the unattached in London. It was such a shock, they were no age at all." She squeezed his hand reassuringly. "I don't think they ever imagined the clause would be invoked. I guess they thought we would be married and have given them lots of grandkids before that time came."

"Ok, so potentially you are a millionaire. That doesn't change who you are. I'm still happy for you to move into The Cottage with us if you are."

"I was worried that you would think I only wanted

to be with you and to marry you in order to access the money. I wanted to be honest with you. But the longer I waited, the more complex the situation became." She took a moment to take in what he was saying. She sipped her tea which had cooled considerably in the time they had spent talking.

"So, what you are saying is that you are worried people will think me a gold-digger or you just married me to gain access to your inheritance…" He shrugged at her ability to summarise the bane of his existence.

"Basically, yes." Rhys agreed.

"So what would happen, if we did get married but you didn't claim the inheritance. What would happen to it?" A light seemed to flash in her eyes.

"Well, just marrying would automatically make the money mine, but I could put it straight into a trust for all and any future children we might have."

She drained the last of her tea from the cup and placed it back on the table beside them. "The thing is, I don't much care about the money, unless I've been written out I'm likely to inherit a small fortune myself anyway."

His eyebrows raised, "Ooo my very own sugar-Mumma!" He tickled her until she began to squeal.

"Stop, stop, someone, will come in."

"You," he kissed the tip of her nose, "are," then his teeth grazed her earlobe, "mine!" he kissed her full on the mouth and she seemed to melt at his touch.

"I am yours, money or no money."

He rested his head against hers. "How did I get so lucky?"

She shrugged as they walked back along the

corridor to the ward where Tabby was still sleeping. "I haven't said yes yet!"

Rhys released a deep boom of laughter, "I haven't asked you yet!"

Her eyes twinkled, "but you will, one day and you know I'll say yes and it won't be because you're rich, because I will be too one day!"

Chapter Forty-one

Rhys

Nearly two weeks later, on the twenty-seventh of December, Rhys walked into the marquee alone. The Christmas fayre was in full swing, and although Sadie chose to stay with Tabby, Rhys had promised to show his face and support in her stead.

He was barely there two minutes before a queue of well-wishers had formed. Each showing their love for the girl that would soon be his daughter in a matter of months.

After a while the Reverend approached and announced that they would be having a service for Mr Smithers on Sunday. "The three of us will be there, and I'm sure that Tabby would like to pay her respects." The Reverend nodded his agreement and then went on his way.

Near the centre of the marquee next to the platform that had been erected in place of a stage, Mr and Mrs Mirada stood, both haughtily looking down their noses at the proceedings going on around them.

Rhys approached them and wished them a Merry Christmas. "Rhys, old chap, Merry Christmas!" Mr Mirada boomed warmly. He noted that neither asked after their grand-daughter's well-being and frowned deeply at the lack of love they seemed to have for their family.

"What a great turn out, you must be so proud of all that has been accomplished!" The pair nodded but showed no emotion or any sign that they were genuinely impressed. "I am sorry about your driver, Mr Smithers. I hope that Mrs Smithers is bearing up. Would you please pass on our regards and let her know she is in our prayers."

"She has decided to take to retirement early and will be moving back into the village. A most inconvenient time of year!" Mrs Mirada declared for all around her to hear.

Rhys ignored the statement and moved on, "The flowers you sent Tabby were lovely. Thank you. I was surprised that you hadn't come to visit in person."

"Tabitha has snubbed our efforts to provide her with an education befitting a young lady." Mr Mirada was growing purple in the face and clearly was not happy about her returning to her previous school. "She has grown up to be wild and head-strong, just the same as her mother. We had hoped that we may have been able to steer her on a more suitable path…"

"I'm sorry, it sounds to me like you haven't visited your grand-child in the hospital because you don't agree with her decisions." He was shocked that they were being so forthright in their displeasure. "Please correct me if I am mistaken."

"Tabitha is just like her mother!" He boomed louder still. "She will turn out just as much of a disappointment." Rhys opens his mouth to retort back, but was cut across by Ewan.

"Tabitha is the light of this community. She is good and strong and kind-hearted. All of the things she got from Sadie!"

The Miradas seemed to ignore the jibe made about their parenting and instead boasted about the Knights taking up lodgings in their family home once more. It was clear that the only thing they respected more than status was money. The news that Ewan had managed to secure their ancestral home was like music to their ears. He never understood why his own amazing parents were friends with these people.

By now, Rhys had heard enough and cut in calmly yet assertively, "Look around you… your daughter did all of this. She has managed to set this up, they came because of her, the person she is. Thoughtful and generous, loving and full of compassion for others. All the traits I love about her!" Either stunned at being spoken to like this of having no desire to argue their point, Sadie's parents stood still and remained reticent.

"Tabby is an amazing kid because she has an amazing parent who understands what it really means to be a part of a community." Rhys paused for a breath not realising that those around them had stopped to listen.

"Sadie might not have followed the path you set out for her, but look at the path she forged for herself. Despite all that happened… You both were horrible to her, and then Darren breaking her heart before he died, becoming a single mum at such a young age. Your daughter is the best type of person and one day you will hopefully see that too." Ewan was trying and failing to stop Rhys now that he was on a roll.

"But if you do not. You can be sure, that I won't be letting this toxic relationship persist anymore." Rhys continued to stare them down.

"I don't think they'll be attending Sunday dinner for a while. I think you need some time to think before they are ready to let you back into their lives."

Sadie

"Rhys." Her voice was soft, yet in control. The group between them turned towards her. Sadie had been pushing Tabby in a wheelchair. "What's going on?"

Mae and Jacob were standing next to them, Rhys looked unsure what to say. She smiled at him briefly before suddenly and quite loudly, Mae called,

"Well said!" Then JJ nodded and said about time. Another person to their right announced their agreement and so the wave of ascent continued including both Mrs Grimshaw and Mrs Figg who was standing behind the nearest stall handing out the last of the plastic flutes filled with all manner of non-alcoholic beverages.

Mr Mirada seemed to be finding his voice as Sadie pushed the wheelchair closer. She reached out her hand and squeezed Rhys' affectionately. "You, told them?" She whispered.

"Now, Rhys. We've always respected you and your family. But I won't tolerate myself or my wife being spoken to this way, on our own land no less, this is an outrage!" Blustering and flustered, his sentences weren't fully formed yet the message was heard loud and clear.

Ewan stepped in front of Rhys as though to protect his brother from the older man's words and actions. "Mr Mirada, Edward..." The older man grunted though did not make any attempt to leave. "What Rhys has said is the truth. It might not be pretty, and I can imagine you might feel both embarrassed and maybe a little hurt. But the rest of the village agrees and are also voicing their opinions. Perhaps, this is an opportunity to start a new?"

Mrs Mirada whimpered, her eyes were glassy as she stared at her daughter and granddaughter.

"I will not be spoken to in this way! The festival is over!" At his words, the villagers began talking as though hundreds of tiny insects were clicking their pincers.

"Grandfather, no, please." Tabby looked devastated.

"There will never be another Christmas fayre in these grounds!" With that he nodded curtly at his wife and marched off towards the exit of the marquee.

"Mum!" Sadie had called out and Mrs Mirada stiffened. "You don't have to do this." Their eyes met and Sadie tried to put all she could into that one look.

"I have to follow, I am so pleased you are out of the hospital Tabby." Her voice had been sweet and soft, then when she straightened up she declared in a carrying and haughty voice. "You may finish the festival as planned, but please ensure everything is packed up before morning." Her shoulders seemed to sag slightly, "Thank you all for coming." And with that she exited the tent just like her husband.

After the silence had descended again, the Reverend's booming voice came over the speaker system. "Right folks. How about we wrap this up early!" There was only one more hour left of their allotted time and his voice contained no contempt or malice and quite strangely there appeared to be no hurt or unhappy faces in the crowds. No one argued. They just went on their merry way as though this had been expected to happen all along.

Rhys buried his face in his hands, muttering how sorry he was. Meanwhile, villagers came and patted him on the back and offered their Christmas wishes.

Ewan offered to take them all back to the village, but Sadie said she wanted to stay and help with the clear up.

She leaned in and kissed the tip of Tabby's nose. "Love you."

"Love you too mum." They hugged before Mae turned her away and then headed towards the car.

"Thank you." Sadie was now gently coaxing his face free, "Thank you for all the wonderful things you said!" They embraced and she pecked him affectionately on his jaw. "So, you love me huh?" Her smile broadened.

As though instinctively, his arms encircled her and drew her body to his.

"I have always loved you!" He whispered before leaning in to kiss her softly.

"Well, I'm happy to hear it," she laughed. "Rhys, I have something I need to tell you…"

Epilogue

Rhys

Rhys had just become a dad for the second time in his life and he couldn't be prouder of the family they had become.

"Oh my gosh, I'm so excited!" Tabby had looped her arm through his as they had walked the corridors of the hospital. The car seat would soon be holding the newest member of their little ensemble. "Dad," Tabby tugged a little harder and finally gave up on patience all together, dashing forward and opening the door to the maternity ward. He would never tire of hearing her call him Dad. His heart felt so full and he couldn't imagine being capable of loving anyone as much as he did his two girls.

"Mum!" An exaggerated whisper erupted from Tabby as she swooped down and kissed her cheek. Cradled in her arms, only a few hours old was Freddie. He squirmed at the noise around him and flexed his fingers before settling back to sleep.

Tabby looked between her parents, her eyes

glistening. "Can I hold him..." She was cautious, so Rhys pulled out the chair next to the bed encouragingly.

"Come on, take a seat." He kissed his wife briefly on the lips before carefully scooping his son from her arms. It had only been about fifteen minutes since he had last held him, but already he felt that he was heavier, was that even possible? He placed a solitary kiss on his head, breathing in the smell that was intoxicating before he positioned him in his daughter's arms.

He went back around the bed and sat with Sadie. She was exhausted but looked stunning as always. She was amazing and he couldn't be prouder.

Tabby stared at her baby-brother transfixed and completely at a loss for words. "Darling, talk to him, tell him a story..." Sadie leaned back against Rhys and sighed.

Tabby began cooing away at her little brother, telling him all the wonderful things he was going to be experiencing. How he was so precious, and she couldn't wait to watch him grow. Once she started there was no stopping her. The love on her face was paramount and his chest squeezed watching his children together for the first time.

Rhys felt a pang of longing, he knew that in a few short months she would be off to university. He knew it was selfish, but part of him wished she would stay this way forever. Already he had seen such a change in her and he knew that she was a force to be reckoned with, regardless of what she decided to do with her life.

"Penny for them," Sadie whispered into his ear.

He chuckled, "I'm just thinking... how did I get this lucky?"

"You aren't getting any brooding ideas are you husband," she smiled coyly up at him.

"We do have that big house to fill," he joked. Tabby's eyes shot up before realising he was jesting her mother and settled back to watching her brother sleeping.

He pulled Sadie into his side and gave her a gentle squeeze "Nah, I'm pretty sure this is as perfect as it gets..."

About the author

Hannah lives near Bourne in South Lincolnshire where her novels are inspired by the fens to the east and the rolling hills to the west.

After university, where she studied Primary Education, she taught for several years as a teacher of Key Stage Two. Hannah loved being in the classroom and was inspired by her pupils to follow her dreams.

She now runs a Tea shop, where she gets to bake, and drink copious amounts of tea with a lovely slice of cake.

Hannah returned to her writing roots during the long days of the first, second and third lockdowns in England. Since rekindling her passion for the written word, she can be found typing in the corner of her shop between making flat whites and encouraging kids to draw on the enormous chalkboard wall.

She hopes to one day purchase her narrowboat and sail around the British inland waterways, writing, baking and knitting lots of odd socks.

Hannah enjoys walking in the countryside but loves nothing more than enjoying a good book with a cuppa in front of a roaring fire.

Printed in Great Britain
by Amazon